THE ICE CREAM
SHOP
DETECTIVE

RONNIE LEVINE

ISBN-10: 0692204482
ISBN-13: 978-0692204481
New Views Press

ACKNOWLEDGMENTS

The events in this book are completely fictional. However, Nick would not exist if not for the time I spent with Detective Sergeant Eugene Buonanno of the Tarrytown (New York) Police Department. Like Nick and Lissa, he and I sat and talked and I painted in the cozy ice cream shop, Main Street Sweets, run by his family. I was impressed with his dedication, compassion, and his ability to move freely between fighting crime and serving ice cream cones. I was lucky to find the Hudson Valley Writers' Center in Sleepy Hollow when I began to think seriously about going from "I'd like to write a mystery someday" to "It's time to write my book." There I found a positive and productive atmosphere in workshops led by the wonderful mystery writer Joanne Dobson. She helped me expand my work from purely academic to something much more fun to write, and, I'm sure, to read. The Writers' Center was founded in 1983 by the multi-talented Margo Taft Stever, and it has attracted many talented, intelligent and accomplished people for its board, its staff, and as fellow workshop participants. Years before I discovered the Writers' Center, The Art Students League helped me find my way as an artist, in classes and in the suggestion that doing copies of great paintings at the Metropolitan Museum could be an important learning tool. Many thanks to my sister Fran for her encouragement, and for starting me on this path many years ago by passing along her Nancy Drews and Agatha Christies. I owe immeasurable thanks to my kind and brilliant Uncle Harold for his lifelong example of accomplishment, and for his unwavering support of my efforts.

PROLOGUE

When Danny didn't answer the door, I was annoyed. It didn't feel ominous at all. It was so like him. He'd practically begged me to come to his studio, and now he was leaving me out on this dark, cold, deserted side street?

Where *was* he?

I hesitated, then tried the door, which opened easily. "Danny?" I called out, then again, then louder the third time.

Silence.

Paintings were everywhere, on easels and stacked along the walls. Tables covered with paints, solvents, and mediums made the small room a maze. The piney, fruity aroma of turpentine mingled with the pungent smell of anchovies on a discarded slice of pizza. There was something else in the air, maybe some spoiled food. Not unusual for Danny, I thought.

Strips of frame moldings shifted as I walked, and I winced when one hit me in the shins. A small heap of pastels and paper sat next to a palette with blobs of paint that appeared to have been freshly squeezed, not yet mixed to use.

1

"Danny?" I tried again. My voice sounded a little shaky.

Now it was beginning to feel wrong. He'd been so eager to talk to me.

No answer.

I could see books, stretched canvases, six-foot-tall rolls of canvas waiting to be stretched. I could see brushes and buckets and shelves and taborets crammed with god-knows-what.

The only thing I couldn't see was Danny.

I went past a standing screen that I knew some of his models used when they took off their clothing. It wasn't that nude models are shy, of course, but most don't want to do a striptease.

And there he was. Lying on his back on the floor, his face contorted, lips curled back, skin blue, staring blindly at the ceiling like the old-fashioned doll my grandmother had once given me. It had sparkling blue eyes that used to close when you laid it on its back, but eventually the connecting bands had snapped, and the doll could only stare into space. It had scared me. It was horrifyingly unresponsive, dead.

Now Danny was unmistakably, unblinkingly dead.

Or was he? With legs turning to jelly, I looked again. Danny was just the kind of immature guy to play some dumb trick. For a brief moment I told myself it was staged. A tableau. Performance art, just for me? *Please let it be that?*

But no, Danny wasn't having fun tonight.

Danny would never have fun again.

Dizziness overwhelmed me. I wanted to run, but I couldn't. I managed to find my cell phone, but I couldn't speak.

How could this happen? It had to be some terrible freaky accident.

My knees began to buckle and I grabbed onto a table to keep from falling. Tubes of yellow and red paint went flying.

I turned around so I couldn't see Danny's horribly transformed face. I focused on the paintings until I could feel my legs again. I made it to the door.

Once outside, in the dry, crisp night, my shaking hands somehow found the directory entry for the Tarrytown P.D., and I made the call.

A calm, deep voice answered, "Police, what's your emergency?" Anyone with a voice like that could handle this a lot better than me, I was sure. I wanted him there, right away. And Nick too.

"Hurry!" My voice was barely audible. Could he hear it? "Someone's dead." I gave him the address.

I walked a few feet and looked toward Main Street, where things seemed impossibly normal. People were coming out of the hot dog place, steam rising as they unwrapped their small packages. Distant, barely audible voices murmured in front of the Tarrytown Theatre, punctuated by a burst of exuberant laughter. People strolling down the street stopped to look in store windows.

None of them knew that a young artist was lying dead in his studio.

I wished I didn't.

The sirens started almost immediately. Police cars filled the tiny street from both directions, slamming to a stop in front of me.

"Where is he?" I'd seen the young officer a few times at Bellini's, talking to Nick. I pointed to Danny's door, silently instructing myself to breathe in, breathe out.

CHAPTER ONE

When is a Monet not a Monet?

Maybe when the colors are a little drab and the faces are without personality. When you study masterpieces for a long time, you learn to feel them as well as see them.

You become a danger to a forger. And you'd better have someone like Nick Bellini in your life.

The day Nick told me something was going on had started out like any other. I got to Main Street around 11 A.M., picked up a hazelnut coffee at the 7-Eleven, and made my way through the light coating of snow to my studio. We'd had one storm after another and I was getting tired of it. Snow can be beautiful, but too much of it can strand you at home, and I'd much rather be at my studio. I unlocked my door, picked up my mail, and wondered how many weeks were left until spring.

I checked for messages. A routine day: just a robocall with a new approach to scamming me out of my hard-earned money, and a student postponing a class. As I walked towards the area in front of the windows where my easel was set up, I breathed in the pleasant fragrances of turpentine and linseed oil. Settling into my painting chair, I got out a fresh palette for working on my portrait commission.

It's never easy to earn a living as an artist, especially a traditional one, but between teaching at my studio, writing about art for a local news website, and acting as my own sales agent, I was squeaking by. My current painting was of two children playing in a park on a beautiful autumn day. It was a commission, to be a birthday gift from the children's father to their mother. I wished I had such a thoughtful guy in my life. Still, anyone who's been burned in a relationship knows that it's a lot safer to focus on work.

I began to squeeze my paints onto my palette. I started with white, then yellow, then through the rest of the color wheel, in the same order every day. I'd gotten as far as ultramarine when the phone rang.

"Hey, Lissa, how ya doin'?" It was Nick's comfortably rough voice, with more than a little New York in it.

Not such an ordinary day anymore. Nick had never called me at this hour on a weekday. As a lieutenant with the Tarrytown P.D, he was always busy, whether at the police station or out dealing with some crime somewhere in town.

"Fine, Nick," I said. "What's up? Anything wrong?"

"No, no, just wondered if you'll be at the shop tonight. I need your take on something."

"Uh, oh," I said, my tone light and teasing. "Did you buy another artist's painting?"

He laughed. "No way. I'm sticking with you, kid," he said. "It's something else…something important."

"Okay, sure," I said. "Around seven?"

"That works. See you tonight." He hung up abruptly.

Nick is the kind of guy who makes it seem like life is manageable. He can tackle problems and stay cheerful. My sister is a "no-can-do" defeatist, and though we're close, it drives me crazy. Nick is refreshingly positive and capable. I'd met him when I'd come to Tarrytown not knowing anyone, had sat down on the street, set up my easel, started painting. He was among the many people who came along to see what I was doing.

I tried to force myself to concentrate on my painting, but I was distracted by the call. *Damn!* I'd almost ruined the little girl's shiny hair. I took a swab, dipped it in turpentine, and repainted the section. I had to focus. There was no time for screwing up. This painting was on deadline.

CHAPTER TWO

I waited for Nick in my favorite spot in Bellini's, way in the back, where I could see the whole place and, out the front door, the street. Even though it was winter, there were a few customers and lively music. The walls were painted a warm gold, and everywhere you looked there were colorful displays: menus, artwork, several glass-fronted freezers with a dazzling array of ice-cream choices. I watched for Nick's dark curly hair, energetic walk, and his familiar moss-green windbreaker, which was usually the first thing I spotted when I saw him at a distance. I knew he was beginning to mean too much to me. He hadn't shown anything but friendliness on his side. If it hadn't happened by now...

Bellini's was always bright and cheerful, full of sweet smells and laughing children. I felt good there. Outside, as you approached the building at night as I just had, spotlights threw a warm glow over the façade, revealing the charmingly irregular pattern of nineteenth-century bricks under the yellow paint. Inside, it was completely renovated, clean and bright, with a colorful mural that went the whole length of one wall.

It was an unlikely backdrop for the stories Nick told me about his work.

Promptness wasn't one of Nick's hallmarks, but that evening I didn't have to wait very long. He greeted the teenage ice-cream scoopers as he walked in, his smile so warm that it made me feel good even though it wasn't directed at me.

He saw me, waved, and headed towards me.

"Lissa, good," he said. "I'm glad you made it." His voice was strong and deep.

"Anytime," I said. "You've got me wondering."

"Give me a minute to change into my work clothes," he said.

I could barely make out his words now, since the kids behind the counter had just turned up the music, as if it were a party. Nick disappeared into the little private office. I went on sipping my coffee, watching the customers and the movement, and thinking about him.

Nick is a complex man. His days are spent investigating assaults, burglaries, and car accidents, but when he comes to the ice cream shop he transforms himself into a genial host and energetic scooper. He had to be tough, I knew, since a detective has to handle trouble, but I'd never seen him be anything but friendly.

He came back dressed in a Bellini's t-shirt. "Can I give you an espresso?" he asked. He was already holding a small cup in his hands, extended towards me. Again, not the usual. Offering espresso was a special-occasion thing for him.

"I'm fine," I told him. I tilted my coffee cup to show him it was nowhere near empty. He lowered himself into the seat across from me. Nick was muscular and agile, and his movement was a welcome sight. He took the espresso for himself, his powerful hands wrapped around it as he took a quick gulp. I took in the sight. Michelangelo must've had a model like him when he sculpted his *David*.

Not that I was acquainted with as much of Nick as I was of *David*. Unfortunately.

"You belong to the Tarrytown Artists' Guild, don't you?" he asked.

"Yes," I said, "I go to most of the meetings." I could see the seriousness in his eyes, and yes, it made me feel a little concerned, but it was only the tiniest clue about how big--and dangerous-- this case would become.

He started to fill me in. "We just got information that some pretty successful phony big-name paintings have been coming out of this area," he said. "I figure you know a lot of artists."

I was surprised. "Forgeries in Tarrytown?" Did he want this to be public knowledge? I looked around to see if anyone was listening, but I realized the loud music kept our words private. Two feet away, no one would hear a thing.

"Looks like it. I can't say why."

"What kind of paintings?"

"At this point we're looking out for a Monet, a Renoir, a Van Gogh, some Picasso prints, and possibly a Velazquez," he said, tapping his cup on the table to punctuate each name.

"Top tier," I said. "Some forgers go for lesser-known artists. To imitate artists so famous, someone has to have balls."

"You know a lot about that kind of art, don't you?"

I nodded. "I've done my share of studying. Twenty-first century artists are supposed to worship Andy Warhol, Jeff Koons and Damien Hirst, but for me there's nothing like a Monet, Rembrandt, or Vermeer. You've heard of pushing the envelope?"

He looked like he hadn't. I didn't wait for an answer. "It's the postmodern dictate for artists that if they want to make it, they have to do something no one ever did before, or at least something no one ever before said was art. Novelty has become the most respected thing in art, and traditional skills are scorned."

"That doesn't sound like your work," Nick said.

"It isn't. I don't play that game. The people who make up the art establishment make it sound like their value system is based on fact, that weird and crude are better in some provable way, but really it's just opinion. I don't love that art, I love the best figurative art of the past, the pictures that have intellect and feeling as well as pleasing color and line. I try to analyze what made those works great, and aim for that quality in my own art."

"It's lucky for me that you feel that way," Nick said. "What we need is someone to help us spot fakes from a distance, so to speak, without tipping off the artists or owners that we're looking at them. You and I have known each other long enough for me to believe you're the one for it."

I gulped. Hard. And then again. I hadn't seen this coming.

"Me?" I finally managed to say, in a voice that sounded more like a croak. "I don't know. Wow. Authentication is a tough business, tougher than ever. A painting may not look exactly right, but plenty of times nobody wants to say anything. You don't want to tell private collectors they've been duped. They may have they overestimated their own knowledge of art, or they may have been over-eager for a suspicious deal to be legit. Either way they'll be very unhappy."

"We think even galleries and museums may have some of these," Nick said.

"If they honestly think they're real, the quality has to be pretty good."

Nick nodded. "Somebody put it over on a lot of people, we think, for a while," he said, his voice now barely audible. "But we're going to catch up with him. He's not as smart as he thinks he is."

"Who bought them?" I asked.

"I can't tell you that right now," he said. "We don't know whether the owners know."

Crimes in Tarrytown seemed rare to me. People came in from somewhere else to grab some jewelry and run—or try to run, anyway—but this felt different. If there were long-term crimes being done by people who were part of the local arts community, it was a shock. The artists I knew were good people.

Weren't they?

Nick put it out there. "Do you know anyone from this area who might be able to do top-quality fakes?" he asked.

"No, I can't think of anyone who's that good," I said. "Or that corrupt."

"Lissa, do you think you could tell a real Monet from a fake?" he asked, leaning in close to me and keeping his voice very soft.

I didn't know what to say. *What if I got it wrong?* This would be a huge responsibility. For one thing, a painting was still valuable if it was by a major artist even if it wasn't his or her best. The thought of making the judgment was terrifying. No amount of turp on a swab could wipe out *that* mistake. I could screw up people's lives.

And what if a forger I exposed screwed up *my* life? People who authenticated—or wouldn't authenticate-- valuable paintings got sued sometimes, if what they said made someone lose money. A few experts even got death threats. "Nick, I really couldn't..." My words were drowned out by his ringing cellphone.

While he talked, I thought. I breathed in the sweet aroma of vanilla and browning sugar from the waffle cones they were making up front. I got up and walked over to the mural, which someone had painted before I discovered the place. In front was a quick rendering of Tarrytown, based on photos Nick had given the artist. It was a boldly colorful, simplified graphic of Main Street, as though seen with a telephoto lens from up the hill, with the river and the Tappan Zee Bridge at the top. The back section was the parks and homes of Sleepy Hollow, and the river ran the whole length of the shop, uniting the two sections. Sleepy Hollow, right up Route 9, had been North Tarrytown until the Johnny Depp movie with that name, based on nineteenth-century local resident Washington Irving's *Legend of Sleepy Hollow*, had brought the town new notice. Irving had set his story there but had given it a new name; despite initial griping about printing new stationery, the village's name had been changed to match the fiction. Now, of course, Ichabod Crane and the headless horseman were Fox Network TV stars and their "hometown" was thrilled. And you'd better be lucky if you wanted to find a parking space in Halloween season.

As I paced the shop, waiting for him, my thoughts went back to the day we'd met.

I'd worked my way up the Hudson River from New York City, where I'd painted in Central Park, at the South Street Seaport, and at Wave Hill in Riverdale, where I'd become interested in the river. I started in Yonkers and then headed north. When I was finished with a location and ready to move on, I checked out new spots like a Hollywood scout. I'd been delighted to find that Tarrytown still had several beautiful nineteenth century buildings that I'd seen in a book of Historical Society photos. Nick and everyone else on Main Street had been strangers to me. It had been early April, still chilly, but I'd been elated that winter was over and determined to get some outdoor work done. I was putting the first color on my canvas, which would depict the four buildings across the street from my easel. I'd chosen this spot mostly because of the building with yellow-painted brick walls, muted orange shutters, moss-green accents and a very fresh and happy-looking red-and-white awning over the entrance to the ice cream shop. Richly dark strips framed the large shop windows.

"Do you like that building?" he'd asked, pointing at my underdrawing of it.

"Yes, very much," I'd said. "It's definitely my favorite."

His face had brightened. He'd said, "My family owns it. We did the restoration ourselves."

I stopped mixing my orange paint and looked up at the stranger who would become so important in my life. His rugged face was wearing that warm smile. His eyes were pleasant and confident.

"Wow, you did a great job," I'd said. I imagined the care that went into each color choice, and the effort of the many moments spent polishing the wood trim.

"Come in and see the mural inside," he'd said.

"I'd love to. As soon as I'm finished for the day."

Did I know something important had just happened? No, I had no idea.

CHAPTER THREE

It sounded like Nick's conversation was coming to an end. I came back to the present and sat down with him again.

"All right, then, tomorrow," he said into the phone. "Yes, it's all ready," he added. "See you in the morning."

As he put the phone down, I thought about what my life had been when we met. I'd broken up with a man I'd lived with for six years, who had a nasty temper and didn't treat me the way I felt I deserved. I'd had enough. I'd also grown unhappier about the contemporary art world and what was being considered great. I needed to strike out on my own, to do the kind of art I believed was of greater value to people than what was being traded among multi-billionaires for millions of dollars per painting—or per set of crumpled gum wrappers, if they were touted by some critic. It wasn't easy, though, and I'd been pushing myself to go on. Then Nick walked into my life, bringing warmth and excitement.

What did I have to lose by helping him? Where would I be without him?

I found my courage. "Look Nick," I said, "all I can tell you is that when I see a magazine article or book about fakes, I can tell which are real and which aren't. So far I haven't been wrong."

"Great! I knew you would do it!" he said.

"I didn't study it directly," I said, as a caution. "But you do look at paintings and learn why they're considered great. That means others aren't so great, and I worked hard to understand why. I did copies at the Met, which helped. I told you, remember?" I asked.

He didn't have to answer because I could already see it in his steady gaze. But he did anyway. "Sure," he said. "That's part of why I thought of you as soon as I heard about this."

It was one of the things I liked best about Nick. He listened and remembered. I'd grown up in a family in which no one ever seemed to be paying attention, so no matter how many times I'd repeat something, it was news to them. It was frustrating. With Nick, I had a sense of a meeting of the minds.

He looked at me for what seemed to be a long time and said, "Just keep your eyes open and tell me if you see anything unusual."

I nodded.

He got up and started to wipe the table. It always intrigued me how easily he could go from intense brain work to physical labor. But despite his outward transformation from detective to ice cream shop proprietor, I was sure he was still thinking about masterpieces and forgery.

CHAPTER FOUR

The annual Civic Beautification fundraiser was in the nicest house on Fairview Avenue. It had a circular driveway and a huge old elm tree sheltering the driveway. Fundraisers are usually held in exclusive locations, to lure you into parting with your money. I'd gotten onto the front porch of Irvington's Octagon House that way, a significant improvement over admiring it from the road. It was one of only a few nineteenth-century octagonal houses still standing in the whole country, a delicate pink Victorian confection, but with a tragic history. A young girl who lived there in the nineteenth century fell in love with a boy who was considered unforgivably her social inferior, and, unable to bear being separated from him, she walked into the Hudson and drowned herself. Stories like that put the pursuit of wealth in perspective for me, and made it possible for me to cope with the precariousness of my life as an artist. I still liked to visit a beautiful home when I got the chance, since it was likely to be pleasing to my artist's eye, but there were limits on what I'd do to own one.

I dressed carefully, adding a colorful scarf and big silver chandelier earrings to my simple black dress to make it a little more festive. My image in the mirror looked okay, if not ravishing, helped out by my shoulder-length red hair and green eyes. I got in the car, being careful not to wrinkle my dress. I lived not far from my art studio, and I passed it as I drove uphill on Neperan Road, then past Grove Street with its gorgeous Victorians, climbing higher, and turned onto Fairview Avenue.

The houses were set back from the street, with lush front lawns and dramatic views of the Hudson River and Tappan Zee Bridge. It was only 5:30, but it was winter so it was already dark. All I could see in the distance were the sparkling lights of the bridge and the homes across the river. In my head I could see what I went out of my way to see every morning: just down the hill were Grove Street's big old homes, then Archer with its mix of fabulous and ordinary ones. Beyond that was Broadway and streets of nice, if not all elegant, homes and charming small shops, the streets descending ever more downhill until they reached the star of the show, the river.

The Hudson changes every day with the light and season. Beyond it are the cliffs of the Palisades, thousands of trees interrupted every once in a while by warm brown rock formations. In daylight the colors are vivid nearby and get paler and bluer as they recede in the distance. From the right places you felt like you could see almost to Bear Mountain. I never got tired of looking at this world-class view, every bit as beautiful as Montmartre or a Tahitian sunset.

I arrived at my destination, a creamy palazzo with an orange-tiled roof, set well back from the street. The front garden was covered with snow, but you could still see the shapes of interestingly manicured hedges. How good life might be if you have a beautiful home like this. Under the right circumstances.

The owner, Jim DeWitt, was visible through the window. He was carefully groomed, every bit the bank executive. He had intense amber eyes, sandy hair and a mature but athletic build. His white shirt contrasted with his winter tan, enhancing it. I'd read that he had some sort of art collection, though it wasn't clear whether he really loved art or just the money one can make buying and selling it like any other investment.

Diana, his wife, was always in the local press at some event or other. She was one of those tall, slinky, size-zero blonds, a few decades younger than her husband. Her features were Barbie doll to the extreme. I had serious doubts about whether Mother Nature had made that perky a nose. The physical perfection helped balance the fact that she was reputed not to be the deepest thinker on the block. It also helped that she was from a prominent San Francisco family. She had come east several years ago to work in the fashion industry, and was usually demanding and condescending to people in town. I wasn't at all sure I wanted to know them better.

Just the house.

The door was open, and when I went in I found people standing in small groups, talking and drinking wine. I spotted a few people from the Artists' Guild and walked up to two of them who were having what looked like a lively conversation. I thought about what Nick had told me, but these people couldn't do anything criminal.

Could they?

"Alissa, you made it," said my old friend Anne Sutcliffe. "You tore yourself away from your easel."

"For this, of course," I said. "You know I love to snoop into these old houses."

Anne had been a childhood friend of mine until her family had moved away while we were in high school. When I joined the Tarrytown Artists' Guild we'd met again, and become friends despite the fact that her main focus was now on raising her family and mine on career. We were standing in an entry hall with walls of intricately patterned honey-colored wood, warm and cozy with golden lighting.

"Well, what do you think so far?" she asked, and I nodded my approval. Anne was tall and slender, with an aquiline nose I envied, and long, straight blond hair. She was feminine but muscular, partly from sculpting in stone. She was cool and professional, not one to get into arguments or backstabbing. Standing with Anne was Connor, a singer and songwriter who, unlike his usual state of perpetual motion, this night looked a little tired. With thick brown hair and good strong physique, he was definitely attractive enough for show business. I thought he deserved a lot wider success than he'd had so far, but at least he was busy in town. It helped, he'd told me, that he got royalties from his one big hit of some years before. He loved his work, and he was out there no matter how many obstacles were placed in his way. I patted him affectionately on the arm.

"Anything up, Connor?" I asked.

"Doin' great," he replied, his face filled with pleasure. "My agent's keeping me busy, with two gigs a day sometimes. Kids, restaurants, senior centers. I love it."

"Lucky man," I said. "And lucky audiences, too."

"Has anybody heard from Paul?" Anne asked. She was talking about Paul McGill, who'd become an art star. He lived in Tarrytown before I got there, and I'd heard about him—who hadn't-- but I'd never met him. Before I'd arrived he'd moved to an area upstate where he was able to buy a Victorian mansion for a fraction of what it would cost in Tarrytown.

I didn't like his work very much, but the critics did.

"Not me," Connor replied. "Maybe Danny has. They used to be pretty close. Van Gogh and Gauguin, only they have all four of their ears. Is our Van Gogh here?"

Anne shook her head. "You couldn't drag Danny to one of these things. He doesn't like having to be a good boy, even for an hour."

"That's Danny, all right," I said. "Did you see the review of Paul's show at the Contemporary Arts Museum in *Art in America*? They loved it."

"Yeah, he's big. I wonder how Danny feels about it. Especially since they're not in touch anymore. Our Gauguin made it and our Van Gogh didn't."

"Don't write him off yet," I said. "He's still young." Not that I thought Danny was a great talent, but neither was Paul as far as I was concerned. Danny had just as much chance at winning over-glorification as anyone else in the bizarre twenty-first century art world.

"Hey, did you see the paintings in the living room?" Connor asked me. "In the sunroom they've got the contemporary stuff, the things that look like the maid hasn't thrown away the trash, like the crumpled cigarette packs and braided wires, but the living room is strictly Classical and Impressionist. Just what you like."

"Sounds like it's worth a look," I said, and I decided to do it right then. On my way I stopped to join the group around our hosts, Jim and Diana DeWitt. They were holding court along with the mayors of Tarrytown and Sleepy Hollow. Whenever I saw politicians I tried to put in a pitch for more support of traditional art, but so far it hadn't done much good. Our various projects were always under-funded. Still, you had to try.

Diana, standing next to her husband, her carefully made-up, black-lashed blue eyes a good four or five inches above his, was wearing a scarlet satin dress and looked a lot more show-biz than suburban banker's wife. Her short, straight and sleek blond hair clung tightly to the contours of her head. Her facial features were delicate, but the look in her eyes wasn't. Jim's left arm was around her, and he held a drink in his right hand. He looked the very picture of

20

respectability and contentment. They were talking about the booming new development in the village, and the soaring retail rents.

"So the antique shops have to move out," he said, "the important thing is that the property values are going up. We can go antiquing anywhere we want," he said, with the assurance of a man whose SUV couldn't guzzle any more gas than his wallet could handle.

Diana smiled adoringly at him like a politician's wife on a TV interview show.

"I like to go to Manhattan," she said. "I like to go to Bergdorf's."

"The antique shops are not so expendable to me," I said. "They're part of what made me settle in Tarrytown. They set the tone, especially when they're in nineteenth century buildings, surrounded by other old buildings. They look good and they attract people who care about the visual arts."

"That's very true," said Peter Giovanni, the mayor of Sleepy Hollow. "But you have to consider the broader picture. The new condos at the riverfront are bringing in a lot of money. So it's a little more crowded and you lose a few views of the Tappan Zee Bridge, well, that's life. The important thing is economic growth."

"Here's to money," said Diana, holding up her champagne in a toast. Soft laughter filled the air.

Many times I'd driven down Beekman Avenue just to enjoy the sweeping river scenes, now partially obscured by new buildings. Before, as you approached the river, the houses, though modest, had a resort-town feel, I suppose in part because you could see open space and river beyond them. Now it's town and more town. Still beautiful, but I worry about the future.

"I understand that money is important, but art and architecture are too," I said.

"I like art, too," said Diana. "I like that man who paints the soup cans. Who is that, darling?" she asked her husband.

"That was Andy Warhol, dear," he replied. "We have one in the den, don't you remember?"

"Oh, yes," she said, giggling. "It's hard to keep track sometimes. We have so much."

"We support the arts," said Jim.

"I know that," I replied, but I also doubted that any local artists benefited from his investments. I bit my tongue and walked into the next room to check out the paintings.

The room was far beyond what I would expect in this beautiful but unpalatial home. I think I gasped audibly, but no one was there to notice. Was I committing a *faux pas* by coming in here alone? I soon forgot about manners as I took in the collection.

Jim's money had certainly put him in an enviable position as a collector. The room looked like something out of the Lehman wing at the Metropolitan Museum, only still lived-in. To my astonishment, on one wall was what appeared to be a Monet, of his middle years, after his first wife, Camille, had died. He'd gone traveling to find new subjects that could help him deal with his grief. This was not my favorite period of his work. My personal reading was that even though he remarried quickly he never completely recovered from losing her. He got more into the decorative aspects and somehow the work didn't have as much life for me. Still, it's highly regarded by the market and is worth a fortune. If this was a real Monet it was a piece of him, touched by his hands, an incredible thing for someone to own.

On another wall was a Dutch scene, a village in the woods that looked like a Hobbema. He was a delightful seventeenth-century painter with a distinctive style; his work possessed the capacity to transport you in time and space. You looked at it and you were there. I couldn't imagine being able to sit in front of this painting every night. How lucky Jim was. That is, if he could feel it. There was also a small Guardi, I thought, a lovely Venice scene, and an English portrait that looked like it might be a Hogarth. I sat down on a couch to take it in. This was an incredible collection, and I'd only seen part of it. As beautiful as the house was, it was dwarfed in value by this collection.

I sat staring at the Monet. Actually, even for his bereavement period it didn't seem exactly right, once you really looked. The colors were good. They looked like they were mixed with the complimentary color, plus blue, not dulled down with black. Still, the child's face looked like an unseeing doll. Trees drooped unappealingly, their branches didn't vary much in size or shape from each other, and they didn't have very many twists and turns in them.

I started to wonder. Already? Could I find a suspicious work so quickly?

"I see you found our treasure." I jumped at the sound of Jim's voice right behind me, so close I could feel his breath on my ear. I turned and saw that he still had a drink in his hand, but it was in a different glass. He'd been fine a few minutes ago, but now he was beginning to slur his words. I was surprised, but of course it wasn't the first time I'd seen this sort of thing.

He finished the drink, took a bottle out of a lacquered cabinet, gave himself a refill, and downed that one just as quickly. "Isn't it something?" he asked, gesturing at the Monet.

"It's amazing," I said. "I never thought I'd see one outside a museum."

"Life is full of surprises, isn't it?" he said, with an ironic tone.

"It's wonderful that you allow the Civic Beautification Committee to have their fundraiser here."

"Well, you've got to give a little back, don't you?"

The drinks were having a cumulative effect, and he was now unmistakably over the line, lurching and leering. He came over to me and bent to speak face-to-face. I've never had any patience with drunks, no matter how wealthy or connected. One moment they seem like bullies and the next they're pathetic, needy little boys. Still, I knew I'd better watch my step with Jim.

"It's wonderful," I lied. "Have you had it for a long time?"

"It's new," he said. He laughed raucously, his mouth open so wide I could see his throat. I backed into the couch cushions as far as I could. "A new Monet! Isn't that funny?" he asked. Then, as if *I* were the one who was only half-conscious, "How could a Monet be new?" He roared with laughter again.

"I congratulate you," I said, a little formally and carefully. "I've never met anyone who owned a real Impressionist painting."

"You're an artist, right?" he asked, touching me on the shoulder. "I've seen you at your easel on Main Street."

"Yes," I said, moving his hand away and trying to distract him by turning it into a handshake. "Lissa Franklin. It's nice to meet you. I've seen you around town and in the local media. I didn't see anything about this painting, though."

"You can't go around telling everyone everything, Lizbeth. You can't let the bad guys know about everything you've got. Or the taxman." Once more the empty-sounding laughter filled the room. He sat down next to me. Right next to me. He put down his glass and took my hands. His were cold and wet from the drink. I pulled away but he took them again. "Liza, what's the matter?" he asked. "Don't you know who I am?"

I started to stand up but he pulled me back. "I can do things for you, Liza," he said, his eyes narrowing to slits.

"That's okay, I'm fine," I said, my stomach turning. In a conversational tone I asked where he'd gotten the painting.

"Trade secret," he said. "Let's just say it was a private sale."

"Around here?" I asked.

"You paint people, don't you, Lizbeth?"

"It's Lissa," I said, though with little hope that he'd notice. "Yes, if you'd like to have a portrait done..."

"A portrait? Where's the fun in a portrait?" he asked. He leaned in close and whispered, "A nude, now that's fun. That's something I'd pay for. I can be there tonight. Where will I be when I'm there? When will it be, then, there?"

I stood up abruptly, catching him off-guard long enough to make my getaway. Just as I reached the other side of the room Diana walked in, accompanied by several guests. Jim, facing the maybe-Monet, didn't turn around.

"There you are, darling," she said as she came into the room. "Our guests want to see the new painting. I told them how pretty it is." She didn't show any signs of having heard any of our conversation.

"Fabulous."

"Wonderful."

"Amazing."

The voices boomed out, overlapping into a rumble of appreciation as they looked around the room.

"This one is my favorite," said Peter Giovanni, taking a position in front of the purported Monet. "Look at all these colors, and the swirling clouds. It looks like a real Monet."

"It looks like a real Monet," said Jim, following up with a hiccup, "because it is a real Monet."

Peter smiled. "I can't believe I'm seeing it right here in Tarrytown. Jim, you old dog, I never thought when we were kids that you'd have a place like this."

Jim smiled, a little sadly, I thought. "I'm a lucky guy, all right," he said, raising his glass and drinking deeply. "Beautiful, beautiful life."

No one reacted to the irony I heard in his voice.

"Elizabeth likes my painting," he said.

"Who is Elizabeth?" Diana asked.

"She is," Jim said, pointing at me.

"Alissa, actually," I said, again not expecting it to do much good. Diana turned and looked at me, vacantly but politely.

"A lot of people like this painting," said Diana, "and we have these others," she said, pointing to the Hobbema and Guardi canvases.

"Excellent, charming, superb," said various people.

"Who were they painted by?" somebody asked.

Everybody looked at Jim, but Jim was looking at his empty glass. Diana opened her mouth to answer but appeared to be short on knowledge. "The names of the artists are on little plaques at the bottom of the frames," she said after a brief pause. "Aren't they glorious?" she asked. "These are Jim's babies. Jim brings them home, and Jim takes care of them. And I take care of Jim. Isn't that right, baby?" she asked breathily.

Jim looked up and nodded. He looked a little more focused now. "Don't be modest, Diana," he said. "You were part of buying the last few. Since you met that what's-his-name."

"Let's not bore everyone with the details, darling," she said. "We're here for the Beautification Committee today. Shouldn't we announce the special donations now? Come back into the other room where I have the list, everyone."

Amid a lot of murmuring, the group headed out the door and I turned to join them.

Jim's voice was barely audible. He said, "I'll be seeing you, Lizabeth."

It was a simple enough statement.
Why did it sound slightly menacing?

CHAPTER FIVE

I was uncomfortable with the idea of telling Nick what I had thought about the Monet. My self-doubts had come back. Jim and Diana were powerful people and they wouldn't be happy at all if Nick started investigating their collection. Maybe I'd hold off.

And I did, for two days. On Saturday, when I came home, the answering machine was flickering to indicate a message when I got home. "Call me, Lissa," was all it said.

It was Nick. I didn't. I wasn't sure what to say. I turned my cell phone off.

The landline rang five minutes later. I knew it had to be Nick, but I checked the caller ID anyway. "Unavailable," it read.

"Don't taunt me," I said to the phone. I took a deep breath and picked it up. It was him, all business.

"How's it going, Lissa?" he asked. "Did you think about what I said?"

"Nick, what if I had an idea that something I'd seen might be a fake?" I asked. "What would you do?"

"We'd just keep our eyes open for now," he told me in a reassuring tone. "What do you think, we're gonna go bust down someone's door just because you said something looked wrong?"

I felt like I was about to do something irrevocable, to take a step that might lead me off a cliff.

But what if I could put right a criminal wrong?

I took that step. "Jim and Diana have a Monet," I said, "only it doesn't look exactly the way most Monets look."

"Really!" he exclaimed. "What was wrong with it?"

I told him about the lifeless face and the too-simple trees. "It's good, but it's not quite right," I said. "It lacks charm, it lacks the "family" resemblance to his other work."

"You saw it at the fundraiser?" he asked.

"Yes."

"Did anyone say anything?"

"Everyone admired it. It looks okay when you just glance at it."

"I'm sure you didn't say anything?" he asked.

So why did he ask? "No, I'm not going to, at all," I answered.

"Good girl."

I winced. Okay, he wasn't perfect. Who is?

"When's the Artists' Guild meeting?" was his next question.

"On Monday. It's at one of the studios," I told him. "Right in town. Near the Chinese restaurant."

"China Palace, on Main Street?" he asked.

"Yeah, that one. The meeting is right around the corner, on Kaldenberg," I explained. "Danny's got a studio in that little building that used to be a garage."

"Danny? Isn't he one of the wilder ones?" Nick asked.

"I guess you could say that," I replied.

"Is he a full-time artist?" Nick asked.

"I don't really know. But he could be. I don't think you have to bring in big bucks to pay for that place, as good as its location may be. It's pretty basic."

"Call me afterwards," he said. "My other phone is ringing." He hung up abruptly.

Our conversation was the only thing I thought about for the rest of the evening.

CHAPTER SIX

Damn these morning people, I thought when the phone rang at 10:30. *Saturday morning, give me a break.* I took a couple of deep breaths and picked it up.

"Hello?" Amazingly, I sounded almost alert, at least to myself.

"Lissa?" the deep voice said. It was Nick. I was suddenly wide awake. I sat up in bed and ran my fingers through my hair, as if he could see me. I was suddenly aware of how soft and sweet-smelling my bed was.

"Listen, I've been thinking," he said. "Everybody stops to look at your two paintings in the back of the shop. You know the mural?"

"Of course," I said.

"We'd like you to repaint it," he told me.

I was surprised. "I thought you were so proud of that mural," I said.

"We like it. We want you to add to it. We'll keep the design the way it's laid out, and you can make it more detailed, and use the colors you like."

"Great," I said. It would be fun to paint at Bellini's. A lot of work, too. "I'm almost finished with my portrait commission. But--are you planning to pay me?" I asked.

"Hey, artists have to eat, too, don't they?" he answered.

I smiled at the phone.

"Come in later in the afternoon," he said, "and we'll see how low I can get you to go on your fee if I throw in an espresso and a little friendship."

I laughed. "Ten percent off for friendship," I said. "With espresso on demand."

"Tough negotiator," he replied. "I'll have to run it past my accountant."

I hoped he'd be there when I got to Bellini's, but it was his sister Gina I saw, up front near the coffee. I sniffed the fragrant air, saturated with the scent of freshly-made wafer cones. I looked around but didn't see Nick.

"He's coming," Gina said. "He called a few minutes ago." She was there just about every day, including weekends, and her energy and enthusiasm had to be a major part of the success of the place. Gina was tall and slender, with vivid brown eyes like her brother. Her long dark hair surrounded a pretty, heart-shaped face. I envied her delicately arching eyebrows. I usually didn't have the patience to do anything with mine. We'd become friends as I'd worked across the street on the paintings that now hung in the back of the shop. "He wants you to work on the mural?" she asked.

"Yes. Like the idea?"

"Sure, why not," she said. "You're good." I liked the way this family got along with each other. No drama for the sake of drama. My family was loving, but stormy every day, no exceptions for birthdays or holidays.

I took a steaming coffee to a table in the back, where I found Katie, Gina's two-year-old, covering pages of a circus coloring book with corner-to-corner diagonal blue and orange stripes. The ringmaster, the clowns, the elephants all sat under the stripes. Katie was clearly enjoying manipulating the colors. I sipped my hot drink slowly, savoring it. The tiny, curly-haired junior artist quickly made it clear that she expected some attention, so I put my cup down and took her on my lap, admiring her artwork and pointing out the two paintings of mine on the back wall. Gina sat down with us and Katie reached out for her mother. I transferred her from lap to lap.

"You're good, with her, Lissa," Gina said. She smoothed Katie's hair and kissed both of her little hands. Then she turned towards me. "So what's with you and Nick?" she asked.

"Nick's my art friend," I replied. "He acts like what I do matters. And he's good to talk to."

"I don't know if you think about it turning into something more," Gina said. "You know about his wife?"

My heart stopped. I guess I'd still been hoping for more, after all.

"His ex, I mean."

My heart started again. "No. He's never said anything about her," I said. "Is she here in town?"

"No, not now," Gina replied. "But she grew up here. We met on our first day in Tarrytown Primary School.

"She and Nick were already close when they were kids?" I asked. "Were they a couple from school days?"

"No, she and I were friends, but we're both four years younger than Nick. To him we were children."

"When did he change his mind?" I asked. I was aiming to sound curious and friendly, not too interested.

"When she was a nursing student. She got a part-time position in the ER at the local hospital. He would bring emergency cases there, and he'd have to hang around for around for paperwork. He started noticing her."

"How long did it last?" I asked.

"Six years. They had a big wedding, just like we dreamed about when we were little girls. A fairy tale," Gina said, bouncing Katie on her lap. Her eyes seemed to be looking somewhere else, I suppose into the past, and Katie began to cry. "She turned on him," Gina said. Her face looked as though she was still surprised, years later. "He was always there for her, and suddenly she started acting like she was too good for him."

"How awful," I said. "Did they have kids?" *I would know if he had kids, wouldn't I? People divorce their spouses but not their kids. People like Nick, anyway.*

"No, he wanted to," she said, her voice quiet, "but she kept saying she wasn't ready. And then she left. She left him and moved away."

Nick seemed like a man with deep feelings. A betrayal like that definitely wouldn't be shrugged off. I didn't have much time to think about it, though, because just then he walked in the door, and the atmosphere changed as though an energy field had been switched on. The air was suddenly more breathable.

"My favorite girls," he shouted as he strode in. Katie was soon swinging in the air in his strong grip, screaming with pleasure. "My girl," he sang in a deep voice, "ba da, ba da, talkin' 'bout my girl." He kissed her on the forehead, then cradled her in his arms.

"I love that song," I said. "The Temptations, right?"

"You know your classics, I see," Nick said. "It's one of my favorites. I guess it means happy times." He put Katie down in front of her coloring book and turned to me. "So what's the word?" he asked. "Are we going to have a new Lissa Franklin masterpiece on our wall?"

I smiled and did my best to play agent for myself as we worked out the plans for the mural.

CHAPTER SEVEN

The coffee was always hot and full-bodied at the Olive Tree Diner in Dobbs Ferry. As I sat there a couple of days later, I alternated between my pleasure in the coffee and my pain at reading the newspaper account of the latest nominees for one of those big art prizes in England. Who had won it last year? Wasn't it some artist who had cut off the tip of his nose as homage to Van Gogh? Cutting off his ear wouldn't qualify, of course, because that would be mere imitation; but the judges had felt this was more creative. With contemporary art you couldn't always tell reality from craziness. The artist who'd had his poodle groomed—he hadn't even done it himself--with the map of the Milky Way shaved into its fur had been the expected winner, but at the last minute Mr. Nose (yes, he'd had his name changed legally) had pulled to the front of the pack. I got so involved in reading about the contemporary arts follies that the deep voice saying hello had to repeat it three or four times until I realized it was directed at me

"Elizabeth," the man said. Then more insistently, "Elizabeth!" I looked up and there was Jim.

"Lissa," I said yet again, wishing I had gone elsewhere for lunch.

"Jim De Witt," he said. "You were at the fundraiser the other night, weren't you?"

It was surprising that he remembered. Apparently he hadn't reached the blackout stage, yet. Good for him, not so good for me.

"Yes," I admitted reluctantly. "What brings you to Dobbs Ferry?" I asked.

"I had a lunch meeting here. I'm on my way out," he said.

He didn't look at all pathetic today. He looked fit, well rested and tanned, as he had at the fundraiser before he got drunk. He looked like a man I'd like to know. I had to remind myself in detail how he had behaved. Better to spend your time with ordinary sane people than to get into some soul-destroying game with the rich and crazy. Still, I knew that Nick would be disappointed if I didn't take this opportunity to find out more about Jim's Monet, so I invited him to sit down.

"I enjoyed seeing your collection," I said. "It's wonderful that you have an appreciation for such a variety of artworks."

"Thank you," he said. "I have to give Diana credit for some of them. Even though she calls it 'my' collection, she's had a hand in some of the recent acquisitions. Tell me, Elizabeth, what's your favorite style of art?" he asked.

"Impressionism," I told him. "Hands down. It combines feeling, intellect and respectable technique. I think people who put so much importance on the novelty aspect of art are missing the qualities that really make it so wonderful. Sure, it was new and different, but it wasn't only that."

"I think you're very clever to see that," he said. Somehow I felt I should be cautious about taking his praise at face value. "Peter told me that you do some writing about art."

"Yes, I write for InTarrytown.com."

He looked very serious. "What kinds of things do you write about?"

"Sometimes technique. I share my experiences painting outdoors or doing... um, mixing colors," I said. I had almost mentioned doing portraits, but I caught myself just in time. I didn't want to go there again. "I've also written about art shows and paintings that can be seen locally, such as the collections at Kykuit and Sunnyside."

"I think I might have seen some of those articles," he said. "It's that local news website?"

"Yes. I'm very flattered that you remember them," I said. Damn. He wasn't going to be nice, I hoped. Never trust a drinker, I thought, because they can be nice enough until you're on the hook, personally or professionally, and then turn mean or childish. Or both. But sometimes the good things about them make it tempting.

"I do," he said. "They're very good. And have you written about private collections?"

His tone and challenging facial expression told me that wouldn't be a good thing. So that's what this was about. Better this than the nude painting. "I won't say anything about your home. I only write about collections open to the public," I assured him. "What would be the point of arousing curiosity about something they could never see?"

"Yes, yes," he said. "You are a clever woman. And anything else that's not intended for the public, you also know that it wouldn't be a good idea to write about that?" He looked a little threatening. Not embarrassed in the least. So much for being nice.

I gulped and said, "I certainly have no interest in betraying anyone's trust in me."

He looked approving. "Yes, one has little to gain from that. I'm glad you understand." He got up to leave. I hadn't had a chance to ask anything about the Monet.

He walked up front to the cashier, who at the moment was George, the owner. They spoke for a few minutes, and I noticed twice that Jim turned around towards me and George also looked in my direction.

When I asked for my check, the waiter said it had already been paid.

CHAPTER EIGHT

That night was the monthly meeting of the Artists' Guild. We didn't have a regular meeting place, so members offered their homes or studios on a rotating basis. Tonight it was at Danny Bogart's studio. When I knocked on the door, he opened it almost immediately.

"Hey, Lissa, Lissa, Mona Lissa." He made it into a little off-key tune. "Come in, Mona Lissa, let nothing stand in your way," he sang loudly and tunelessly, slurring his words.

Great, now Danny was high on something. I wasn't even going to speculate about what it might be.

"Hey, Danny," I replied, "I guess I'm the first one here again. Can I help you with anything?" Danny hadn't been much of a host in previous meetings, but at least he was centrally located. His studio, the converted garage on Kaldenberg, didn't come with amenities such as adequate heat. We'd talked about meeting in one of the restaurants this time, but he'd insisted that he had something to show us he couldn't bring anywhere else, so here we were.

"Nah, just sit down. You don't want a beer, do you?"

"No thanks," I answered, "but it's cold. I could make some coffee if you'd like. I brought cookies."

"Cool," he said. "Do you have any coffee?"

I sighed and said I'd run down to the grocery. This meant not only laying out the money for coffee and milk, but having to face re-entry into the world of Danny Bogart. Once you were there for a while, you built up some tolerance, but going in took some stamina.

Danny was the wild man of the Artists' Guild and his work reflected it. I didn't consider myself the least bit prudish and, despite my caution at Jim's approach, under the right circumstances I had no problem painting nudes of either sex and any age. Still, I recoiled at Danny's garish 10-foot-wide and 6-foot high canvases with their unhappy, sick-looking nudes. Their roots seemed to be some sort of marriage between the subject matter of Lucian Freud and Francis Bacon, with some of the cloisonné technique of Van Gogh. It wasn't a happy union.

When I got back Anne and Johnny had arrived, to my relief, and so had Miles Armstrong and Margaret Merriweather. Miles was an Ivy League grad who until recently had worked at the local museum doing the graphic design of their exhibitions. He did matting and framing, made the informational labels for each artwork on the computer, and stenciled the large text that went directly on the gallery walls. He was very tall, with sandy hair and classic features, and I usually considered him very attractive. Unfortunately, he'd recently lost his job and become unpleasantly sullen. Margaret was fiftyish, short with black, curly hair. She was a librarian and clay sculptor who disapproved of nudes but didn't try to get anyone to stop painting them. Every once in a while I saw her look at one of Danny's paintings and visibly shudder. Tiffany Grimes, a performance artist, came in shortly after my return. She was a bubble-headed blond (literally, with poufy yellow hair, as well as figuratively like Diana) wearing a short, tight blue dress that showed an abundance of cleavage. I had no idea how she could make it through the winter so bare. Her career had taken off at the same time she'd begun sleeping with a museum official. Strictly coincidence, of course. Sure.

Ramón Baleras came in next, with a booming "Hola, amigos." His voice was much bigger than he was. From New Jersey by way of Mexico, he was a young guy with a toddler and a very pregnant wife who called him constantly on his cellphone. "I am her courage," he'd explained with a smile at the last meeting. Though he hadn't been in Tarrytown for long, he'd gotten to know a lot of people quickly in his job as waiter in the nearby Tarry Café, and the owner was showing some of Ramón's attractive, life-affirming folk-art pieces.

Mandy and Jack Terwilliger, both photographers, were supposed to come but Mandy called to say Jack was on deadline for a magazine piece, and she was staying home to help him. Charlie Fischer, a dancer and teacher, had scheduled a performance for his children's group, so that left us with just a small group.

"The primary thing we need to discuss tonight," said Margaret, "is the Outdoor Art Fair. We've got the list of artists and performers from last year and we need to start contacting everyone to see who's coming back."

Anne volunteered to take part of the list.

"Anyone else?" Margaret asked. She looked around the room, but no one spoke up. "Come on, folks, I can't do everything. I've got family coming in this weekend and then we have special events all month at the library."

Ramón said, "Okay, I will take some. I can call in the morning before I go to work."

Tiffany raised her hand and said, "Did the funds come through for my belly-dancing? Everyone loved it last year. I want the posters in color this time."

Margaret made a face and said "Not yet, Tiffany. And nobody's the star here. We're all pitching in."

"But Roger told me not to do it this year unless I got more publicity. He said I have to be careful and make decisions that will advance my career."

"Well, that's your decision," said Margaret, in her firmest librarian voice, as if reprimanding a noisy child. "I know they liked you, but I can't deal with this right now. I'm sure we can work something out later."

Danny broke in, saying "I didn't think the Fair was so good last year."

Margaret flinched. "What was the problem, Danny?" she asked in an icy tone.

"The no-nudes policy really sucked. What's the difference between a belly dancer and nude paintings?"

"Well, it is in a public park in the middle of the day. There has to be a limit. Okay, I'll grant you Tiffany's dancing wasn't aimed at the kids, but she was far from nude. Couldn't you do something else for it, just to make a few sales that day and get the families interested in art?"

It went along like that for a while, with Danny raising objections to everything. Finally Miles said, "Give it up, Margaret. You're wasting your time. Why don't we get out of here and finish the meeting at the café?"

"You're both full of it," yelled Danny. "Neither one of you is a real artist. What do you know? Don't tell me what to do." He sounded like a four-year-old.

Miles stiffened. Margaret sniffed contemptuously. I was not eager to sit through a nasty clash of egos so I tried in my most soothing voice to calm things down. "Look, we're all talented people here," I said, looking first at Danny and then Miles and Margaret. "Let's try to get together on this festival. It does give us a platform for our work. None of us is doing so well financially that we can afford to miss the opportunity."

Danny took a long drink from a beer mug, burped, grunted, and stared at the wall. Then he got up and walked over to his easel, picked up a two-inch flat brush, and started going at his latest creation. Margaret began talking again, listing the musical performers and their various fees and demands, and my attention started drifting. I watched Danny work on the background of his painting, swirling with too many colors as far as I was concerned, and then the legs and then between the legs. Having done so many nudes myself it shouldn't have bothered me, but somehow the pubic seemed too public while we were talking about business. Then he went to the face, switching to a small filbert brush, and with a shock I saw him dip it in black paint and then put the tip--paint and all--in his mouth.

"Danny, what are you doing?" I shouted, and everyone jumped. "Some people think Van Gogh used to do that, and it might be what made him go mad. Paint is toxic."

"Ahh, don't worry," he said. "This is ok. It's just bone black. It's no worse than those little burnt pieces you eat when your hamburger gets overcooked. It helps me get the shape just right."

"Not a good habit, Danny, really," I insisted. "You might forget and do it with one of the cadmiums or a lead white. Try rolling the brush on your palette instead."

He grunted and said, "Maybe for the next painting. I have to finish this one the way I started." His voice had that same childish defiance.

"We're not going to get anything done here," Miles said. "Why are we here in the first place? What was it you wanted to show us, Danny?" he asked. He sounded harsh, I suppose annoyed. "Bring it on."

Danny got up slowly, maybe reluctantly, and walked towards the back of the room. He brought a chair with him and placed it in front of a high cabinet. He climbed on the chair and reached as far back as I could see. Then he pulled his hand out, empty, and got down.

"Never mind," he said. "I don't think I want to do this now. I'll show you some other time."

"I think that's a wise choice," Miles said.

I wondered what he meant, but I didn't ask. The meeting broke up on that awkward note.

CHAPTER NINE

"We're here to see Juliana Le Grande," Nick told the guard at the front desk. "We have an appointment." He'd asked me to come with him so he could get an idea of what was so special about Paul McGill's work that it had made him famous. I'd shown him the review in *Art in America*, but he wanted to see some in person and talk to the curator. I wasn't impressed with the type of work Paul was doing. I didn't think I could explain his success to Nick or anyone else in terms of quality.

I looked around at the lobby, which was glass and more glass, including the elevator. It might have looked like a hotel except for the number of sculptures, most of which looked like construction fences or supplies, or just debris. One or two were mildly interesting. A woman walked up to us, tall and cool, dressed in a straight black sheath and boots with tall spike heels. Her hair was long and straight, nearly black, and her makeup was dramatic, with black eyeliner and long lashes above cheeks carefully accentuated with crimson blusher. Her lipstick was vivid crimson, like Alizarin straight out of the tube. The image of her taking a tube of paint and applying it to her lips popped into my head. Of course she didn't do that. I'd spent too much time with Danny.

"I am Juliana Le Grande. You are here to see the work of Paul McGill?" She spoke formally and enunciated every syllable.

I let Nick confirm.

"Please come this way," she said. "We are fortunate enough to have some excellent examples of his creative intelligence." We walked down a long hallway lined with prints and photos. Juliana set a formidable pace with her long legs. Nick could match it, but I struggled to keep up. There was no time to look at the works on the walls, but at a glance they were too severe for me. I found it ironic that, in an age where pleasure is avidly pursued in sex and possessions, a lot of art is considered "great" if the average person wouldn't like it. Curators and gallerists don't actually say that, of course, but the more difficult it is to appreciate the work, the clearer it must be that if you say you love it you're part of the "smarter" elite.

I was definitely a resister.

We walked into the gallery. Nick's expression made it obvious that he was not impressed. There was a pile of glass chips on the floor on one side and a group of orange wood boxes on the other. An assistant approached Juliana and held out a paper for her to sign. While they were talking, I turned to Nick and whispered, "Great, all the wisdom of the ages reaches a crescendo with this."

Juliana turned back to us. I was sure she hadn't heard me, but she seemed to sense our reaction. She probably encountered the same thing all the time. "These are two of the most respected artists in the New York area today," she said in a stern voice. "Art has changed and we have to follow the lead of the innovators," she added.

"Where is Paul's work?" Nick asked.

"Over here," Juliana said, and we followed her to the next gallery.

We walked through a narrow hallway hung with black-and-white hand-drawn prints of various weapons, from Colt 45's to AK37's. Someone had sublimated, at least for as long as it took to so lovingly depict these death machines. "Did he do these?" Nick asked.

"No," replied Juliana, "these were done by Maxwell Grace, who lives in Woodstock." I imagined how happy the people of that small artsy town must be at having such a violence-loving person among them. We walked into a large gallery at the end of the hall, and were faced with several large canvases that were each untouched except for one barely visible dot or line on each. Variety apparently came from choosing a different spot on each canvas. I imagined two collectors discussing whether theirs had a dot on the top right or near the middle. One of them might gasp with envy at hearing what the other had managed to acquire.

"This is it?" asked Nick, since Juliana had stopped in the middle of the room.

"No, no," she said, following our gazes. "*This* is it," she said, turning and gesturing towards a small stack of jars of olives, nuts and cherries on the floor behind her.

"Where?" I said, and she pointed again at what I had taken to be supplies arriving for an evening reception.

"Yes," she replied, "this is Paul McGill's most significant work."

I decided not to offer my critique. She wouldn't be interested, anyway. Instead, I asked, "Where did Paul study?"

"He did his undergraduate work at Columbia and of course he got his got his MFA at Yale."

"Of course," I echoed, and gave Nick a look. With all due respect for the other departments, I thought Yale Fine Arts was just sad and wrong. I'm sure they'd feel the same about me, and they'd laugh at my lack of worldly success. I was happy with my choices, though, and sure of my views, born of years of independent, unbeholden-to-big-tuition-bills study.

"He was a rebel," Juliana continued, ignoring the tone of my interjection and any inferences that might be drawn from it. "He was considered a genius at Yale, and was snapped up by a major New York gallery before he got his diploma."

"What's so special about this?" asked Nick.

"Fair enough," Juliana said. "We're not all educated in the fine arts." I had told Nick to expect attitude and he didn't visibly react to her condescension. "Paul's work, of course," she began, "draws attention to the very nature of consumption. Much like Andy Warhol in his time, Paul draws us to the consideration of the very nature of gathering and sharing. He has an unerring instinct to do enough and no more to draw out of us what he does not put in the work himself." She began to sway a little, as though overcome with the emotion of seeing the divine light. "We are like his puppets, under his control," she said. "The power of art is unrivalled," she added.

I wondered if this might be true for people who were heavily under the influence of drugs, but personally I considered myself free of Paul's presumably colossal power. Nick showed every sign of having avoided the bonds as well.

"Was this the type of work he always did?" asked Nick. "Did he ever do more traditional artwork?"

I knew he was wondering if Paul could be skilled as a forger.

"He did some paintings early in his career, but they were not considered to be ground-breaking," Juliana said. "They were very competent in their understanding of art history, of course, as you would expect from a genius."

"Do you have any examples of these?" Nick asked.

"No, they would not be images we would be interested in giving our limited gallery space. All of the work we own by Mr. McGill is installation, conceptual art."

"Do you know where I might find some of his paintings?" asked Nick as we followed her through three more rooms of art whose power was not lighting my world. She led the way to a small, barely visible white door and opened it onto a tiny, surprisingly cluttered office. I had imagined that it would be almost as minimal as Paul's artwork, but I wasn't even close. She removed some *Art in America* magazines and some newspapers from a couple of chairs and gestured for us to sit.

As she sat down, I saw just a flash of a Monet calendar as she whisked it behind a stack of books.

I felt a warm, brief pounding in my chest. It wasn't because she owned a Monet calendar, so unlike the work she was promoting, because anyone could have given it to her. It was the surreptitiousness of the movement and the fact that she didn't look us in the eye for what seemed like a long time after.

Could it be that Juliana was the living confirmation of one of my speculations in my art opinion pieces? Could it be that she really didn't care for the work she had to deal with on a daily basis but had to accept it to work in the field? Mere curators, I felt, couldn't fight the businessman-backed twenty-first century commercial "fine art" machine. Some of those businessmen were the same ones selling derivatives and other hyper-cerebral products with un-confirmable value. Like the artworks, they were worth a lot because the experts said so. As they prevailed, others followed, investing in work because it was likely to increase in financial value, simply because they were in vogue. Maybe the Monet calendar revealed her personal art interests and she was afraid that her taste for the traditional would become publicly known. That would be a career "crime" well outside of Nick's jurisdiction.

I didn't say anything, but I wouldn't forget that moment.

Juliana went to her file cabinet and pulled out a large number of clippings in a folder labeled, "McGill, Paul." She placed them on a small table near us and said, "Be my guest."

We looked through them in just a few minutes. There was nothing to suggest that Paul had ever had a significant interest in the work of past master figurative painters. I noted the references just in case I wanted a second look, and we were on our way, with things no clearer than before.

CHAPTER TEN

Nick pulled up to my door and I got in the car. "I'm not sure where Johnny's studio is. Do you know?" I asked. We were looking at more local artwork, this time the decidedly un-famous productions of Johnny Giardelli's studio.

"Hey, this is my town," he said, "I know every inch of it. He's in a building on the grounds of a garden apartment complex near the Sheraton, in a section they use for community activities. In the back they have a couple of rooms they rent out at below market rates for workshops and storage. Semi-finished, like garages or basements. Your guy has the one farthest from the road. Nice and quiet, for whatever he wants to cook up."

"He's not my guy," I protested mildly, figuring Nick didn't really think he was. "I just know him from the Artists' Guild." Nick smiled. I sat back and enjoyed being with him, despite Gina's cautions. I thought of the time I'd made him laugh hard, and it was a billowing sound from deep inside that expressed great pleasure. I enjoyed that. He was undeniably masculine and still he felt that art matters. What more could a woman want?

We arrived sooner than I would've liked, parked and walked down the path behind the building until we reached a large red door. Nick knocked and soon the door swung open with a loud groan. I could smell turpentine and garlic.

"Yes?" said Johnny. He was short and stocky and almost stereotypically the disheveled artist, with long, curly dark hair that hadn't seen a shower any time in the recent past. "Oh, hi Alissa, what can I do for you?" The words were pleasant enough but the tone was grudging.

Although Johnny had always been well-behaved with me, I was cautious and kept him at a bit of a distance because I knew he had a dark side. He'd confided in me about arguments and relationships that had threatened to turn physically violent. Still, I gave him the benefit of the doubt. I hoped and mostly believed that he would always stop short of physical confrontations.

"This is my friend Nick. I was telling him about the paintings you had in the Artists' Guild show last month and he's hoping to see some of your work," I said. This was true, of course, but not exactly as it sounded. I felt a little guilty, but if I was going to continue being part of the investigation I was going to have to get used to role-playing.

"Are you interested in buying something?" he asked, suspicious and hopeful at the same time. Buyers didn't drop out of trees these days. The world was full of artists without sales, and the Van Gogh legend of eventual recognition was embraced by millions to keep their spirits up.

"Could be," Nick said, "I buy paintings if I like them, from time to time. I haven't bought anything for a while and I wondered if you might have something special."

"OK," said Johnny, but it took a minute before he stood aside to let us come in.

A few Chinese food containers on a small table near the door explained the garlic smell. "Moo Shu Pork?" Johnny offered.

"No man, but thanks," Nick said. I let that stand for me, too.

"Pretty cool," said Nick as he looked around at the paintings, and he made a little whistling noise. I couldn't help feeling a twinge of jealousy at Nick's interest. The artwork was pretty good, and seemed to show an absence of inner turmoil. Johnny had a good classical sense of proportion, composition, and subdued color. To my eyes it meant that he was in control of his emotions, at least when he was at work.

It might also mean that he was capable of doing forgeries.

Nick walked around the studio, commenting every once in a while, especially when he came across a recognizable local scene. Johnny visibly relaxed.

"I did this one last summer," he said, pointing out a small lake scene with a glassy reflection of tasteful sap green foliage. "And this one is brand-new," he reported, "larger than I usually do." It was a wide canvas with a sunny Hudson River/Palisades scene. You could tell it was a windy day by the choppy water that didn't mirror the sky or the Palisades. Waves break up reflections, so in this work the overall color of the Palisades had found its way into the water only in small, well-distributed bits of color. It's harder to do than a scene with mirroring water, and Johnny had handled it well.

We stayed for about 15 minutes, looking at various paintings and drawings and chatting about pigments and oils. We walked past closets and cupboards that might conceal a few "private" works in progress, but Johnny didn't seem any more nervous than the average rarely-paid, unrecognized, highly-skilled professional. If anything, I'd say that he was sorry to see us go. Nick can be a charmer.

He left the distinct impression that he would be back to make a purchase.

"So what did you think?" Nick asked when we were back in the car.

"There was some pretty nice work there."

"Do you think he's capable?"

"Artistically or ethically?" I asked.

"The art is your department," he said. "I can handle the rest."

"Artistically, yes, and I'll tell you anyway that my guess is that Johnny gets enough satisfaction out of making the work to keep him honest. It looks like he's at peace when he paints."

"It has nothing to do with that. We're not talking about satisfaction, we're talking about money. How does he pay the rent?" Nick said.

"There was something that bothered me, although I'm sure it wasn't him. Johnny told me he'd been questioned once by the Greenburgh police, and I couldn't tell whether he was a witness or a suspect. He said that someone he worked with had been found pretty badly beaten. He seemed very upset and frightened."

"When was that?" Nick asked.

"It must be a couple of years ago, so I guess he must be in the clear," I said. My voice sounded a little tentative to me, and I knew Nick would pick up on it.

"But you wonder if they just couldn't make it stick?" he asked.

I nodded. "If he could live with himself after doing that--and I don't think he was the one, but just if—he could certainly live with being a forger," I said. "I've read that some of them are resentful about lack of recognition for their own original work, and use that to justify the crime. 'If people are too stupid to recognize the value of my work they deserve to be tricked.'"

"I'll see what I can find out," he said.

CHAPTER ELEVEN

The minute I saw Nick the next day I knew something was wrong. I rushed to Bellini's to work on the mural as soon as I finished with my afternoon students. The heavenly sugar-and-vanilla fragrance of the freshly baked cones met me as usual, and I inhaled it with pleasure. Nick was in the back, wiping tables intently. Way too intently, I could see when I got close, since the tables were already sparkling clean.

"Hey," I said, trying to ignore the queasy feeling in my stomach. A man in a dark, expensive-looking suit was the only customer at the moment. He was all the way in the back, sitting in front of one of my paintings. I noticed him right away because of the suit, and after that I noticed that he looked pretty attractive in it. He was probably around forty-five, with broad shoulders and wavy, honey-brown hair. Everything else about him seemed arrow-straight and chilly. I thought I'd seen him around, but not at Bellini's. Not dressed like that, anyway. Almost everyone who came in was dressed casually and looked like they were relaxing.

"Lissa, um hm, hello," said Nick, looking uncomfortable.

"I think I'll start Village Hall today," I said, gesturing towards the mural, lamely attempting to wish away whatever the problem was.

Nick glanced at the man in the suit, who nodded, and then turned towards me.

"Lissa, I'd like you to meet someone," Nick said. "Would you like a coffee?"

"Sure, thanks," I said. I'd already had three cups, but it would postpone whatever was coming. I went up front, looking at the completed sections of my mural as I walked, drawing some strength from what I had accomplished. I poured myself a cup, too nervous to stop pouring when it was full. I slammed the cup down and withdrew my hand in pain as the coffee overflowed onto it. I wiped it off and walked slowly towards the back, trying not to spill any more, with about ninety-five percent success. The other five percent gave me the opportunity to head to the front again for more napkins. Finally out of ideas about how to stall, I joined them. They were sitting together. At least they were on opposite sides of the table, which meant that I could slip in next to Nick.

"Lissa, this is Chief Mercer," Nick said.

"Chief?" I asked. I'd managed another stall, since I already knew the Fire Chief and this guy was unlikely to be head of an Indian tribe.

"Chief of Police, Tarrytown P.D." the man in question answered crisply, in a strong, deep voice. "I've heard quite a lot about you," he added.

"Good, I hope," I said, trying to sound confident.

"Well, you've certainly made a friend in Lieutenant Bellini. But I would be lax in my duties if I didn't get to know more. We've got an active investigation going on and I hear that you've been playing quite a role in it. I want to make sure the Lieutenant here isn't being taken in by a pretty face."

"Thank you for the compliment," I said, though well aware of the unpleasant implication. "You know, I'm sure, that I'm working on the mural here?" He nodded. "That's what I do," I continued. "I like to think it's a good job. I hope my skill is visible." I gestured at my work along the wall.

He made a non-committal gesture with his head, not quite nodding but not shaking it either. "Tell me a little about yourself," he said. "I'm not an old townie like Nick. I've seen the mural, I've seen you on the street painting, and I know you're a writer, but that's about it. Are you from this area?"

"No, I'm from the city. I painted my way up the river and fell in love with Tarrytown." I looked at Nick. Why was he so tense? I was on the level, he must know that. The coffee wasn't sitting in my stomach all that well. I could feel its heat coming back up. Did I have an antacid with me?

"I heard you spent some time at the Metropolitan Museum. It was in one of your articles," he said.

"Yes, I spent a couple of years at the museum," I said, "doing copies of master paintings and then two original paintings of the galleries."

"Why did you spend so long on copies?" he asked.

I gulped down some more coffee in spite of the burning and churning of my stomach. Clearly this could go somewhere very unpleasant if he didn't get who I was. My own hard-won expertise could be used against me. "It's a traditional educational step," I explained. "It helps you see how the masters worked."

"Didn't you have teachers for that?" he asked.

"Claude Monet and Edouard Manet weren't teaching at my art school," I said. "The teachers who were there were okay, but not geniuses."

"So you made copies?" he asked, in a mildly friendly tone that didn't reduce my discomfort at his suspiciousness.

"For a while. Only for a while. If you're a serious artist you need to find your own voice. If you turn around and look at the canvas on the wall behind you, or the finished section of mural up front, you'll see that I have found my own style, and the discipline to produce a very complex painting."

"I congratulate you," he said, in a tone that might have been just a little sarcastic. "And what did you do with the copies?" he asked.

"I sold some of them at the Museum," I told him, "in full view of the public and the security guards and any curators who might be wandering by. There's an Education Department there. Everybody supports the artists who come there to do copies."

"Lissa told me all about this," Nick said, "and there's nothing wrong with what she did. She's a serious professional."

"So copying art is a good way to make money?" the Chief asked.

"No, no, no," I said quickly. Did he have to belabor this? "I didn't make much at all. I was there to learn. I left there far more capable than when I arrived." I wondered if I could ask for a hot-fudge sundae. There was a bar next door that a lot of people might think about in a situation like this, but when things got tough my mind went for the sweets.

"The museum must have concerns about forgery," he said.

"I'm sure they do, but that has nothing to do with me." I looked at Nick. He nodded encouragingly. I felt a little better.

"How do you know?" he asked.

"They were very supportive. They made it pleasant for me to be there. They wouldn't have done that if they'd thought I was doing something wrong."

Nick broke in. "I know Lissa," he said. "She's okay."

I smiled gratefully and went on, "I spent a lot of time talking with the guards. They know a lot more about art than most people realize. That's why they've chosen that particular job. They're not just human burglar alarms. And they could tell I was a serious artist," I told him, hoping I didn't sound too defensive.

"Okay, okay," the chief said abruptly. "We'll continue this another time. I've got things to do." He turned towards Nick. "She'd better be what you say she is," he told Nick, "or it's both your heads." The tone wasn't as hostile as the words, I thought. Maybe it was just bluster. He turned back to me and said, "We'll be keeping an eye on you, and don't ever doubt it." Was it wishful thinking that I saw a hint of approval in his eyes?

Nick walked him to the front door. I couldn't hear their conversation. When he came back he offered me a package of cookies, sat down across from me, and told me not to worry. "He'll see who you are, if he's got half a brain in his head," he said.

"Does he?" I asked, still a little concerned. No one had doubted me like that before, but of course the subject of forgery had come up among my fellow copyists at the museum. Not that anyone had declared a career path in that direction, but the reality was that there were some who might use their skills that way.

"I hope he does," Nick said. "Anyway, he's only temporary. My chief is on sick leave. He could be back soon. He wouldn't have the least question about you, Lissa. He knows people and he knows my judgment is solid."

"Has this guy been with the department long?"

"No, he just showed up a couple of months ago," Nick told me. "He's some politician's brother-in-law."

"Does he know what he's doing?" I asked.

"He's got lots of degrees," Nick said, without enthusiasm. "He didn't work his way up through the ranks, so I don't know him. Maybe he's okay. He gets his face in the news a lot at charity events. He may be a good guy."

I didn't like the subtle undercurrent of anxiety coming from Nick. He was usually full of confidence and *joie de vivre*.

"He's got a lot of power?" I asked.

Nick visibly pulled himself up. "You'll be okay. I'm with you 100 percent," he said emphatically.

That was more like it.

I wasn't sure I should work on the mural after all, feeling a little shaky, but I got out my paints and started squeezing out my little bits of alizarin crimson and French ultramarine onto the palette. A group of children came in and made a beeline for me, bubbling with excitement about what I was doing. By the time I had all my colors out, I was ready to get to work. My art served a purpose to the community. Even the chief would have to admit I had no need to turn to forgery when I could do my own valuable works.

Wouldn't he?

CHAPTER TWELVE

The phone rang at 8 A.M. the next day. I'd gone to sleep at my usual late hour and knew that something must be up, because no one who knows me well would call so early. It wasn't even time for most offices to open. Art isn't just a deeply-felt calling for me; I also like the hours.

I reached for the phone with some trepidation. Probably American Express reminding me how much they'd like some money from me. "Hello?" I mumbled, trying to sound awake.

"Alissa?" a man's voice asked.

"Yes, who's this?" The slightly whiny voice was familiar, but I couldn't place it.

"It's Danny, Danny Bogart," he said, sounding nervous.

At least it wasn't a family emergency. "What can I do for you?" I asked politely, though I really had been enjoying a very pleasant dream about running my fingers across the dark hairs on Nick's muscular arm and I was pretty annoyed at the interruption.

"Could you help me with something?" he asked. He might be a wild man but his voice sounded a little childish. Maybe even frightened.

"What's up?" I was coming fully awake and starting to be interested. Maybe this had something to do with the case.

"You remember I was going to show something at the meeting? And then I didn't do it? Could you come by for a few minutes tonight, like 7:15?" he asked, almost pleading. "There was something you said. I'm in a jam and I need advice."

"Ok," I said, though still a little reluctant to get involved with Danny's problems. Wasn't I just helping Nick with assessing the art? "Can you give me some idea what you're talking about?" I asked, but even as I finished the sentence I realized that there'd been a soft "click" and he'd hung up as soon as I said ok.

I tried to go back to sleep but I couldn't stop wondering what it was.

I was working on the portrait today. I showered and headed to my studio.

Danny kept popping into my mind all day, but I managed to make some progress despite him. I stayed with the simpler sections of the painting, the landscape areas that I was doing in a loose, Impressionist style. I didn't attempt to work on the girls' faces. In portraits, the facial expressions sometimes come from the artist and not the subjects, and that's *not* the mark of a master. Maybe tomorrow.

That turned out to be way too optimistic.

I washed my brushes around 6:30 and set up the easels and tables for the students who would be coming the following afternoon. I decided to go in for a cup of coffee on my way down the block to Danny's, at a popular hangout for the caffeine and music crowd. I could have gotten the coffee at Bellini's and looked for Nick there, but it was out of my way and I didn't have much time. Coffee Masters was right near Danny's studio. I had a quick latte there which failed to either relax or energize me, but I grabbed my purse and my cellphone and headed out the door.

The night was moonless and dark, but Main Street was well-lit. The air was clear and crisp. I walked slowly past the antique shops and the entrance to the Tarrytown Theatre, already bustling with people arriving for the evening concert. I wasn't as high up on the hill as when I'd been at Jim and Diana's, but the warmly-lit houses and bridge in the distance were still beautiful. If I could reach out and capture a solid replica of the image of the bridge from this spot, it would be the right size to wear as a jeweled lapel pin. It was a night scene begging to be painted, and I'd have to find a way. Art for me is at its best when used to celebrate and preserve life's pleasures and treasures. I was always happy when, because of my work, somebody told me they had stopped taking the beauty of the area for granted.

At the end of the block I turned to my right, just as the tantalizing garlicky aroma emanating from the Chinese takeout restaurant filled the air. I managed to ignore its temptation and keep walking another half-block to Danny's place.

I opened the gate to the path beside the house, and walked towards the former garage. Rock music was blaring. Danny was going to have to turn it down or I wouldn't hear a word he said. The big swing-up former car door looked like it had been opened recently and not placed completely correctly back in its closed position. Danny used it sometimes for moving very large canvases, but people came and went by the side door. He didn't answer when I knocked, so I tried again, louder. My knuckles hurt by the third try, and it was much darker on this street. Tarrytown is a pretty safe place, but you can never be sure these days.

I tried the door and it opened.

I went in.

CHAPTER THIRTEEN

And that's when I found him.

Dead eyes staring at nothing.

Soon after my call to the police the small studio swarmed with officers looking at the body, at the things on the tables, at the easel. There was a swirl of activity that couldn't be real, it seemed. I expected to wake up and find that the only thing wrong was that too much steam heat in the bedroom had given me a nightmare.

The young policeman who'd arrived first said, "I've seen you at the ice cream shop. Do you remember me?"

I nodded, even though my memory wasn't really up to the task at the moment.

'We've called in Detective Bellini," he continued, "and I know he'll want to talk to you."

"Yes, of course," I said. *Hurry, Nick!* I needed him. "How long will he be?"

"We got him at home, Ma'am. He's just a few minutes away."

"Oh, good," I said. "Can I sit down?"

He found me a chair near the door and I sank into it and kept my eyes off Danny's still face.

In three or four minutes Nick burst in and exclaimed, "What happened, Lissa? Are you all right?"

"I'm ok," I said, "but I've had better days. So has Danny. I don't know what happened. He asked me to come, and I walked in and there he was."

"Did you see anyone on the street when you came?"

"No. Not nearby. In fact, it was because it was so dark and deserted that, when he didn't come to the door after I knocked and knocked, I tried the door and let myself in."

Nick walked over to the body and bent down. "He's still warm," he said. "It's lucky you didn't get here a little earlier. If you'd walked in on it..."

I felt sicker. "Couldn't it be natural causes?" I asked hopefully, although that would make the situation only a little bit better.

"We'll see. Jeez, this place is a mess. These paintings are awful. How did he look at these all day?"

"You know, artistic freedom. It's certainly not my taste," I explained. "Maybe a critic did him in," I said, slightly hysterical, my voice high-pitched and wobbly.

"Take it easy," he said. "You were here before, for the meeting you told me about. Are things are out of place?"

I took a deep breath and got up to walk around, looking and trying to remember how things had been arranged.

"Don't touch anything," Nick said. "Look from here."

"I knocked over those tubes of paint tonight," I said, pointing at the area near what had been Danny. I gulped hard. "It was them or me. I don't know what else might be different. We were all talking about a lot of things that other time, and I didn't look around that much. I'd been here once or twice before that, but the only thing I really remember about the physical setup was that at one point he went over there to his easel and started working. He took a paintbrush, loaded it with black paint, and put it in his mouth to shape it."

"In his mouth? That sounds a little crazy."

"I think so, too, but he's not the only one who's ever done it. It's called pointing. I warned him that some people think Van Gogh's madness may have been a result of doing that, but he shrugged it off. He said it was ok. He said it was just charcoal pigment, like burnt bits in food."

"They'll be looking for any possible toxins with someone this young," said Nick. He looked around some more, put on crime scene gloves, and started carefully looking through stacks of paintings and sketchbooks. "His style," Nick said slowly, as though thinking it through as he spoke, "is it all his own? Does it look like any famous artist's work?"

"Lucien Freud, Francis Bacon, certainly," I replied, "with a touch of Van Gogh. But it's derivative, not imitative of any one artist. I can't see an intent to deceive, especially since he shows—showed this work under his own name."

"Do you think he could have had other work that might be more deceptive?"

"I wouldn't know everything he did. Of course there could. I don't think it could be connected, but he did bring us here for the meeting to show us something he said he couldn't bring if we had the meeting in public, and then he decided not to. But he wouldn't show us a forgery, would he?"

"Unlikely," Nick agreed. "Not the whole group. Any idea what it might've been?"

"No, none. All I know is that he called me today and said he wanted to show it to me. That's all."

"Any idea where this thing was?"

"Maybe. At the meeting he went over to that cabinet in the back, stuck his hand in, then pulled it out empty and said he'd changed his mind. He didn't actually say it was in there. Maybe he was doing something else and then was going to get the thing to show us afterward, until he decided against it."

We looked at the cabinet I indicated. The door was wide open and the top shelf, where Danny had reached in that day, was clearly empty. Nick gestured to one of his men and he went over to the cabinet with an evidence kit.

"Do you see any materials that could be used to paint a forgery?" Nick asked me.

I looked at the surface of the worktable. Tubes were strewn all over it, in no particular order. They were Grumbachers, not the best quality but certainly quite common and thoroughly modern.

"Anything look wrong?" Nick asked.

"Not that I can see," I answered. "You can't do 150-year-old paintings with these Grumbachers. Some paint companies go back that far, but these are commercially made and will have all kinds of modern pigments and fillers."

"Okay, keep looking."

I looked at the shelves above the table, and saw some jars and a ceramic bowl. "Can I see those things?" I asked, indicating the shelf.

Nick told the photographer to record the exact positions, and he took several photos from several different angles. Then Nick put on gloves and brought the bowl to me. He held it out but didn't hand it to me. I saw an object inside it.

"That *is* interesting," I said. "It's a mortar and pestle, which can be used to grind pigments to make paint the old way."

Nick placed each object in an evidence bag. He brought over one of the jars from the cabinet and opened it. The smell of linseed oil was obvious. It was red paint, in the scarlet family.

"It could be something he ground himself," I said. "I don't know. It's not a particularly unusual color, but I can't say it's *not* a Grumbacher or a Winsor Newton."

The jars of paint went into evidence bags as well.

Suddenly I had an idea. I didn't know if it would go anywhere. "Can I see those tubes again?" I asked. "I wonder if someone could have put some paint in them that didn't belong there."

"It's pretty hard to get something in a tube. Unless something was injected from the top," Nick said.

"You can buy empty tubes, too," I said. "These tubes are folded and crimped at the bottom, not sealed."

"All right," he said. "Look at them as long as you like."

The tubes had been bagged and he let me handle them through the plastic. I looked at cadmium yellows, pale and deep, cadmium reds regular and deep, ultramarine and pthalo, crimson, burnt sienna, burnt umber, titanium and bone black. Nothing looked wrong. I shook my head and began to hand them back to him.

"Take your time," Nick said. "Does anything look even a little odd?"

"It all *looks* right, I don't know…," I said, thinking furiously. "I wonder if…"

"What have you got?" So much for the "take your time." Nick was breathing down my neck now.

"The label on the black," I said, fingering it through the plastic bag. "It feels a little thick."

Nick grabbed the bag and felt the tube. "You may be right," he said. He asked the photographer to turn on a high-intensity light.

We both saw it at the same time.

Under the strong light, the faint images of another label were barely visible. The print was in Chinese.

Danny wasn't working with ordinary charcoal-pigmented paint at all, at least not today.

"Good work," Nick said. "Ok, we'll take it from here. I'll have someone take you home."

CHAPTER FOURTEEN

Nick gave me the news at the shop the next day. I was painting a store window on the mural, filling it with tiny vases and mirrors with gilded frames, when he came in.

"We got lucky," he said, face much grimmer than the words. "In two ways. First, we know what killed Danny. They found hydrogen sulfide, a small but deadly amount, in his stomach."

"Horrible," I exclaimed. "But how?"

"Like we thought. You spotted it," Nick said. "It was in the relabeled tube, all right. The translation of the Chinese characters is 'antimony black.' Not the harmless pigment he thought he was using. He must've been too addled—or too unaware that he was in such danger-- to pay attention to the thickness you noticed."

I put my palette down on a nearby table, and sank into a chair. "I was looking for something," I said. "He wasn't. But wouldn't he smell it in the paint, or taste it right away?"

"Maybe it had a funny taste, but we'll never be able to ask him. But it wouldn't have been obvious until it hit the stomach," Nick explained. "It forms a gas after it's eaten, and that gas has a nasty rotten egg smell."

"At least we know for sure. It's better to know," I said, and silently wished I didn't have to. "What's the other bit of luck?"

"It's a damned good thing the amount was minimal. We'd all be in trouble, because even inhaling it from the body could've been highly toxic for anyone there."

It began to sink in how dangerous this had become. Not an academic project at all. "Nick, how awful!" I said, "I can't believe this is happening. I can't believe anyone would do such an ugly thing. It had to be someone who knew that Danny put his brushes in his mouth. It had to be someone he trusted. Maybe someone I know."

"We'll get the filthy bastard, Lissa. No one gets away with something like this in my town." His face was full of determination.

I believed him, and I felt a little better.

CHAPTER FIFTEEN

Nick and I were still visiting studios, but now the situation was far more serious.

We arrived at Anne Sutcliffe's just after lunch. I led Nick to the basement entrance at the side of the house. I'd been there several times. We could hear the repetitive, rhythmic noises of hammer meeting chisel. Anne was expecting us and answered our knock quickly.

"Come in, come in," she said. "Just excuse the mess. Stone dust, you know. Quite unavoidable."

Anne was not only a friend, but also stable and reasonable. I'd explained to Nick that I knew her well and would vouch for her absolutely. We walked into a small, low-ceilinged room, extending probably about half the footprint of the house. Several sculptures of various sizes stood in various states of completion, most of them on separate stands. Nick approached one near the door and expressed admiration for its rough-textured form.

"That one's a portrait of my younger son a couple of years ago, when he was seven," she said.

"I've always loved that one," I said. "You really captured his spirit. You know, Nick, that's pretty difficult because kids don't sit for these things very long."

"You're right," she said. "I was lucky to get him to pose for a few minutes while I took photos. I take them from all angles, so I can do a solid form that's right from all sides."

Anne Sutcliffe was a woman who seemed to have it all together. Married to the same man since a year after college, her two children were old enough to take care of themselves in many ways, but young enough to still live at home and need Mom as chauffeur and cook. In between tasks, Anne retreated to her stone-sculpture studio in the basement of her house and got a surprising amount done.

"Are you still working with marble?" I asked.

"Yes," she replied. "It's not the easiest to work with, but it's worth the effort."

"I like it," said Nick, running his hand over the sculpted child's head. "Are you going to keep it rough like this?"

"No, said Anne. "Some people do that, but it'll be like this one." She pointed to an elegantly tall and slender nude. "You start with the cruder chiseling and you get the basic form, then you refine it."

Nick seemed interested. He wandered around for a while, and of course he lingered near the female nudes. I guess for him it was one of those "tough job but somebody has to do it" moments.

"Nice," he said. "Did you know Danny well?"

"We all knew Danny," Anne said with a sigh. "All of us in the Artists Guild. He was a pain sometimes, but I tried to help him. He did have talent and I thought if he were more successful he might calm down and stop getting himself in trouble."

"What did you do?" Nick asked.

"I gave his name to a collector I know from Katonah. I met him when I was in a group show in Peekskill. I don't remember him that well, but I know he was into the wilder things, and as you can see my work is not particularly wild, so why not help a fellow artist?"

"Did they get together?" I asked. I hadn't heard anything about this before.

"I'm not sure," Anne said. "I think so."

"Do you have his name and number?" Nick asked.

"I don't remember his name," she answered, "but I probably have it in my file box. I'll recognize it when I see it." She went over to a desk and pulled out a drawer, then looked in a little file box with cards and notes. "There are so many things I've stuck in here. I guess this is really important?"

"Could be," said Nick. "We can wait."

"I've intended to neaten up this box and divide it into categories, but I just haven't gotten to it yet." She unfolded several pieces of paper and placed them back in the box. She shrugged her head after several tries, and then her face brightened.

"Here it is!" she said. "Gerald Parker. I remember him a little better now. He spends a lot of time and money on art and artists. He told me that he's not just in it for the investment potential. When he gets home from the city at night he takes off his business suit and morphs into someone else he'd much rather be."

Nick copied the information into his cell phone. He thanked her and we made our way out through the maze of sculpture stands. When we got outside, he asked me if I'd ever seen the rest of the basement.

"No, I don't think so," I answered, surprised. "It's probably utilitarian. Laundry, furnace, all that. Why?"

"Just wondering. There was no door from the studio. I just thought that was a little odd."

"I never thought about it," I said. "But I'm sure it doesn't mean anything. Why, you think she's got a forgery studio on the other side?"

"Probably not," he said. Even the small bit of doubt in his voice drove home to me how poisonous this crime could be to innocent people.

CHAPTER SIXTEEN

"Jeez, this house is as big as a hotel," Nick exclaimed softly.

We were standing in front of a massive concrete-and glass structure, two floors high, with a large swimming pool visible through a courtyard next to the front entrance. The shade umbrellas were the only touches of color, folded and tied, but still showing a rainbow of oranges, blues, reds, and purples. In the spring the foliage would add some vivid greens.

"And just as impersonal," I said. "Actually, it reminds me more of an office building. I don't understand why one-percenters like this sort of thing. Unless it reminds them of where they make their money."

The door was opened by a quiet, red-haired maid paradoxically wearing a traditional uniform, complete with frilly apron. She led us through an elegant foyer with immaculate polished hardwood floors, past a curving staircase, to the rear of the open-plan first floor space. In front of a glass and metal wall facing out onto the pool, a man sat on a white leather sofa. He stood up as we approached.

Gerald Parker was aging gracefully, if you like the marionette Botox and dyed-hair look. He was probably around 60, from what I'd read, but his face was unlined and almost childish. You couldn't call his hair blond; yellow was the only word for it. His white linen suit had an Old West dandy look. "Gerald Parker," he said in a strong voice with a western twang that sounded totally phony. "Sit down, sit down," he intoned.

The red-haired maid asked in a soft voice if she could get us drinks. Nick and I opted for coffee. Parker asked for a bourbon and water.

"I didn't know you were bringing a date," he said. "I could have found a cute blond too. Course my wife sometimes gets a little pissy when I do, especially when I bring them home. Thirty-five years of marriage, you'd think she'd understand. But it's nothing a new bracelet can't fix." He winked at me.

"This is Lissa Franklin," Nick told him, "whose artwork is well known in Tarrytown."

"Can't say I've had the pleasure," Parker replied. "You're not here selling anything, I hope, Miss Franklin."

"Far from it," I replied, blushing.

"We're looking into the local art scene," Nick said. "Lissa knows her stuff, so she's helping us. After this we go to Peekskill where she'll show me around the galleries. I heard you're a regular visitor yourself."

Parker stretched his arms and made an encompassing gesture, indicating artwork on the walls. "The gallery scene is my relaxation. Get away from the grind. Tiresome business, sometimes, just dealing with money and more money."

"Art's not an investment for you?" Nick asked.

"I don't have to buy my pieces for their future value. Been lucky with my day job, for sure, can't complain. I pay my dues every morning when I head down to Wall Street on the 5:40 train. .I'm not going to be waiting tables anytime soon, if you know what I mean," he said with a guffaw. He looked a little delicate, but it was clear when he spoke that the testosterone was still flowing. "You can't take it with you, so you might as well do something with it while you're here," he added. "My wife used to drag me to the art shows and I ended up getting hooked."

"So Anne Sutcliffe is right. She told us you're the real thing," I said. "A collector who buys out of genuine appreciation for the work. She said you've been helpful to a lot of local artists. Even a patron to some."

"Anne Sutcliffe, yes, I think I remember her. A lovely woman. Yes, yes, she knows her stuff. I've encouraged a few talents. Financially," he acknowledged. "Anne's not one of those. She doesn't need it. Husband's got a good job. And her work's a little tame for me."

"How about Danny Bogart?" Nick asked. "Did you have any involvement with him and his work?"

"Heard about that awful thing, of course," said Parker. "In Tarrytown, of all places. Yes, I knew him. Guy didn't know when to keep his mouth shut. I finally dropped him and so did the galleries here. He made a scene at a reception for his last show. It probably would have been his last altogether, if not for this terrible business. Now they'll show them."

"What was the problem at the exhibition?" Nick asked.

"Oh, one thing after another. He didn't like the way they hung his pieces. And he made a big mistake opening his mouth to a critic who wasn't impressed. But I don't know anyone who'd be angry enough to get rid of him completely."

"Did you buy much of his work?" I asked.

"No, just two paintings, but they were pretty large. Take up most of a wall. Show you later, if you like. I gave him a lot more money than he deserved. Maybe they'll be worth more now," he said with that hearty guffaw that in this context made me cringe. Art is the only field in which you can earn more money after you're dead, and Parker, despite his declarations of being a pure-hearted angel, wouldn't regret benefiting from Danny's misfortune.

Could he have had a role in bringing it on, though? So far I couldn't see it.

Nick jumped on it. "Are you planning to sell them?" he asked.

"Nah," said Parker, taking another sip of his bourbon. "Not me. I'm strictly trying to help the struggling artists. And the paintings aren't bad. I've got them hanging. Not in the living room, of course, the subjects are a little, shall we say, too exposed for that. I've got them in a room I use as a combination library and gallery. If I get bored with what I'm reading I look up and they keep me awake. Sometimes I'll bring guests to see them, other times I know they wouldn't go over very big."

"Not very good for the ladies?" said Nick.

"For the ladies and for some of my men clients, too," Parker replied. "It's best not to give away all your little secret passions when you're dealing with peoples' money. They want you to be stodgy and conservative. You play the game, plain old suit and tie when you're in the city, and all that."

The drinks arrived. Parker downed his drink in three gulps. The coffee was very good, strong but not bitter.

"Did you think Danny was a skilled craftsman or just a run-of-the-mill worker?" asked Nick.

"He had some talent," Parker said. "If he'd had a little discipline, if he'd had the chance to mellow with age, maybe something could've happened. This way I don't really expect to make anything substantial on my investment, even with the big bang at the end. A flash in the pan, if anything, and if you miss the moment, the work goes back to the three-or-four figure category. I don't think anyone's going to make a killing, if you'll pardon the expression."

I felt a little shock at his coldness, but of course Danny hadn't been very cuddly.

"Hey, come and look at my Bogarts!" Parker said it so loudly and emphatically that I jumped.

I should have seen it coming. *What do I do?* I wondered. He had said the "ladies" find them offensive, so would I look cheap or unfeminine if I went?

I looked at Nick, who seemed eager enough.

I had to go. I was a professional. Not a lady, at least for the moment.

Parker led us back to the curving staircase, and then what must have been the equivalent of a midtown Manhattan block. We passed white sofas with black end tables, black sofas with driftwood coffee tables, an area with a wet bar and several stools, and a section with a computer and large-screen TV. Finally we were at the far right corner of the house, and there were the two big Danny Bogart paintings.

I couldn't look at Nick or Parker. The paintings were too much for me, crude multi-figure orgy scenes in lurid colors, with everything showing.

I heard Parker's voice as though from a distance, but he was practically at my ear.

"What do you think, Ms. Franklin?" he asked, his voice amused at what must have been a clear discomfort on my face.

I looked at Nick, hoping he'd jump in, but he looked like he was enjoying the situation too.

I cleared my throat twice before I could manage what a reasonably sophisticated and educated response. "Obviously he was influenced by Lucien Freud," I said. "Maybe a little Francis Bacon, too, without the violence."

Parker roared with laughter, although I hadn't said anything funny. He slapped me on the back. Too hard. "As good an answer as any gallery flack," he said, an admiring look on his face.

"Lissa knows her stuff, all right," Nick said, but I thought the look on his face was a little mocking. Never let them see you see you sweat, I thought, so I put on the iciest face I could manage.

"What I don't know, though," I said, remembering the reason we were here, "is whether this was Danny's *chosen* style, or whether he could only paint this way. I know that he used to do museum copies, but some people who are good at that can't make original paintings in a classical or Impressionist style at all. It seems that when they have to start from the beginning, they just don't know how."

"I can't tell you about what I haven't seen," Parker said, "but I will say that I think Danny had his share of cleverness. No manners, but brains, yes."

"Who might know more about his skills?" Nick asked.

Parker hesitated, then replied, "Why don't you talk to Babette Young at her gallery on South Division Street in Peekskill," he said. "She's the one who knows everything that goes on in this town when it comes to art."

Nick and I walked to the car in silence. I felt more awkward with him than I ever had, and at the same time more aware of him as a man. Had he found the paintings exciting?

CHAPTER SEVENTEEN

It was Saturday and the galleries were open late, so we went right to Peekskill. It was a sunny day with a brisk wind. I concentrated on looking out the car window, but Nick was right there, only inches away, and I couldn't keep the image of his muscular body from superimposing itself on the landscape. Every time I looked his way he grinned, and I pretended harder to be not the least bit interested.

"Oh, come on, Lissa," he said after we went through the same look-and-look away business three or four times. "Didn't you like those paintings just a little?"

"Too gross!" I replied, and Nick smiled.

When we got there we found streets lined with galleries showing everything from demure classical landscapes to huge, garishly colored abstracts and installations of the piles-of-junk type. Eating places had artsy names like the Brushstroke Bistro.

We parked right near the Young Art Gallery, where Danny had had his blow-up, according to Gerald Parker. Nick stopped to look at the window display.

"Do you think they have anything of Danny's now?" he asked.

"I don't think so," I replied. "I think they dropped him entirely after the solo show last year. They probably gave back any work they were holding for him."

"He reminds me of those Pekinese you see yapping in the faces of Rottweiler," said Nick. "Next thing you know they're dinner."

I cringed but I laughed too. "What an image. Poor Danny."

Nick squeezed my arm and then caressed it briefly. "Let's go in," he said.

Everything in the gallery was beige except for the paintings. The furniture was minimal and the huge windows let in a dazzling amount of sunlight.

A formidable woman with soft, long orange hair, a flowing dress and a sharp face approached us immediately. Nick got right to the point.

"We'd like to ask you a few questions about Danny Bogart," he said.

"Oh, yes, Danny," she said. "Wasn't that unfortunate?" she asked without much expression. "Are you interested in buying some of his paintings?"

Her face fell as Nick introduced himself.

"I always do what I can to help," she said, but didn't show any sign of meaning it. "We don't carry his work anymore. We dropped him a while ago. He just wasn't selling much. You know how it is with artists, though. After what happened I got several inquiries. If I had any of his paintings I could do something with them now."

"Are you the owner?" he asked.

"Yes, I'm Babette Young. I've owned this place for the last ten years. I've represented many local artists, and done well for them."

"I've heard it said that gallery owners would enjoy their work more if only they didn't have to deal with artists."

83

"I suppose it sounds unfair but it is true in some cases," she acknowledged with a half-smile.

"What happened in Danny's case?" asked Nick.

"Danny isn't—wasn't—a regular member of our roster but we still have to consider what went on here as a private matter."

"I can respect that, of course," said Nick, "but we're on Danny's side. Was the work he had here similar to this?" he asked, indicating with a sweep of the arm several large canvases grouped on one wall, each with a single triangle on a brightly colored background. Apparently the artist's idea of inventiveness was to vary the colors of triangles and of the backgrounds from painting to painting.

"No, no, Danny was a figurative painter in the Lucien Freud sense of heightened color and form."

"Was he strictly modern," Nick asked, "or did he ever do things that were more like say, Monet or Degas, or even earlier artists?"

"Not that I ever saw," Babette replied without hesitation. "I can't imagine Danny being so graceful or precise."

"Did he study classical technique at all?" I asked. "Did he show any interest in restoration or the chemistry of old paintings?"

"Why would you ask a thing like that?" She sounded really surprised. "Danny just went with the expressive nature of painting, as far as I knew. I can't imagine him as a disciplined student of chemistry. I can show you a catalogue of the last show we had for him," she said reluctantly, "if you can give me a minute to find it. But after that I really must get back to my work for the spring show."

She walked to a door in the back of the gallery and disappeared inside. We heard rummaging noises and Nick leaned towards me and asked "Is any of this good?"

"Question of taste. Is it worth money? I guess so, as an investment. You might do well if you resold it in a few years. Does anyone enjoy living with this? If there are people who feel something good when they look at it, just from the image itself, well, I don't know what they're seeing."

Babette came back with a thin booklet showing Danny's name in large type on the cover. "Here you are," she said, "it's an extra copy and you may take it with you." As soon as possible, she clearly meant.

"This is very different from what you have here now," said Nick. "It must be a tough job, choosing from all the artists who come in. You must have a very good eye. And a lot of training."

"I do what I can," she said, her face softening just a bit.

"You've always been in the art field?" he asked. "You've had this place for ten years, you said—what about before that? Did you train in a museum? Or one of the big auction houses?"

"I did some museum work," she confirmed. "I was a curatorial assistant at the Contemporary Arts Museum for two years just before I bought this place. I have an MFA and an MBA."

"Which came first?" Nick asked, but didn't wait for the answer. "Did you already know you wanted a gallery when you went for the MBA?" He made it sound like it was the most fascinating conversation he'd ever had.

"I'd always dreamed of having my own gallery. My mother used to take me to the galleries in Soho when I was a child."

"I give you credit," he said, flashing a dimply Nick smile. "Very few people make their dreams come true. And at such a young age." On top of that he piled on a compliment on the beauty of the catalogue and asked, "You

85

didn't do this yourself, did you? It's so elegant, so professional."

"Well, yes, I designed and wrote it myself."

"No kidding!" he exclaimed. "You're really something."

He had her. "Jeez, I'd really like to know what happened with Danny," he said. "You've got the eye for talent, you make a beautiful catalogue, and you put on a great show, so what went wrong?" he asked.

"Can this be just between us?" she asked.

He nodded and gave her a reassuring smile.

"A lot of things. He was fine when he first approached us with his work, but once the show was set and publicity started appearing, he complained about everything. He didn't like the color of the walls, to start. He actually wanted us to repaint them black. Then he objected to where we placed each and every painting. He even objected to the hors d'oevres for the opening. He was like a spoiled little kid who felt he had the upper hand. He seemed to take pleasure in twisting the knife."

"Did anyone seem particularly upset with him?" Nick asked.

"Well, I almost lost a good assistant. But I gave her a bonus for her patience and she stuck it out. We did make some money on the show, after all. She wouldn't hold a grudge against a crazy artist."

"Anybody else?" Nick prodded. "We could really use your help."

"You didn't hear this from me," she said, leaning in. "He made a terrible scene with a critic, Alexander Leighton. Leighton came with his wife, who is a curator, and they are used to being treated like royalty. Leighton made some comments to his wife about one of the portraits and Danny overheard them. He went over to Leighton and told him straight out that he was a fool."

"Jeez," Nick said, "how did he take it?"

"He turned as red as one of Monet's poppies and started reeling off a long list of criticisms. The work was naive, the colors were abominable together, and the forms were repetitive and lifeless. It was far worse than what he'd said originally. Everyone had stopped talking when Danny started his rant and they hung on to his every word. He screamed at Leighton, told him he was a no-talent mother-you-know-what, and didn't know enough to judge his work. Leighton slammed his wine glass on the nearest table. It was one of my finest Steuben stemware. It smashed and the wine went all over the table and onto the carpet. It was a terrible mess, but at least it was *white* wine. Leighton told Danny he was washed up, finished. He'd never sell another painting; then he turned around and stormed out. His wife followed him without a word to anyone."

"Did he print the criticisms?"

"He didn't print anything about the show. He shut us out entirely. The only thing worse than a bad review is no review at all."

"But you still made money?" I asked.

"A little, but nowhere near enough to chance another show. I haven't heard about any reputable gallery getting involved with Danny since then."

"Sometimes you don't get another chance," I said, and she nodded.

A worried look came on her face. "You didn't hear any of this from me. They wouldn't want this to be known. Even though Danny was not a power nobody likes these ugly scenes repeated."

"Of course," said her new "best friend" Nick.

"What's Mrs. Leighton's name?" I asked.

"She doesn't use the 'Leighton' professionally," she replied. "It's Juliana. Juliana Le Grande. She's at the Contemporary Arts Museum. That's how I got a critic to even look at Danny's paintings. I used to work for her at the museum."

I gripped the arm of the chair. I hadn't seen this coming. Why was I so surprised? Everyone knew everybody else. Somehow it made me feel we were on the right track, and I guess I hadn't expected that feeling to come so soon.

Nick and I looked at each other. "Yes," he said, "we've met her. Thanks very much for your time. Love this one," he said on the way out, pointing to what appeared to be a six-foot by 8-foot depiction of fraternity bed sheets the morning after a big beer bash. It was as off-putting as Danny's orgy scene, but in a different way. That would no doubt add to its cachet among those who would claim to "understand" it.

We got outside. The air was fresh and cool. "You're buying that painting?" I asked Nick. We both laughed.

"I'm mortgaging my house to get it! Who could ask for a more beautiful thing to see every morning and every night?"

"Now you're catching on!" I said. "Sophistication comes to Nick Bellini."

"Yeah, right. Jeez, I wouldn't buy that thing at gunpoint."

"Maybe she has a gun in there. Maybe that's why she does so well. Can we get a search warrant?"

"Sure, sure. I'll just tell the Peekskill chief that nobody would buy this stuff without coercion. He'll have us in there in five minutes." We laughed. He went on, serious now, "So Danny was pushing Juliana to show his work at the museum even though he'd made a scene with them at the gallery."

"Maybe it was denial," I suggested. "Or he may have felt so powerless that he didn't understand his words would have an effect on them. Like some of the viler comments you see online. Healthy people hold back the venom when they realize their words can really hurt, or change the course of things in a negative way."

"Let's get Juliana's version of what happened," he said, and we got into the car and headed home.

CHAPTER EIGHTEEN

Yet another wake-up call the next morning. There are disadvantages to making your own hours. It was Nick. "You're not still in bed, are you?" he asked at the sound of my mumbling voice. "It's 7:30, for God's sake. Juliana is meeting us at the museum café at noon," he said. "Get up and meet me there."

I sighed. Nick was a morning person. That was clear enough. I had worked on my painting until about 10 the night before, and didn't get to bed until around 1:30. I wasn't ready to face the day.

We were incompatible.

Except in every other way.

"Lunch?" I asked, rousing myself as best I could. "Can't we just go to her office?" I felt like I had to dress better for the museum restaurant and I didn't have anything to wear.

"Better to make it look informal," he replied. "I told her we wanted to look at some of the exhibits we'd seen briefly when we walked through last time."

"Okay, okay," I said, after managing to sit up most of the way. "I'll be there. Are you going to tell her what Babette said?"

"Would I lie to Babette?" he asked in a boyishly wounded and quite phony voice. "I gave my word that I wouldn't."

"Scout's honor, right?" I said.

"You got it," he replied. "We'll talk to Juliana about artists and critics. We'll see if she mentions Danny's scene. Sometimes it's important to know what someone's *not* talking about."

Two minutes before noon I was standing at the entrance to the Starving Artists Café, a slick, cool space filled with lacquered wood and silvery metal. Arrangements of white flowers in silver bowls and vases were placed at the entrance and on tables at the far side of the room. Its cool elegance belied its insensitive name. The rich seem to be amused at the financial plight of artists. We'll all be famous when we're dead, supposedly, and the work itself should be reward enough. Of course people don't expect brain surgeons or politicians or CEO's to work for next to nothing, even if they enjoy their jobs.

It would be awful if I got stuck alone with Juliana here, I thought, but I was relieved to spot Nick at a table about halfway across the room. Escorted by a stick-thin, unsmiling hostess in a white micro-mini dress, I joined him.

"You made it!" he said.

I yawned as I sat down. "I hope I can stay awake," I said. Luckily the coffee arrived quickly.

"Lissa, Lissa, Lissa," Nick said. "You're staying up too late. Morning is the best time of day. Don't miss it."

"Yeah, yeah," I said. "Morning is great. It just doesn't work for me." I buried my head in the menu. "Omelets for twice the price of the ones at the diner," I grumbled. "Now I see why they call it the Starving Artists Café. All I can afford to get here is coffee."

"It's on me," he said. "I guess you deserve something for coming. Just make it the cheapest thing you can find," he said with a big boyish grin.

"You're lucky I like cheap people," I said. "And grilled cheese."

"Too bad they don't have pizza," Nick said. "Listen, when we get this wrapped up I'll take you anywhere you want," he added. "We'll have a special night. I promise."

"Well, I don't know," I said, "I'll have to see if I can fit you in. I'm pretty busy these days." But of course it was good. Really good.

The sound of Juliana's heels on the wooden floor got progressively louder and brought me back to the reason we were there. Nick stood up when she arrived but didn't go so far as to pull out her chair. She looked tired under her blusher and mascara, but her dress was an immaculate ice blue that made her hair look even blacker.

The waitress came over and we got the ordering done and settled into small talk about the museum.

"How many of those large sculptures do you have altogether?" asked Nick. "I mean, like the ones in the first gallery?"

"We own about 300 sculptures over six feet in their largest dimension," she said. "And there are four negative space sculptures upstairs."

"Negative space?" he asked. I'd heard of these but of course I let Juliana answer.

"Negative space is the removal of matter from ground or floor. Negative space retreats rather than projects."

Nick looked blank for a minute, then said, "You mean holes? You're showing holes?"

Her face filled with what looked like a mixture of scorn and practiced patience.

"They are space as much as projecting sculptures are space. Artists such as Peter Gensen and David Hawthorne make us think about the presence of absence."

"Yes, of course," Nick said. "I can see that. How interesting. I'm going to be thinking about space in a whole different way. Oops, no pun intended."

I smiled but Juliana was dead serious. I wasn't about to start anything.

Nick mentioned a few photos he'd seen last time we were at the museum, even remembering two or three photographers' names. I was impressed. Our entrees arrived and we talked about the food for a few minutes, and finally he got to the point.

"Do you work directly with artists?" he asked.

"I work with ones who are having a solo show, or are participating in a group show of just a few artists," she said.

"What about artists who are trying to get their work into a show?" I asked.

She looked at me a little suspiciously. I wondered if she thought I was trying to sneak a meeting with her about my own paintings.

"Artists submit digital images. Anita and Bruce, my assistants, look at them and bring notable works to my attention. If the situation warrants it, I will invite them to show something to me in person."

"Was Danny Bogart one of those artists?" Nick asked.

"No, I'm afraid Danny's work was not up to our standards," she said, and busied herself with her salad, cutting and moving things around on the plate. She didn't seem to be eating much.

"Had he approached you personally?" I asked.

"He called a few times. I told him to be patient. And to submit work over the Internet in the future."

"Did that upset him?" Nick asked.

"I don't recall any problem," she said, studying her coffee and taking a long sip.

"Artists can be very temperamental," he said. "Sometimes," he said, looking at me as if to say "don't get angry." I smiled and nodded.

"I didn't have any problem with Danny," Juliana repeated. She turned to me. "You're from the same area, aren't you? Did you know him?" she asked.

"Yes, we were both members of the Artists' Guild in Tarrytown," I told her. "It's so sad. Danny tried so hard. And his work was definitely on the way to something."

"Did you think so?" she asked, with just a touch of scorn.

"You didn't think he'd grow?" I asked.

"Maybe so," she said. "He certainly hadn't arrived yet. Unfortunately we'll never know."

"Did you have any dealings with him outside the museum?" Nick asked. "Did you ever see him at openings or special events?"

"Not that I recall," she said, finishing her coffee and looking at her watch. "I really can't stay much longer. We're preparing a retrospective of the work of Delaney Jefferson and I have to contact several people regarding terms of loan for the work they own."

She stood up to go.

"What about your husband?" asked Nick.

"My husband? What about him?"

"He's a critic, isn't he?" Nick said.

Juliana looked surprised. "Yes, that's right," she confirmed. "Alex is a professor at Westchester University and a critic. Chairman of the department, in fact. He had nothing to do with Danny. He's too busy to deal with artists like Danny who've never had a significant show."

"But did he know Danny at all?" Nick asked.

"Not to my knowledge," Juliana said slowly. "Now I really must go. If there's anything else please see Anita or

Bruce." She turned and took one or two steps before Nick's commanding voice stopped her.

"Have you ever been to the Young Art Gallery in Peekskill?" he asked.

Juliana stopped and turned to face him.

"Not that I recall," she said slowly.

"Your husband didn't have a scene with Danny there?"

"Who told you that?" she asked, clearly less confident than before.

"Did they have a scene?" Nick asked, looking intently at her.

"Was that Danny?" she asked in a cold, bored voice. "Those nuisances are best forgotten."

"You forgot that Danny publicly attacked your husband's reputation and then came to you for artistic recognition?' Nick asked.

"We meet aspiring artists daily. They all want their work here. They get petulant or they plead, or they try to ingratiate themselves. It all blurs together after a while. We are perfectly capable of looking at their work and judging it on its own merits. Danny's work didn't break new ground and wasn't very successful by traditional standards. Artists like Danny are routine. He didn't stand out in any way, good or bad."

She turned and walked away. This time Nick didn't stop her.

"Let's give a call to the professor," he said.

CHAPTER NINETEEN

Compared to Alexander Leighton, his wife might seem sweet and generous. He didn't greet Nick and me with any enthusiasm, but he did sit down with us in his office at Westchester University. The department chair's office was small but elegant, though it was showing signs of age. Dark wood paneling and bookcases were everywhere. It was all very traditional, but instead of a scholar in a suit with elbow patches, he looked more like a man who spent most of his time looking good. His blue and white striped shirt was elegant, possibly Armani. It fit his slender frame snugly. He was an attractive man, probably around 40, maybe six foot three, with longish, golden blond hair. If he didn't look so arrogant he'd be handsome. He gave the impression of someone who came from money and worked for his own amusement.

He sat down behind his desk and motioned Nick and me to side-by-side leather chairs opposite him. I sank in comfortably and looked around.

His diplomas were impressive. They took up a fair amount of the wall above his desk. His PhD in Fine Arts was from Yale, and it left no doubt that he was an acknowledged authority.

"I don't have much time for this," he said as soon as we walked in. "I'm afraid I have an important speech to finish writing for tomorrow night and it just can't wait very long."

"Thank you for seeing us," Nick said formally. He was always polite and well-spoken in situations like this. It must be part of the detective training: fit in wherever you need to be. His blue-collar New York roots, which I found endearing, were more obvious when he was in casual company.

"It's a sad thing, of course," Alexander said, "but it has nothing to do with me."

"We just need to ask a few questions. You and your wife both knew Danny Bogart?" Nick asked.

"Barely. Danny was an artist in a world full of artists," Alexander replied. "There's nothing I know about him that can shed any light for you with regard to his tragic end." His fingers probed a small metal sculpture on his desk. It was made up of several interlocking sharp diamond shapes, possibly tight loops of barbed wire, like the ones you see at the top of a fence to keep people from climbing over it.

"I'll be the judge of that," said Nick firmly, eyeing Alexander's fingers on the sculpture. "We were told that things weren't always pleasant between you and Danny," Nick continued.

"Me and Danny? There was no me and Danny," Alexander said, waving his hand as if to brush away the idea from where it had appeared out of thin air. "He was a little nobody who tried to get my attention once. He failed. End of story."

"And then he tried to get your wife's attention?" Nick asked.

"It happens a hundred times a day. Juliana is used to it. She has assistants to keep these people at bay," Alexander answered.

"Was there anything at all promising about Danny's work?" I asked. "Anything you might have suggested he could try in the future?"

"I barely know his work, but from what I remember, there was nothing that I could work with," Alexander said. "Danny wasn't a student. He wasn't old but he was already set in his ways. Stubborn and egotistical. There was no point wasting my time with him."

"If he had been your student," I persisted, "would you have had ideas for enhancing his work?"

"I would have told him to use it to line birdcages and housebreak puppies. I would have educated him in contemporary art expression and concepts of aestheticism. He hadn't a clue. All he knew was the dead art of the past."

"Ouch," I said. "You have no use at all for traditional art--other than what you just mentioned?"

"It is acceptable in certain museums," he replied. "People need to see the infancy of art, the various stages before it evolved into the thought-provoking field we have now. Traditional paintings, done by hand, are a waste of time. They're just not needed any more, in the age of digital pictures and video."

"You don't think feeling is important?" I asked. Nick's foot nudged mine and I realized that I was getting off the track he wanted to be on. I sat back.

"We were told that you and Danny had at least one heated, public exchange," Nick said.

"The heat didn't last very long," Alexander replied. "I hardly even remember it."

"Did you ever go to Danny's studio?" Nick asked.

"Why on earth would I go there?" Alexander replied. His face became even more arrogant, although I would've said that wasn't possible.

"So you never set foot in his studio?"

"Absolutely not," he answered in a firm, authoritative voice.

"Not for a meeting or anything at all?"

"No, no, I told you," Alexander insisted, sounding annoyed. "I don't even know where it is," he said in a tone that clearly implied that to even know the location would be to place undeserved value on it.

"If I said that you were seen there?" Nick asked, eyes penetrating and voice authoritative.

"I'd have to say that you were misinformed," Alexander said, returning Nick's gaze with equal force. "I have never been to Danny's studio and neither has my wife."

"Where were you the night Danny was killed?" Nick asked.

"When was that?" Alexander asked. His voice was cold.

"Thursday night between 5 and 7 P.M." Nick replied.

Alexander fingered his calendar. "I was here," he said, "working on my speech."

"Did anyone see you during that time period?" Nick asked.

"I'm sure my secretary was here. I told you it was an important speech. We were working on it then, too. I'll check with her."

"Don't bother," Nick said. "I'll do it."

Alexander's fingers tapped the sharp barbed-wire sculpture. Despite the absence of visible injury, it reminded me of stories about ultra-macho men who hold their hands over a candle flame to prove they can do it without flinching. He seemed to be telling us that if he was going to have a lot of heat coming his way, he could handle it. Was he underestimating Nick?

I followed Nick's lead and stood up to go.

"We'll be in touch," Nick said.

Alexander didn't look too happy at the thought.

CHAPTER TWENTY

I arrived at Bellini's the next day about four paces behind a fashionably dressed young woman with short blond hair. She asked the girl behind the counter if Gina was in, and followed her gesture to one of the tables in the rear. A happy scream was the result, followed by a warm embrace. I walked by them and went to the closet to get out my painting things, mildly curious. No point in even greeting Gina right now, she was so intensely involved in their conversation.

The woman was small and perky, with high cheekbones and green eyes. "I'm back for good," she said. "I'm at White Plains Hospital, in Pediatric Care."

"Wow," Gina replied. "How long have you been there?"

"Two months. Long enough to know that I love it."

"It must be so hard. I mean, seeing kids sick all the time."

"It is, but the flip side of that is we get to send most of them home healthy. It makes me feel I'm doing something good. Maybe it makes up for mistakes of my youth."

I looked at Gina. Her face was serious, even sad. "I thought we'd never see you again," she said. "Does Nick know you're back?"

What about Nick? They had ninety-nine percent of my attention now, and with the other one percent I began to lay out my palette.

"I know," said the woman. "I loved London, but...the place where you grew up...the people who mattered so much to you..."

"Have you seen him?" Gina asked. Her voice implied caution.

"No, not yet," she, whoever she was, replied. She sounded a little defensive and a little defiant. "How do you think he's going to react?"

Oh, please, let her be a felon he'd had deported, I silently begged the universe, knowing full well that it wasn't going to comply.

"Oh, Nancy, I hate what happened between you," Gina said. "And you were *my* friend first."

"I know," Nancy replied. "I thought we'd be family forever."

My palette was ready and I had no choice but to make my way to the mural. I'd been planning to start on a complicated building, but that would require more concentration than I had available. Instead, I began throwing strokes of blue on the lake, on top of other strokes of blue. No one was looking anyway.

"Sisters-in-law should never stop being family, no matter what happens," Gina said, getting up and hugging her. Both had tears in their eyes.

Oh God, I thought. *Nick's ex. Nick's ex had come back, eager to rejoin the family.*

"Don't tell him you saw me, okay?" Nancy asked. "I want to call him. I know how angry he was at me. Do you think he still is?"

Gina shrugged. She patted Nancy's hand and said, "He was hurt. We all hated what happened. But I can't speak for him. Call him."

"Maybe. I have today off. Then I'll be on duty through the weekend."

"I don't know how you do it," Gina said. "Being a nurse must be the hardest thing."

Damn, I thought. *It's not enough that she's pretty and perky, she has to have a conscience and a brain also.*

"It's rough sometimes," Nancy confirmed. "But it's worth it, at least to me."

"You have no regrets?" Gina asked. "I mean, about moving to London? And the other thing?" Her voice was a little shaky.

"I know I paid a price," Nancy said, looking down. "Nick was hurt. I didn't want that to happen. But it was the chance of a lifetime, working for one of the greatest medical innovators in the world. What a fluke that I met him! Lightening wasn't going to strike twice. It wasn't about Nick."

"I know, but Nick didn't want to be irrelevant," Gina said quietly.

This was sounding a little better to me.

"It's so sad," Nancy said, "that you can't have everything you want. Did you ever tell him about...?"

"No. If it had been anyone else but you...But it wasn't my place to tell him. Call him," Gina said. "I can't speak for him. Maybe he's over it. Maybe you can start again. Maybe this time it'll work out."

Maybe, maybe, maybe. Maybe I can stop painting the same one-square-inch area with the same blue dots on top of the same color that that was there already. Meaningless dots, raining on the wall one after another. I knew Nick saw me as just a friend. Why should I care so much about the return of the prodigal wife?

CHAPTER TWENTY-ONE

The Metropolitan Museum is a maze of hallways and wings, staircases and courtyards, but I knew my way around. Nick and I were there so I could show him some masterpieces full-size, in the flesh, so to speak. On the way to the galleries I often liked to stop by the decorative arts section and soak up the atmosphere of the Venetian palazzo room. I decided to show it to Nick.

"In the back, through the Medieval Hall," I told him.

"Lead the way," he said, with a sweeping arm movement.

We went past the Great Hall staircase and into the dark, cool medieval area. I showed him some of my favorite sculptures as we walked, people carved out of wood or stone.

"When I first started coming to the museum, I wasn't too interested in this period," I told him, "but after I passed through a few times on my way upstairs I had to stop and look. I fell in love with these 'people' and their palpable sadness and kindness."

"I think I know what you mean," he said. "I see it."

I led him through doorways and galleries and around corners, and then I motioned to an alcove on our right. We stepped in as far as we could, limited by a low Plexiglas barrier.

"Oh, it's a bedroom," he said. "All kinds of things happen in bedrooms."

"No kidding," I said. Too bad that, thanks to Nancy, I might never know how it felt to be in Nick's.

It was a dark room with jade green flocked wallpaper and a big bed with a red silk bedspread. A doorway on the left now presumably went nowhere, and a window on the right let in dim, yellow light that, since we were nowhere near the outside wall of the museum, must come from a hidden lamp. It was part real, part stage set.

"I imagine different stories when I come here," I said. "One day I might think of a woman hiding her lover under the bed or behind the curtains when her husband comes home early, another day maybe a woman giving birth without modern medicine. You know, this was really part of someone's home."

"This was someone's real bedroom?" Nick asked.

"Mm hmm. Well, it was from a real palazzo, but it may not have been where they really slept. For some reason royalty had business visitors in bedrooms. I've no idea why. If you read the notes over there," I said, indicating a stand on the other side of the alcove, "that's what it says."

"Interesting," Nick said. "I wonder why.

"Let's go upstairs," I said. "I'll show you a shortcut."

We headed back toward the Great Hall, but as we approached the back door to the gift shop, I said, "In here."

"Oh, Jeez," Nick said. "We just got here. Can't you go shopping another time?"

"Have faith," I said, and I maneuvered us through the aisles, and around the bargain tables. I admit I gave them a quick glance; after all, unlike the good people of the Medieval Hall, I'm not made of wood or stone. I led him into a small alcove. "At this time of year we can avoid the crowds," I said, "although in the summer people are everywhere." We got into a tiny, empty elevator and rode to the second floor. We exited through the children's bookstore, past vividly colored puzzles and games, and I led him through the European Paintings section until we reached one of my favorite galleries.

I brought him to a Sir Thomas Lawrence painting called *The Calmady Children*. We were lucky—a large easel was in front of it, with a paint-spattered copyist hard at work. It looked like the new version was almost done. "Take a good look at it," I said softly to Nick.

We stood just behind the artist. "Nice work," I said. He thanked me without looking up. I pulled gently on Nick's arm and we walked to the other side of the room. We could see both the copy and the original behind it.

"Not bad," he whispered.

"Pretty good, in that it's the same features and the same clothing. What do you see in the expressions?" I asked.

He didn't answer right away. Then he said, "Well, the kids in the copy look like they're uncomfortable. Their mouths and noses are a little pinched, and their eyes aren't open as wide as in the original."

"Yes, that's exactly right! It doesn't come even close to capturing the vivacity of the older girl and the sweetness of the baby," I said. "Think of it this way: it's like Hamlet performed by a class of average seventh grade kids. The story is the same, they may be the exact words Shakespeare wrote, but is seeing it the same experience as being in the audience when it's performed by the world's best actors?"

"So they're not worried that copyists working here are going to try to pass off forgeries as real?" Nick asked.

"Well, yeah, they are," I answered. "The Met has rules you have to follow. They don't let you do them the same size as the real ones, you have to leave them here until they're finished and photographed by the museum, and before you take them home they stamp the backs so that the guards know you haven't managed a switch. The museum allows it because it's a time-tested method of learning how to paint."

"Jeez, it would take guts to try to walk out the door of the museum with one of their paintings," Nick said. "Did anyone ever try it?"

"Definitely not me," I said.

He laughed. "Why does that not surprise me?" he said.

"Sometimes I almost hoped they'd insist my work was really one of their masterpieces. I mean, who wouldn't be flattered? These guards are very observant. Of course it didn't happen," I said, smiling at the thought, "but one guard did delay me at the exit once."

"He did?" Nick asked. "What did he say?"

"He called over a couple of other guards to check out my painting, claiming to be suspicious. But I think they were teasing me. I was friendly with some of the other guards and they probably set it up," I said. "They knew I wouldn't be tempted to pass my work off as the real thing."

"Never?" he asked. "Never even a little?"

"No, no. Even if I thought I could get away with it, I think doing fakes is a failure."

"How do you figure that?" he asked. "These guys can make a lot of money."

"Yeah, I know, but I'm too stubborn to admit that I can't create my own great work someday. I suppose that sounds egotistical, but that hope is what keeps me going."

"Good attitude. Stick with it," Nick said with a smile. "Otherwise, you know, Sing-Sing is just a few miles up Route 9," he said in a mock-threatening voice. "They could make it co-ed someday."

"Thanks so much," my voice dripping with as much sarcasm as I could muster.

Next I brought him to a painting of a dimly lit room with a woman in a chair, a Vermeer. "There was a famous forger, Van Meegeran, who was very successful for a while with what he claimed were early Vermeers. They say he got away with it for a long time because people wanted to believe."

"I've heard of that case," Nick said. "He finally went to prison, didn't he?" I nodded. "How did they break that one?" Nick asked. "With a chemical analysis?"

"Yes, but it's not foolproof," I said. "People can buy old canvases in antique shops, scrape them down and reuse them. And with a little research they can make sure the pigments and varnishes they use were available to artist they're forging. There are ways to quickly age a painting, although they usually wouldn't fool an expert. One problem is that experts honestly delude themselves sometimes, when there's a lot of money at stake and a lot of excitement about the painting. That's what they say happened with the Vermeers, but eventually they couldn't ignore the poor quality of the work."

"Here's another important thing," I said, pointing at the Vermeer. "*Craquelure*," I pointed to the Vermeer. "I told you about it. There's a particular way that old paintings crack that is extremely hard to fake. You can use old canvas, hand-ground paints with pigments that were available at the time you claim the painting was made; you can give it a coat of mellow yellow varnish, but you can't get it to crack in the particular way it cracks from genuine aging."

Nick studied the Vermeer. "There are a lot of cracks in it, but not everywhere," he observed.

"Yes, exactly. You can heat and then chill a painting but the pattern you get will be even and everywhere. *Craquelure* from aging usually has variations in pattern and only happens in parts of the painting."

"Is that how it's faked?" Nick asked. "With temperature extremes?"

"That, or you can break the rule of painting with oils, which is never use a thin, low-oil layer over a dry, thick well-oiled layer. It's known as "fat over lean." If you do it wrong, you'll get cracking over the whole surface, again evenly. That takes a longer time and it still won't look right. Or instead of that, you can use a varnish that's made to crack. You'll fool only the unenlightened. When you study the painting, you'll see that the cracks don't go all the way through."

"You really have to be a scientist to pull it off, don't you?" he remarked, as much to himself as to me.

"You're thinking about who we know that could do it?"

He nodded. "I can't see Danny sitting down to study the chemistry of painting, can you?"

"No, he was more of a slap-it-on guy. Emotion as art," I said.

I wanted him to see the Impressionists, but I was having trouble pulling myself away from the Dutch galleries. I showed him my favorite seventeenth century Hobbema country scene with the little cottage visible between the trees.

"Cute," he said.

"Isn't it like going back in time, looking at this?" I asked, expecting more. "Didn't you ever want to do that?"

"You mean before they had DNA databases?" he asked. "Or even fingerprints? Not me. You're a romantic, Lissa."

"Maybe I am," I said, feeling a little disappointed that he couldn't feel what I felt. I led him into the Rembrandt gallery. It would be an even tougher sell.

Sure enough, the first thing Nick said was, "Not my taste. So dark and all the ruffled collars…"

"I know," I said. "It took me a while to see how they're special. Forget about the fact that they're framed canvases and just look at the faces. Definitely forget what they're worth in financial terms. Take this one," I moved over to a self-portrait that Rembrandt had done when he was young. "Doesn't he look like a 1970's hippie?" I asked. "Or this." I led him to my next favorite. Nick stared at the prosperous seventeenth-century merchant for a few minutes.

"Look at the whole thing," I said. "Look at his hair, his chin, his mouth, his cheeks, everything. Don't be in a rush."

"It's okay, I guess," Nick said. "They were big shots, weren't they, if they had a portrait?"

"Yeah, it's a show of success, but that's for the historians. Really look at it," I said, wanting him to see what I saw. "Look at all the different skin tones, hard and soft lines, and effects of light. Look into the eyes. The person has a mind and a soul. It's almost alive, not just a frozen likeness. You can imagine the things you could discuss with a man like this."

"Okay," Nick said. "Okay, I see—it's like with the painting of the little girls, and how they had so much more expression than the copy. I see intelligence in his eyes. If I talked to him on a case I'd know before he said a word that he's an educated guy."

"Yes!" I exclaimed so loudly that the other visitors and the guard all turned towards us. I realized I was making too much of it, as if this were a sign that there was a chance for us. There was that Nancy problem, of course. Damn.

"I like the way you talk about these, Lissa," he said. "None of that fancy art language that makes you want to call an interpreter."

"I hate that too," I told him. "You mean 'artspeak.' It takes all the pleasure out of it for me. Makes it clinical instead of joyous or sad or vivid. Art should be human. But that doesn't mean it has to be as tightly rendered as this. Let me show you the Monets."

Nick put his arm around me as we walked. It felt like a perfect fit.

I greeted several of the guards along the way, casual friends from the time I'd come every day. My friend Elio wasn't there any more, I knew, but I still kept expecting him to be around the next corner. I'd heard two different stories, one that he'd gotten a better job, and the other that he'd been sick. I hoped it was the job.

We walked through the long hallway that exhibited drawings, prints and photos. I pulled Nick towards a balcony where we stopped briefly to look down onto the Renaissance courtyard, and after a few quiet minutes we walked the short distance towards the bright, skylit Impressionist section. I led him past the nineteenth-century French salon art, which was on my list of the most boring art in the museum. It was against these drab, overly precise, and often sentimental academic works that the Impressionists had rebelled.

"Jeez, this is your favorite gallery?" asked Nick.

"No, no. Be patient. We're almost there."

His face changed as we came into the small gallery off the main hall. There they were, *Regatta at Sainte-Adresse* by Monet with its beach with water that was so beautifully transparent close to the shore, and *Boating* by Manet, with the virile man moving things along with his big forearms, and presumably with his female companion. In the next room were a couple of Pissarro city street scenes of Paris and nearby was a Van Gogh full of luscious blue-greens. I wanted him to see the Monets most of all. I brought him over to *Camille Monet on a Garden Bench*.

"This is how you use color, right?" Nick observed right away. "And the brightness?"

"Mm, hm," I said, pleased. "Meet my friend Madame Monet," I said, indicating the woman in the fashionable, billowy black-and gray outfit in the painting. "We're looking at faces that are really very sketchy," I said, pointing at her and her dark-haired friend, still leaning over the back of her bench with his sardonic smile, as he had since 1873. "So the magic of it," I said, "is when someone creates life and character out of blobs of paint, whether carefully drawn and layered like Rembrandt did it, or sketched with few tones and much psychology like Monet."

"And that's not something your average forger can do, is it?" said Nick, not needing an answer.

CHAPTER TWENTY-TWO

As Nick unlocked the door to the Kaldenberg Place studio early the next afternoon, the image of Danny's staring, dead eyes wouldn't leave me. I was there at Nick's urging. He wanted me to take another look at all the artwork to see if anything would link Danny to the forgeries, and I couldn't say no.

"Take it easy," he said, looking closely at my face. "You're with me. We're helping Danny."

I nodded and we went in. The studio was mercifully corpse-free this time. As I looked at the artwork that was on the walls, tables, and floors, my emotions began to take second place to my professional training.

"I don't see anything that looks out of the ordinary for Danny," I told Nick.

"Yeah, it should be that easy," Nick replied. "We're going to have to look at everything. Everything in every closet and cabinet." I must have shown my discomfort, because he said, "Hang in there, Lissa. Just focus on the artwork. We can start in the back, where you said he had something the night of the Artists' Guild meeting," Nick said.

"You looked there that night," I reminded him. "The shelf was empty."

"We're going to look at the rest of it," he explained. "There are some sketchbooks and small canvases on the bottom shelf. We're not looking for a specific object or disturbance. We want you to look for signs that Danny could have been the kind of artist who could attempt forgery."

"I don't know everything about his work, of course, just his recent ones. He might even have other people's works too, like his friend Paul McGill," I suggested, beginning to concentrate. "They were pretty close for a while."

"See what you can find," Nick said. "Take your time, take it all in, think it over. We'll come back if we have to. Do it right, not necessarily fast."

I opened the door to the first cabinet and began. Most of the small paintings were on canvas board. I held one up for Nick. "This isn't a professional surface," I told him. "These are thin pieces of wood with canvas glued on."

"It looks okay to me," he said. "What's wrong with it?"

"Look at this." I placed a board on the table to show him that it didn't lay flat. "Everyone worked on wood a long time ago, but it was good quality. These mass-market canvas boards are cheap. They warp often and quickly. Only students and people who can't afford better use them. No one would try to pass these off as supports for master works," I told Nick. "Plus the pictures aren't in the style of any master that I know about."

"Interesting," he said. "Keep going. See what else you turn up."

It looked like Danny had saved everything he'd ever done. The earlier works—everything was dated, though it was obvious anyway—were simpler and even a little childlike. He'd benefited from his studies, though, with increasing complexity and even a touch of sophistication -- if you defined sophistication as knowledge of what was currently considered good.

There were stacks and stacks of large, recent paintings, leaning against the walls. There were notebooks, canvas pads, and visual diaries that held little sketches and color notes.

"I now know much more about the work of Danny Bogart than I ever expected—or wanted-- to know," I told Nick wearily after two hours.

"And?" he asked.

"Nothing that suggests a special focus on Impressionism or Baroque or any era of classical art," I told him.

"So far," he said.

I groaned. "You want me to look at more?" I asked. "Now?"

"Come on, Lissa, this is important," Nick said.

I looked at him, ready to say I'd had it. His brown eyes, surrounded by long black lashes, were intense. His mouth was tense, jaw jutting. "One more shelf," I agreed reluctantly.

I sat down on the hard couch with some large sketchbooks. I went through two and then three more.

"Nothing different," I said. "All Danny, all the time. More landscapes, though."

"Keep going," Nick said. "Would you like me to go get you a cup of coffee?"

"No!" I said, the image of Danny's unseeing eyes returning full-force. "I don't want to be alone here."

"Okay, take it easy," he said. "Stick with it a little longer and we'll both go for a super-special Bellini's cappuccino."

"I'm doing it," I said.

I went through a large box of canvas panels and a box of loose watercolor paintings. "Not archival," I pointed out.

"Not what?" Nick asked.

"The boxes he's got these in aren't acid-free. The watercolors will get stained eventually," I explained.

"Does it matter? If he's doing something to sell now?" Nick asked.

"No, but it's just a little unprofessional."

"I don't see why that matters," he said.

I sighed. He was right. I kept going for another hour but found nothing of interest.

We went at it again the next day and the one after that, and just when I thought I'd drop dead if I had to see one more Danny Bogart painting, I opened a large black box. My breath stopped; I felt a thrill go through my body.

Several pictures that looked at first like big photos of famous paintings at second glance revealed their own signature style.

"Maybe he did spend some time at the Met," I said softly to myself, feeling giddy. "Nick!" I called out with excitement and relief.

"What've you got?" Nick asked from the other side of the room. We'd heard sirens, and he'd gone to the window, cell phone to ear.

"Copies of paintings at the Met," I said, holding a stack of paintings on canvases. They weren't on stretchers, but clearly, from the creases and staple holes around the edges, they had once been.

He rushed over to see them. "Good work, Lissa," he exclaimed.

"They're oils, I think," I said, touching the surface of the top one gently. "I can't tell whether they were done at the Met or from books."

"Are they good?" Nick asked.

"They're okay. Nothing special. Like most copies, you can recognize the subject and the colors, but the emotional content is different than in the real ones."

"Are they signed?" he asked, reaching out to look at them himself.

We saw the initials at the same time: DB.

"They were practice," I said.

"Good work," Nick said. "It's not proof, but we're on the right track."

He pushed buttons on his cell phone. "Is the chief in?" he asked. "Okay, I'll hold." He put his hand over the bottom of the phone. "My girl," he sang very softly this time, "ba ba da da, ba ba da da talkin' 'bout my girl."

I smiled. If it hadn't been for Nancy, and of course poor Danny, it would have been a delicious moment.

"The chief is gonna love this," Nick said, the phone slightly away from his ear.

I loved it too.

CHAPTER TWENTY-THREE

I had told Nick that Connor, my songwriting friend, was a very unlikely suspect, but apparently that was not enough for the Tarrytown P.D. Nick wanted to ask Connor what he knew about Danny and how well he'd known him.

We found Connor in mid-song at the piano in the Andamos Restaurant. He was singing and playing his own catchy, upbeat tune. Nick and I sat down at the bar and ordered coffee for me and a soft drink for him. Connor was a terrific performer. He'd been hired to provide background music, but it was more like a concert. Several people had gathered around the piano, and most of those who'd stayed at their tables were giving him their full attention.

He saw us and waved between notes, and when he was done he came and sat with us.

"How'd I do?" he asked, but his voice was rich with excitement. He didn't need an answer.

"Great," Nick and I both said.

"We've had a full house for two weeks," Connor said.

"Bravo," I said, applauding lightly.

As usual in Tarrytown, there was a wide variety of people: Yuppies, affluent older people, and a few not so well-dressed couples who looked like they might be there on a splurge. The Andamos was decorated in soft and greens. It had a garden-like feel. Much of the food served there originated at the nearby Rockefeller organic farm. Connor seemed at home there. He told us he'd been providing live music on Fridays and Saturdays for several months.

"You were a friend of Danny Bogart's, I hear," said Nick.

"A friend? Who told you that?" Connor asked, looking at me.

"I just told Nick that you're a member of the Artists' Guild," I said, "and that you knew him."

"Knew him, yes," Connor replied. His fingers tapped rhythmically on the bar as we spoke. His rich voice was velvety, smooth and soothing. "I wouldn't say I was a friend if you mean did we pal around or spend all day texting each other."

"Was he a temperamental guy?" asked Nick.

"I guess he had his moments," Connor said. "Never violent, to my knowledge, but yeah, he could be loud and critical."

"You were at the opening of his show two years ago at the Young Art Gallery?" asked Nick.

"Which one was that?" Connor asked.

"It's in Peekskill," I answered. "Babette Young's gallery."

"Oh, that one," Connor said. His eyebrows drew together and his mouth had a set look as though he were remembering something unpleasant. "I was hired to perform at the reception."

"And did you?" Nick asked.

"Yes, I played for about an hour."

"Did it go well?"

"It was fine for me. Not so good for Danny," Connor told us.

"What happened?" asked Nick.

"A pretty big argument," Connor said. "I don't know how it started but Danny really went at it with a critic, I think the name's Leighton or something like that, who apparently wasn't very impressed with Danny's work."

"How bad did it get?" Nick asked.

"Loud and ugly. I felt bad for Danny. I knew it wasn't going to do him any good. At first I stopped playing, but Babette motioned to me to keep it up."

"People were listening to the argument?" Nick asked.

"Yes, and at first I tried to cover the voices by playing louder and faster," Connor told us. "It didn't work all that well, though. Some people actually moved so they could hear the argument."

"How long did it go on?" Nick asked.

"Not that long, but it was pretty nasty on both sides," Connor answered. "I don't know the details, but Leighton, or whatever his name was, looked ready to blow."

"Yes, you're right about the name, Alexander Leighton," I said. "How did Danny take it? I think a lot of artists would want to curl up and disappear."

"I don't think Danny was as upset as the other guy, to tell you the truth," Connor said. "This Leighton dude got all red in the face and stormed out, faithful wife at heel. Danny acted pretty cool. Maybe the poor guy had deluded himself into thinking he'd won somehow because the other guy retreated."

"Did Babette say anything?" I asked.

"She tried to smooth it over and make light of it. Said something about artist's passion making great art even greater, but the evening was pretty much spoiled and she knew it," Connor told us.

"Do you know who the critic's wife is?" I asked.

"Some sort of curator, I think," he asked more than told.

"Yes, right," I said. "She's at the Contemporary Arts Museum."

"So Danny screwed himself with two people," said Connor.

I nodded.

"It must have ticked you off at least a little to have a scene like that go on while you were performing," Nick said.

"It didn't bother me," Connor said. "It wasn't about me, and I got paid, for God's sake. Nothing like that ever happened again. If you're suggesting I bore a grudge about that...."

"Where were you the night he died, just for the record?" asked Nick.

"You've got to be kidding me," Connor said.

"Nothing personal, man, just part of the job," Nick replied.

Connor looked annoyed, but he took his cell phone out of his jacket pocket and began searching its calendar. "Let me see," he said, "Okay, that night I came home around 6 p.m. from a gig at a school in Valhalla," he said. "Four hundred kids in a big auditorium. I remember that. I ended up inviting about fifty of them up there onstage, to sing with me."

"What did you do when you got home?" Nick asked.

"Collapsed! That's hard work, even though I love it. I put my feet up, sipped some iced coffee, and watched the people go by on Main Street."

"From your window?" asked Nick.

"No window. From a chair I always bring outside my building," Connor said. "I changed my clothes, made a pitcher of iced coffee, put out some munchies on a little table, an extra chair in case a friend wandered by, and relaxed."

"Right on Main Street?" Nick asked.

"Right on Main Street," Connor confirmed. "I had no reason to go look for Danny and I didn't."

"And did a friend wander by?" asked Nick.

"Lots of people came by and said hello. Do you need names?"

"No, no, it's cool," said Nick. "Just had to ask."

"I've vouched for you, Connor," I said. "Nick has to question everyone."

"Done with the questions. Let's hear some music," Nick said.

"Any requests?" Connor asked. His fingers tapped out a rhythm on the bar.

"Whatever," Nick said, slapping him companionably on the back. "I'd love to hear more."

Connor went to the piano and started playing some songs I hadn't heard before. Nick seemed more relaxed, and he clearly enjoyed the music. I felt good being there with him, and wasn't happy when he said too soon that he had to get back to work.

I wondered if he'd been convinced that Connor wasn't a suspect, but I didn't ask.

CHAPTER TWENTY-FOUR

It was the first meeting of the Artists' Guild since Danny's death, and Anne's studio felt chilly and isolated. How could she work at home? I needed to be in town, with sound and movement around me, even if it was mostly outside my windows. When I arrived, people were already seated at the large round table. It was made of honey-colored wood that Anne had stained and shellacked herself. I'd been with her when she bought it raw and I knew how much work had gone into the warm glowing surface. I stroked it briefly as I sat down, wanting to cling to the happier things for a moment.

It was a small group again, and everyone was quiet and unsmiling. I knew things couldn't be the same, of course, but it seemed even worse than I'd expected.

"Let's get started," said Margaret. "Whatever else is going on, the Outdoor Art Fair is only eight weeks away and we have things that are not done that need to be done." Her voice was deep and forceful. "The minutes of the last meeting, please," she said, turning towards Miles.

He picked up a small notebook and read, "Anne and Johnny agreed to contact some of the musical performers from last year and Tiffany asked about funding and publicity for belly-dancing. Danny complained about the no-nude paintings policy and just about everything else."

Margaret's head swiveled in his direction. "Isn't that just a little bit callous, Miles?" she asked. "He was a human being, after all."

"Does anybody here miss him?" Miles asked. "Maybe he brought it on himself. If you ask me he was an embarrassment."

"You'd better watch what you say," said Margaret, peering over her half-glasses with a combination of disapproval and anxiety, "at least until they've found out what happened."

Everyone turned towards me. "What's Nick told you?" Anne asked.

"Nothing. And I don't want to get involved."

"Come off it, Lissa," said Johnny. "You're always hanging around Nick's shop. Don't tell me you two don't talk about what's going on."

I felt uncomfortable. These people were my friends, but I couldn't tell them anything. "It's not Nick's shop," I said. "It belongs to his family. He just helps out there sometimes. We talk about art, mostly. What makes it special."

Johnny wasn't looking me at me as he said. "I let you bring him into my studio. He said he might buy a painting. Was he for real?"

"Of course he was interested in seeing your work, Johnny," I said, not lying. "That was before Danny was killed. He had more time to pursue his own interests. Maybe he'll buy something of yours. He's bought mine."

Johnny still didn't look at me. I was a little surprised, because although we weren't great friends, there hadn't been any friction between us before. What was going on?

"Help me with the coffee, Lissa?" Anne asked. I nodded and we went to the small pantry on the far side of the studio.

"Johnny's not himself," I remarked.

"We're all tense. None of us has any experience with this kind of thing," Anne said as she threw some coffee beans into the grinder. Despite the tension, I breathed in the aroma.

She placed several scoops of coffee into a drip pot.

"Are they investigating us?" Anne asked.

"I suppose they're looking at anyone who knew him. But I'm sure nobody has to worry if they're not involved."

Anne handed me a block of cheddar on a large plate, and a knife. "We need this in small slices," she said, waving her hand over the cheese. Ever the careful sculptor, she began cutting the cake into small, meticulously even squares. Finally she asked, "Are you sure they know what they're doing?"

"Nick's a smart guy," I said. "He has the kind of understanding of people and how they think that I've only seen before in psychologists."

"Is he in charge of the investigation?" Anne asked.

"To an extent. He answers to the chief, but his regular chief is away and Nick knows people here better than this guy does. I have faith in Nick. He can handle it." Was I a little nervous? I'd cut my finger along with the cheese. Just a little.

The aroma of the brewing coffee filled the kitchen. When she opened the cabinet to get cups, the door became a wooden barrier between us. I made no move to get around it. I didn't want her to know how involved I was in the investigation.

"I wonder if you're not a little too trusting," Anne said, her voice slightly muffled. "The police get it wrong sometimes. You should keep your distance, even if you're just talking about art."

"Danny called me that day. He wanted my help and I didn't get there until it was too late," I said to the cabinet door, my voice a little choked. "Nick has the power to find out for sure what's going on, the power to stop it. I feel helpless when I see something so horrible, so unjust, and I envy him. And I like being with him."

The cabinet door was closed and out of the way now, and I saw that Anne looked nervous. More nervous than I was, I thought. It surprised me. Did she have something to hide?

"Nick knows how to use his power," I said, trying to reassure her. "It isn't brute force.

She muttered something I didn't catch, and I didn't ask her to repeat it. We headed back to the meeting with trays loaded with coffee, cake, crackers and cheese.

I realized it at that moment: Nick had come to mean more to me than the Artists' Guild, more than my friendship with Anne.

We came back to hear another round of complaints from Tiffany about the publicity for her belly-dancing at the fair. Margaret was getting impatient.

"It's the Outdoor Art Fair, for God's sake," said Margaret, "not the Tiffany Grimes Show. You can do all the publicity you want for yourself, but we can't do any more for you than what I've already outlined."

"It's not just for me. Last year I had the biggest crowds in the park. I can bring people in."

"Good, of course," said Margaret, "but the rest of us are proud of our crafts too. I'm sure it was very challenging for you to learn to wriggle around, but there won't be a diva in this group," she said sternly.

Tiffany pouted and let the subject drop, and the rest of the meeting was business as usual.

CHAPTER TWENTY-FIVE

MEMORIAL SERVICE FOR DANNY BOGART AT THE TARRYTOWN THEATRE: The first message of my e-mail inbox was addressed to everyone involved with the Artists' Guild. I opened it and read, to my great surprise, that golden boy Paul McGill was returning to his roots to say goodbye to his old friend Danny. I would have gone to any memorial for Danny, but Paul's presence certainly upped the ante. It was set for the following Friday at 6 P.M. and I called Nick right away to make sure he knew. Everyone would come. Everyone in the county who had anything to do with art, that is. All the people Nick and I had spoken to and many more.

"I'll be there, of course," he said. "Should I bring Paul a jar of Italian olives?" he asked.

"Only if they're artistically correct," I answered. "Of course, I wouldn't presume to tell Paul which olives in which jars make the most profound statement."

"That's what happens when you don't have a PhD," said Nick. "We're just not qualified. Is it the size of the pimientos? Or the exact placement of the holes? Tall, skinny jars or short, wide ones? We'll never know."

"It's a very complex issue," I said with an exaggerated sigh. "Let's just muddle along as best we can," I replied, "and stick to finding a murderer."

The Tarrytown Theatre had been saved in the 1970's, luckily, from being torn down to make space for a parking garage that would have brought squat modern ugliness to the town's main intersection. A courageous couple had risked everything by buying it when they could ill afford to, almost losing their home. They restored it with their own hands and made it work. Now their daughter and her husband operated it, having mastered the art of grant-writing and fundraising to bring it back to glory and functionality. With its warm Victorian bricks, its towers and its antique stores, it was one of the buildings that had attracted me to the village. Its acoustics were said by the experts to be exceptionally good.

I arrived early for the service. My studio was just across the street, on the other side of Broadway. There was a small crowd under the marquee on Main Street when I got there, waiting for the doors to open, but nobody I knew. It was a relatively mild day, so I was able to sit on the bench across the street for a while and watch people gather. I had done two paintings of the Tarrytown Theatre from this bench and my eyes, by habit, moved from the entrance to the second floor, then the towers, then the shops, then the west-facing facade. The main entrance had originally been on the side street, Kaldenberg Place, and there was still a back door there. A large black van pulled up and a man got out, and I recognized Paul from the newspaper clippings Juliana had shown us. Several other people climbed out of the van after him.

Paul was classically handsome, with lots of tousled, sandy brown hair, and he was built like a football player. He was in his late thirties, and was obviously enjoying the perks of success, with a blonde on his right arm and a redhead on his left. He went in the side entrance with his entourage. None of them looked like they were in mourning.

I looked back at the main entrance, under the marquee on Main Street. The crowd was larger now, and I spotted some of the Guild members. It was time to go in, and I crossed the street, hoping that Nick was on the way. As I passed through the lobby, I checked the glass cases up front for the greeting cards I made, using prints of my Tarrytown Theatre paintings. They sold a few from time to time. I saw that some were gone, as I'd hoped, and I went into the auditorium. The theater was filled with images of flowers and graceful ladies with handsome escorts, apparently done when the theater had opened in the Victorian Era. It looked like a little girl's dream of elegance and romance.

Just the first 10 or so rows were filled, and a lot of the faces were familiar. That was pretty much what I had expected, since Danny wasn't well known outside of Tarrytown.

Martine, who ran the theater along with her husband, was onstage. A slender and photogenic blonde who walked with the grace of a ballerina, she was an elegant emcee. The ceremony began with a song about remembrance, performed by Connor, and then Martine introduced Paul.

"We are honored to have a true genius return to his roots to see off his dear friend Danny Bogart," she said. "Many of us know Paul McGill from the days when he and Danny were fixtures on the streets with their easels and their ideals, and some of us also remember their evenings of shall we say "relaxation" afterward at the Settle Inn." Laughter rippled through the crowd. I saw Anne with a broad smile as she sat half-turned in her seat, in the side section. Many locals had told me they'd met the loves of their lives there in their younger days. I found this out from the unusually brisk sales of prints of my painting *Main*

Street, Tarrytown, which featured The Settle Inn next door to Bellini's. Hollywood obviously liked the bar, too, since it had been selected to be a set for *Mona Lisa Smile*, the Julia Roberts movie.

Martine continued, "Paul's success makes us all proud. Let's give him a warm welcome." She raised her arms and he bounded up on the stage and took each of her hands in his, then kissed her on both cheeks. She led him to the podium and took her seat in the front row.

Paul began, "How wonderful to see all of you again, and to meet new people who care about art. Today is not about me, of course, but about Danny's life and his unrecognized genius." He had a clicker in his hand and slides of Danny's work began to flash on a large screen behind him. "Danny will get his day, I know," he said, "because talent like this can never be ignored. Poor Danny's temper sometimes got in his way. Art gallery owners often say that selling art would a lot easier if they didn't have to deal with the artists." Laughter rippled through the theater. Babette Young had said the same thing when we were at her gallery, and she was sitting not far from me now, nodding her head. "Artists are needy, sometimes, and that causes problems. He used to tell me about the tough times he had as a boy with an alcoholic mother and a father who beat her and sometimes Danny, too. Art was there for him as it is for so many of us, creators and viewers alike." The audience was quiet now.

The paintings went by, each on the screen for about 5 seconds, then fading into the next. Nudes into landscapes, still lifes into abstractions, each done with the bold colors and exaggerated sizes characteristic of Danny's style.

"When I see this work," Paul continued, "I think of Lucien Freud, Van Gogh, Egon Shiele. If Rembrandt were painting today he'd be like Danny."

Oh my God, I thought, but I kept a smile pasted on my face.

"And now we have an exciting announcement. I'm going to yield the honor to the most wonderful curator in the Northeast, Juliana Le Grande of the Contemporary Arts Museum."

Juliana left her aisle seat, her husband Alexander Leighton applauding enthusiastically and the rest of the crowd more perfunctorily. She walked the short distance to the stage and said "Only the Northeast?" Her comically disappointed look at Paul drew a big laugh.

"I am very pleased to announce that the Contemporary Arts Museum," she said, switching to a formal tone, "will be acquiring *Nude # 727* by Danny Bogart." Lots of applause. I wondered what had changed since Juliana told us that Danny's work was not up to the standards of the museum, and Leighton had suggested that it might be useful for lining bird cages. "It will be exhibited in the spring, concurrent with a show at the Young Art Gallery in Peekskill." More applause. I looked again at Babette Young, the gallery owner, who was well enough known in this crowd to be the focus of attention even before Juliana pointed her out. Babette waved both hands to the crowd in response. Juliana, professional and cool, gave the stage back to Paul, and rejoined her professor husband, who nodded approvingly. Because they said so, an inferior work was now a great one.

Paul wound things up, saying "Now please join us up front. We want to share with you some lovely food and drink contributed by our wonderful local restaurants. We all wish that Danny were here with us today, but I know that even under the circumstances he would want you to celebrate his life and his work by enjoying each other's company and all the talented artists we still have here in Tarrytown. Thank you all for coming. I know he's here with us in spirit."

The music began again and people stood up and slowly made their way forward. Anne was one of the first to reach the front and she threw herself into Paul's arms with such feeling that it had to be clear to everyone that they had a past. At least, I hoped it was a past and not a present. I saw Ben, her husband, staring at them. Could their marriage be suffering from his 80-hour work weeks? Anne hadn't said anything to me.

Ben's face was turning an unattractive shade of purple. When other people starting swarming Paul, Anne whispered something to him and turned back towards her husband. I hoped for her sake that the scene was going to wait until they got home. It looked to me like it was going to be a nasty one.

I was watching from a distance when I finally heard Nick's voice behind me and felt his hand on my arm.

"What did I miss?" he asked.

I filled him in on the newly-discovered genius of Danny Bogart and we went up front to mingle and observe the crowd. Nick grabbed a slice of pizza, his all-time favorite food, and chewed very slowly as he stood near the guest of honor. I stood with him, nibbling on some nachos.

Paul was mobbed. People patiently waited their turn to have a moment of his attention. Each of the Guild members took their moment being close to supposed greatness.

Ramón, several inches shorter than Paul, looked up at him as though at a combination of Jesus and Derek Jeter. "Ah, Mr. Paul, I saw at the museum, your work is so, sooo cool," he said. "Could you see mine at the Tarry Café?"

"I'll try," he said politely, "but I won't be here very long."

Margaret's loud, commanding voice broke in. "We'd love to have you do a lecture at the library," she said. Again he wouldn't make any promises.

Tiffany moved in next, and it looked like she might be more successful. Her mini-dress was barely bigger than a one-piece bathing suit, and she didn't seem to mind at all that his attention was concentrated several inches lower than her face. Her boyfriend wasn't with her, and she showed no sign of remembering his existence. "Let me show you around tonight," she told Paul. "I know places you'd enjoy."

"I can think of a few myself," he replied, eyes still focused far below hers. "It's a very generous offer," he said. "I'm staying at the Marriot. Do you know the bar there?"

She did, and they agreed to meet later. He was still watching her walk away when Johnny started making his own pitch, for his artwork. His arms were tightly crossed on his chest in a defensive self-hug as Paul declined to show any interest. After Johnny walked away, Paul hung around for a while, letting people talk at him, most of the time not saying much in return.

Nick stayed back until Paul started looking toward the exit. He approached Paul and introduced himself.

"You have any leads?" Paul asked.

"We're getting there," Nick told him. "I'd like to ask you a few questions about Danny. It seems you knew him better than most of us."

"Yeah, I know what they call us. Gaugin and Van Gogh." His tone was brash. "We had our time together but I've hardly been in contact with him for the last few years."

"You'd be helping us a lot. We can go across the street to Danny's studio."

"Poor Danny," Paul said, his eyes suddenly filling with tears, the first emotion for Danny that I'd seen anyone express. "I don't know if I can."

But he did.

CHAPTER TWENTY-SIX

Paul looked around the studio.

"A lot of stuff I've never seen," he remarked, looking less emotional. He started looking through the stacks of canvases. "Okay, I know these," he said. "Typical Danny." He smiled.

"Was Danny resentful about his lack of success?" Nick asked.

Paul didn't answer right away. Was he too absorbed in Danny's artwork, or was he unwilling?

Nick repeated the question, louder.

"No," Paul responded after a brief interval. "He wasn't into worldly goods or ego trips. I wasn't either. I got lucky, but if I hadn't made it I'd be doing my art anyway, like Danny was."

"Did Danny have a girlfriend—or a boyfriend?" Nick asked.

"Danny liked women well enough, but you have to understand, like I said at the memorial, Danny came out of a tough home situation. He was a big kid. He had a tough time keeping relationships going. He always wanted more from people than they were able to give. Emotionally, I mean."

"Did he have a recent relationship of any length?" I asked.

"I don't know. I told you we haven't been in touch. But I know he used to sometimes pay his models a little extra for a little extra service, if you know what I mean. They were glad to get it. One girl, though, gave him a good smack in the face and walked out on a half-finished painting. Never came back."

"Do you know where she is now?" Nick asked.

"This was years ago," Paul said. "I heard she's married now and has a kid. He got another model who wasn't so uptight, and he finished the painting."

"Do you know anyone else who had a problem with him?" Nick asked.

"No," Paul replied. "Danny didn't look for trouble. Didn't even get out that much."

"What about Juliana?" I asked.

"He met her through me," Paul said. "I told him to take his time with her. She'd come around."

"You were right," I said. "It's too bad he doesn't know."

"Damn, it sucks," Paul said. "Sometimes life really sucks."

"What about Juliana's husband?" Nick asked.

"Alex is a good guy. He just doesn't go for the sort of painting Danny did. I told Danny he had to go with the times. Instead he had to do his Van Gogh thing. A talented guy. He could have done installations, any kind of conceptual. He could have had more but instead he had to walk right into tragedy. Damn!" He made a fist and smacked it into his other hand.

"Did you go to his show in Peekskill?" Nick asked.

"No. I got the invitation but I was stuck upstate. Damn!" he said again. "I didn't know he'd be gone so soon. I didn't know."

"How could you?" I asked in my most soothing tone. He looked a little more comfortable.

"You used to share a studio with Danny, I heard," Nick said. "Was it this place?"

"No, not here. We had a place by the river, in an old industrial building. Near the asphalt plant. Both are gone now," Paul told us.

"Any of these paintings yours?" Nick asked.

"I'd have to look."

"Would you do that, please?" Nick gave him some time to look around. He didn't call attention to the copies, but I knew those were his main interest.

Eventually Paul shook his head. "No, it's all Danny's."

Nick asked him then, "Even these copies?"

Paul picked one up. "It's not too bad, is it?" he mused. "I don't think I could do it anywhere near as well as this."

"He do a lot of these?" Nick asked.

"Not so many. I think it was for a class. You know, some art teachers insist you master the past before you can make the future. I never went for that. Waste of time. You do what's being shown now."

"Do you remember these particular ones?" Nick asked.

"Not really. They may be from the time he went to the Met a lot. He didn't do it that long. He had to get permission to do these, you know, and they only let him work at certain hours. Danny doesn't like restrictions. I mean 'didn't,'" he said, choking a little.

"Anyone else in town you know of who did that?"

"No," Paul said. "Why? Do you think this had something to do with the murder?"

A four-year-old's eyes couldn't show more innocence than Paul's did at that moment.

Was it too much?

I wondered if Nick was thinking the same thing.

Paul stood up and asked, "Is that it? I have to meet somebody."

Nick didn't answer right away, and Paul added, "I'll give you my agent's number. She can always contact me if you have any other questions."

Nick spoke slowly when he finally answered. "You aren't planning any trips, are you? I mean, out of the country?"

Paul's face was hard now, with no trace of childish unconcern. His eyes were cold. "No," he said. "If you need my help you'll be able to find me."

"All right, then," Nick said. He walked Paul to the door and watched him walk away.

CHAPTER TWENTY-SEVEN

Gina wanted to stay home with her little girl, who had a cold, so Nick had promised to place evening manager at Bellini's. We sat over steamy cappuccinos, going over the list of Artists' Guild members. He asked how well I knew Miles.

"Not very," I told him. "He's a little unapproachable, maybe even arrogant. He's from Brookline, I think. He worked at one of the Boston museums. I remember that because he acted a little strange when I asked if it was the Gardner."

"The Gardner? Why would he be uncomfortable with that?" Nick asked.

"That's where they had that mega-theft years ago. Hundreds of millions of dollars' worth of major masterpieces were taken and they're still out there somewhere."

"Oh, jeez," said Nick. "I know that story. You think Miles might've worked there then?"

"It's possible. I think it was around 1990. He would've been really young, but probably old enough to have to a job."

"He could've worked in the shop, or the café, or selling tickets. Some places even hire kids to do security, if they feel nothing is going to happen," Nick said.

"That's right. They never saw this one coming."

"There was a fake cop involved, right?" Nick asked.

"Yes. He came to the door in uniform in the early morning, when the museum was closed, and got the guard to let him in. Then he and another man tied him up, and the second guard too, and they went around taking what they wanted."

"Damn. They should've confirmed before they let anyone in. Rookie mistake. Nobody ever got arrested, did they?" Nick asked.

"Not so far. Some people thought the story would finally come out, more than twenty years later, when they arrested Whitey Bulger, the big Boston crime boss. But so far, no luck. A Vermeer, three Rembrandts, and several other great works are still missing."

"Jeez, what a haul."

"Lucky *El Jaleo* is so big. I can't see anyone stealing that, and it was my favorite when I was there," I said.

"*El* what?"

"*El Jaleo*. By John Singer Sargent. It shows a Spanish dancer with some musicians behind her. With a little imagination you can hear the music and smell the cologne. These paintings belong to the public in a real sense. A theft is a loss to all of us. You can see pictures of the missing paintings, but there's nothing like seeing the real thing full size, and experiencing a sense of being as close to the artist as possible."

"I getcha. What exactly did Miles say about his old job?"

"Not much. He didn't sound like his memories were happy, but who knows, maybe it was just office politics.

Sometimes that can make you miserable even without a multimillion-dollar robbery."

"You think that's what it was?" Nick asked.

"I'm just looking for an explanation for his discomfort."

"It's could be that. I'll look into it." He sipped his coffee, looked down at the table, and tapped his fingers as if playing a little tune. The shop was busy, and two children walked by our table, licking their cones, a girl of about seven leading a boy who was maybe five. Nick smiled at them, said "Good?" and, after they nodded, turned back to me. "Let's try to talk to Miles now," he said. "Do you have his number?"

I looked at the members list. "There is a number here. We could try it. It's not his work number because it starts with 332- and that's here. The museum isn't."

"Which museum?" Nick asked.

"The Contemporary Arts Museum. He did framing and gallery design for special exhibitions. I heard he had some kind of clash with Juliana."

"When was that?" Nick asked.

"In the last few days, I think. I just heard."

"Try calling him," Nick said.

"Does he know you're a detective?" I asked. "I don't know if he'll want to come here to talk to you."

"If he doesn't know, there's no reason to tell him. Does he like you enough to come here for an ice cream with you?"

I felt warmth on my cheeks and knew they must be red. I wasn't the greatest beauty in town but still I didn't want to mislead Miles by pretending I was interested in him. Deception always made me uncomfortable.

"Come on, Lissa," Nick urged. "Danny didn't deserve what happened to him. Nobody should die so young. I'm going to talk to Miles one way or the other. He might as well get a free ice cream out of it."

"Okay," I said, the horrible emptiness of Danny's broken, dead eyes suddenly coming back to me. "I'll tell him I'm planning something for the Artists' Guild."

An hour later, Miles came in for an ice cream on the house and a chat about art--and Danny.

CHAPTER TWENTY-EIGHT

By the time he arrived, Bellini's was as crowded and noisy as on a summer night. The Tarrytown Theatre was having a special early show for kids, and it seemed everyone had to have an ice cream after it. Nick and I were sitting in the back. I watched Miles weave among baby carriages and shrieking toddlers, one of whom kept testing how far away Mom and Dad would let him wander on his little wobbly legs. Miles almost bumped into one father who was rushing to pull his giggling guy away from the mesmerizing swinging top of the garbage pail. Groups of older children, only slightly more sedate, sat together at two tables, the famous Bellini's Blue Monster ice cream visible on their lips. Teens sat at other tables, giggling cliquishly, flirting, sometimes texting, sometimes laughing and squirming in their seats. All the noise and activity would provide us, ironically, with privacy for our conversation, because the buzz would make us inaudible three feet away.

"Sit down, sit down," boomed Nick, the hearty, eager-to-please proprietor. He was playing it that way, I thought, so Miles would relax and talk. He was in full ice-cream shop mode now, completely unthreatening in his bright green Bellini's t-shirt. He interrupted our conversation from time to time to greet the regulars and deal with ice-cream shop emergencies, such as fallen cones. His friendly host manner wasn't false, I knew, just another level of his personality. The fact that he could balance his roles so well, and behave appropriately for whatever situation he was in, was part of what I found attractive about him. Under it all, I knew, he was still a cop, looking for a serious criminal.

"Did they take good care of you at the counter?" he asked Miles.

"Yes, thank you very much." Miles seemed a little stiff and formal. His sandy hair looked even richer in color in contrast to his "casual chic" gray pants and sweater. He looked like he'd stepped out of a Brooks Brothers ad.

"So good to see you again," I said with more warmth than I was feeling, following Nick's lead. If Miles had thought this was a date, he took Nick's third-wheel presence well in stride.

"What did you get, Miles?" asked Nick. "Looks like Bellini's Bold Mint Chocolate Chip?" When Miles nodded, Nick said with enthusiasm, "That's my favorite too," and he leaned closer as though this confirmed them in some sacred brotherhood.

I was prepared to come up with more than a vague reason for getting him there, so I took out my list of Artists' Guild members, which I had previously marked up with notes about each person's work. "I'm thinking about having a Guild show at my studio," I told Miles. "It's small, but a lot of members don't have any place else to exhibit."

"Sounds like a good idea," he said.

"I think I could get our names in the news, and I'd ask just 10 percent of sales to cover expenses."

"That sounds fair," Miles agreed. "I'd do some of the hanging. Maybe some framing, if people need it. I could use a clip of the coverage for my resume."

"Great! I'll talk to the others and let's see if we can pull it off," I told Miles. It wasn't a bad idea. Maybe I'd really do it.

The music had nearly drowned him out as one of the kids behind the counter turned up the volume. A shake of Nick's head got it turned back down immediately. A minute later he jumped up to check out the smell of burning sugar cones. He came back quickly and got right back into the conversation.

"Lissa tells me you're from Boston," he said.

"Yes," said Miles. "Well, the Boston area."

"Yeah?" said Nick. "I've got cousins there. I've been there. Great place. Where exactly?"

"Brookline," Miles answered. "It's been a while. It isn't home anymore—I'm happier here."

"But you go back for the holidays?" Nick asked.

Miles looked a little uncomfortable. "Sometimes," he said. "I'm trying to make it on my own now. To be truly accomplished, that's what one has to do."

"What do you mean? Your family offered to help and you wanted to go it alone? Man, if I had a father willing to pull strings for me..."

"If I wanted to be a banker, it would be great," Miles said. "That's what Father is. He wanted me to follow in his footsteps. I tried—I studied economics in college, but it wasn't for me. I don't want to count money all day and think about how to make more of it all night. So I went to Yale for an MFA."

"It's the best," I said. Although I disagreed with their entire definition of art, this was no time for a debate. "Their program is world-famous. They produce art stars."

"Yes, they do." Miles affirmed. "Unfortunately my family was against it anyway, because according to them, art is for kids and dilettantes."

"That's rough," said Nick. "When your family can't accept who you are..." He shook his head vigorously. "Art is a great pleasure to so many people. Lissa's work adds so much here."

Nick looked at me and smiled, and for a moment he was all that I saw. I almost reached out to touch his hand, but Miles' voice brought me back. I suppressed the impulse.

"There was no big dramatic scene," he was saying. "I just don't speak to them that often."

"I'd think your job at the museum here should be good enough for your folks," Nick said. "Lissa tells me it's very hard to get a job like that."

"It probably looks good on paper," Miles acknowledged. "But Juliana wasn't giving me enough opportunities, and I can do better. Luckily I can take my time looking around."

A customer tried the restroom door, waited a few seconds, and tried it again. Nick jumped up to get the key for her. I chatted with Miles about nothing much until Nick got back. Miles was almost finished with his ice cream, and I figured he might be ready to leave, so I asked in as casual a tone as I could, "Didn't you work at a museum in Boston, too? The Gardner?"

"No, no," he said, suddenly very busy studying his spoon with such apparent fascination that you'd think he'd just noticed an original Warhol painted on it. After a minute he continued, "No, I never said that. I worked at the Museum of Fine Arts. You must be thinking of that."

"Hey, I just remembered," Nick said. "I wanted to ask you--we met that curator's husband--what's his name? Juliana's husband? What a character. You know him?"

"Yes, of course," replied Miles. "Everyone who works at the museum knows Alexander Leighton. He's big. A critic."

"A smart guy. I give him credit for that. You like him?" Nick asked.

"I didn't really have that much to do with him," said Miles. "I just saw him at staff parties."

"Is he involved with the exhibitions at all?" I asked.

"Not in any obvious way," Miles answered. "Of course, there's probably some influence behind the scenes. Pillow talk about the artistic merits and all that."

"I wonder if he ever wrote anything about Danny's work," Nick said. He made it sound like he was just passing the time.

"No, I don't think so. Did he even know about it?" Miles asked. "Juliana wasn't what I'd call a fan."

"I heard they were at Danny's show in Peekskill last year," Nick said. "Were you there?"

"No," Miles replied. "I wasn't interested and it wasn't required viewing. He wasn't big, wasn't expected to become big."

"Why did Juliana and her husband go, then?" I asked.

"Why ask me? I haven't got the foggiest," Miles said. "Maybe they got their schedule mixed up, thought it was someone else showing. I can't imagine either of them taking a serious interest in Danny's paintings."

"Or maybe they know the gallery owner—what's her name?" Nick asked.

"Babette Young. That could be it," Miles answered slowly, maybe reluctantly. "I think so. Sounds possible."

"Jeez, when we met this Leighton guy he was so smug I almost wished I could pop him one myself. But he wasn't one of your problems at the museum?" Nick asked.

"No, no," Miles answered quickly. "I barely knew him. It was just that you have to move on sometimes when they don't take you seriously. Why are you so interested?"

"You're a friend of Lissa's, that's all," Nick said. "I like to find out about people."

"It's hard to imagine that working in a museum could be so unpleasant," I remarked.

Miles' frustration began to show in a bitter expression on his face. "Maybe some are good places," he said. "Not this one. You can't begin to imagine the pettiness and backbiting. It nearly spoiled my love of art. I wake up every morning thankful that I don't have to go there anymore."

"You're lucky you could get out," Nick told him. "There's nothing worse than being trapped in a job you hate. Some people would do anything to escape."

"I'll find something quickly," Miles said, but his hands were tight fists.

"Good for you, man," Nick said, hearty again. "We're gonna be pulling for you. How about an espresso? It's on me."

Miles accepted, and I told Nick I wouldn't mind if he made one for me, too. We chatted for a while about the mural and the work that might be included in the show. When Miles left, Nick turned to me and said, "Your friend isn't telling us everything."

"How do you know?" I asked.

"I know. Trust me. This is what I do. Stay away from that guy until I check him out."

I nodded and tried unsuccessfully to swallow a lump in my throat. The idea that someone I knew could be a criminal was unhappily clear.

Had Miles financed his freedom with forgery?

CHAPTER TWENTY-NINE

I was struggling with the door to Warner Library. I had four giclée reproductions on stretched canvas with me, two in each hand. They were copies of my paintings, made by computer and touched up by hand, and they were going in a show at the busy library's gallery. The door had one of those self-closing mechanisms, and it was difficult to juggle everything to go in.

Suddenly the resistance was gone. The door flew open so far so quickly that I almost fell. I turned around. A man had come up behind me and was holding it open. "Thanks," I said. I looked again.

It was Paul, the artstar.

"Anytime," he said. He scrutinized my face. "Hey, aren't you the one who was at Danny's studio yesterday? With that detective?'

"Yeah, that was me. I'm so sorry for your loss," I said.

"I'm okay. Danny was a good boy," he replied. "Poor little guy. I wish I could have helped him."

We went in and I put my things down, carefully leaning them against the wall, away from foot traffic.

"Did you even know he was in trouble?" I asked.

"No, not a clue," he said.

Did he answer a little too quickly?

I said, "Then how can you blame yourself?"

He nodded and looked like he was about to walk away, so I tried another approach.

"I really admire your work," I told him, "and in fact I took a friend of mine to see it at the museum not too long ago."

"I'm honored," he replied, in such a nice voice that I felt a twinge of guilt about the misleading way I put it.

"So, is this your work?" he asked, gesturing towards the giclée print.

"Yes, I'm still doing the painting-from-life thing," I replied. "I'd love to get your advice. What does it feel like to be in *Art in America* Magazine?" I batted my eyelashes and stuck out my chest.

"Let's have a look at your work," he said.

I could imagine what he'd make of it, given my lack of enthusiasm for his, but maybe if we talked long enough he'd give me some idea of what had happened to Danny.

I picked one up and held it close to eye level.

"Not bad," he said with a broad smile that seemed a little condescending. "But you're not going to make a name for yourself with this kind of thing."

"I know," I said, "I've heard it before. "It's been done. Only innovative work is going to get the grants and museum recognition."

"So why are you doing it?" He leaned in as he said it. His voice was soft and velvety, as if he were offering to let me confide a sin--or at least an egregious error.

"It makes me happy," I said. "A lot of people around here enjoy it."

He laughed. "That's enough for you? Are you happy with compliments? Happy is money in the bank," he said. "Happy is curators kissing your butt and begging for crumbs."

"Did you ever like Monet and Rembrandt?" I asked him. "Any traditional art?"

"Sure, a long time ago. Before Yale. But they taught me what's important. They taught me how to make a name."

"Did you ever really study the masters?" I asked. "I mean, in depth?"

"Yeah, I did some of that crap. 'Draw these flowers like Van Gogh would' kind of thing," he said.

"I saw some pretty good work at Danny's studio. Some copies he did at the Met. Did you ever copy master paintings?"

"Not me. I wasn't going to spend my life painting men with ruffled collars. Danny was really into it, for a while. He wasn't too bad. Pretty pictures. Big deal. Now Jeff Koons, that's art," he said.

"Did you know Danny was trying to get his work into the Contemporary Art Museum?" I asked.

"Yeah," Paul muttered. He looked away, presumably into the past. "I tried to help him. I contacted the curator for him. Too bad it didn't work out before..." his voice quivered a little. "I need a drink," he said.

"You asked Juliana to look at his work?" I asked.

"How do you know Juliana?"

"I don't, really," I told him. "Just from the galleries. The openings. Though I missed the one in Peekskill, when she and Danny had the big fight."

"Artists are a little screwy, that's all. Danny didn't know how to make things happen. He could be too pushy sometimes."

"I have to be careful myself," I said, "because I want to stick with the figurative like Danny did. How do you think he paid the rent with so little success in the galleries and museums?"

Paul looked across the room and pointed to a head-and-shoulders portrait on the opposite wall. "You see that?"

he asked. I nodded. "That's old-fashioned. Old-fashioned. If that artist made any money on that, it would be a miracle."

"I think it's from the Fifties," I said.

"So maybe then you could make a little doing that crap. But now...everyone has a goddamned iPhone or Droid, with not only a digital camera but video too. Who's gonna pay for a painted portrait?"

"Danny did nudes, though," I reminded him. "Like Lucien Freud. Don't you think that's more interesting to collectors?"

"Even that's dated now. You can make your own porn now, for god's sake. I don't know what the hell he was thinking."

"So how did he pay the rent?" I asked again.

Just then Anne came in the door. They looked at each other, and I wasn't at all sure it was a coincidence.

My question about Danny went unanswered. I'd clearly become very unimportant. I went to find the library's curator to tell her I was setting up my show.

CHAPTER THIRTY

Just as I was closing my studio the next night, the downstairs bell rang. I'd been working on the design for the second section of the mural, trying various combinations and relative sizes of the reference photos, when I realized it had gotten pretty late. The street was quiet. Who could be ringing my bell now? I took my time answering, and finally spoke into the intercom. "Yes?" My voice was a little shaky.

"Anybody there?" was the jovial response.

Nick! I relaxed and buzzed him in. I went to the top of the stairs to greet him.

"Come in, come in," I said. He was carrying a large brown envelope. "Got something for me?" I asked.

He brushed against me as he made his way in. I felt his warmth and I reached out and touched his arm in welcome.

"News," he said, holding up the envelope. He spotted the long digital prints I had laid out for comparison.

"Take a look," I said. "They're different ways we could approach the mural."

I pointed out some of the advantages and disadvantages of each design. Some had more of the park scene, others had more buildings. In some there was more foreground and less sense of vast space, in others there was a more panoramic overview.

He looked up from the designs. "Okay," he said. "Let's take our time making the decision. You want to hear my news?" He held up the envelope. "It's about Miles, and the report on the paints we found in Danny's studio. You already heard about the black."

"Tell me, of course," I said. "What did they find?"

"The Gardner confirmed that Miles worked there while he was in college. In 1990. Part-time."

"In what office?" I asked.

"No office. Security," he said.

I gasped. "He was there when it happened?" I asked. I couldn't believe it. This could be so big.

"No, not according to their records. He was off that night."

"So he's in the clear?"

"Not completely," Nick said. "Someone may have given the perps information ahead of time about the security setup. It's a stretch, but we know someone's been committing crimes here, and we have to look at him. For one thing, he admitted he had problems."

"No more than the rest of us," I said, though I really didn't know for sure.

"He told us he couldn't impress Papa. You know what that feels like when you're a kid. If someone starts giving a kid like that a lot of praise and attention, who knows what he'd do?"

"I hope for his sake you're just wasting your time," I told him, "but I understand." I gestured toward the manila envelope he was still holding. "What do you have about the paints?"

"Take a look and see if you spot anything." Nick handed me the large manila envelope.

I looked at some graphs and charts and a page of text. "Traces of paint were found on the mortar and pestle, and the pigments in the jars are hand-ground," I read aloud. "The particles were not of uniform size, as they would be if they had been produced by a machine. Ochres, viridian, cadmiums, quinacridones. Modern. No lead in the white. Titanium. Like we all use."

"No indication of forger's materials," said Nick.

"I see that. They sell these pigments for grinding because some artists like the control and feel of doing it. Since he had plenty of tubed ones, maybe he was just experimenting. The question is, why?"

"There was no evidence of any old canvases or nails," Nick pointed out. "But my gut tells me he was involved."

"Danny was a little crude and a lot temperamental, but I think he was still a decent guy at heart," I said. "Maybe somebody didn't understand that, and tried to get him to do something he really didn't want to do."

Nick nodded. "Could be he tried it on for size, grinding and mixing paints, and couldn't take the next step of actually making a forged painting."

"And when he refused, and maybe even threatened to talk...Danny was so childlike. They must've come to his studio and made a switch of the black paints when he wasn't looking. Oh god, could it have been because someone at the Artists' Guild meeting that night realized that he was going to show something intended to be used for forgery?"

"He was troubled and looking for help," Nick replied. "They knew that."

The thought that someone in the Artists Guild could be so dangerous did a macabre dance in my brain.

"Someone saw that Danny was cracking and didn't wait for it to happen," Nick continued. "Any ideas who it could be, other than Miles?"

"No, none," I said. "If I'd known he was dealing with something so big... Poor Danny. He called me, and I had no idea how much trouble he was in."

"How could you know?" asked Nick. He came closer, placed his hand on mine and looked at me for a long time. "Danny shouldn't have involved you at all. I hate to think what might have happened if you'd gone to his studio a little earlier that night. But I've got your back now."

"I can handle it," I said with more assurance than I felt. It meant a lot that Nick would be nearby.

"We'll manage together," he said. "Gotta go now. Aren't you going home yet?" he asked.

"Just leaving. I'll go down with you."

"Good," he said. He was looking at me and not at where he was going, and he bumped into a stack of paintings near the door. "Sorry. What're these?" he asked. "Are they o.k. leaning against each other like that?"

"Oh, those are just some paintings from my art school days. I like them, but I don't know if they deserve wall space. After all, I didn't compose them from scratch. I painted the models provided by the school."

"Not bad though," he said as he looked through the stack. He pulled one out, stared at it for a long moment, and said, "Oh, boy, are you gonna be in trouble."

"What did I do?" I asked.

"You've got a new one mixed in here," he said. "You're gonna be in it deep if it gets messed up. Diana's not one to forgive anything."

"What does she have to with it?"

"You didn't tell me you were painting her," he said.

"I'm not. It must be a model who looked like her."

"No," he said. "It's her. Boy, you really made her look young."

"Let me see," I said.

He handed it to me. I placed it on the floor, leaning upright against the bookcase, and took a long look. It was a woman in a red dress wearing only a small, fuzzy wrap that barely covered her shoulders. She was sitting in a large, comfortable-looking armchair. "You're right. It does look like her," I said. "But it *is* from art school. What an odd coincidence. I didn't always get the likeness right in those days. They weren't portraits, of course, meaning they weren't being done for the model, so I wasn't always exact about it. It's just a resemblance."

"I don't know," he said. "It's pretty damned close. How could that happen? You hadn't met her then, had you?"

I shook my head. "No, this painting was done long before I came to Tarrytown."

We looked at each other. "Could it be?" I asked. "Diana, the socialite?"

"Anything's possible. I'll start a background check. Leave it to me," Nick said.

After he left I stared and stared at the portrait. Could he possibly be right?

CHAPTER THIRTY-ONE

My second cup of coffee was getting cold. Where was my sandwich? I looked in vain for the waiter. I was sitting in the Olive Tree Diner in Dobbs Ferry, the one where I had run into Jim a few days after the fundraiser. A glorious sun was shining and I was inside, waiting for my lunch, instead of outside, painting. They had to pick today to screw up their usual get-em-out-quick service.

The diner was small, L-shaped, with comfortable booths upholstered in a pleasant turquoise fabric. A homey smell of coffee and bacon hit you as soon as you got within thirty feet of the place. The coffee was the best around, deeply flavorful and not at all bitter. I'd already had two cups and it was time to get moving. I signaled the owner of the diner and he took a break from a lively conversation about last night's baseball game. He was Greek, around sixty-five, gray-haired but energetic and as temperamental as a teenager. His voice was lilting if he was in a good mood and whiny if not.

"Something you need?" he asked.

"Yes, George, please find out what's taking so long. I've got to get to work."

"Always in a hurry," he commented, shaking his head. "Why you so busy all the time?"

"Art's a tough profession," I told him. "The world is full of artists. I've got to work extra hard to be seen above the crowd."

"I help you, sweetheart," he said, "don't you worry. I take care of you." He disappeared into the kitchen and came back with my sandwich.

"You see?" he said. "Anytime you have a problem, you ask for me. I take care of you. See, I give you extra pickle."

"Thanks so much," I said, eying the green sliver that made him feel so generous.

"You sell a lot of your paintings?" he asked.

"I do okay," I said between bites.

"You like old art?" he asked.

"Yes, a lot more than most new art," I told him.

"French art?'

"Yes, very much. The Impressionists are my great inspiration. I love Monet, Sisley, Manet, Pissarro, Degas very much," I said.

"All right, all right, enjoy your lunch. I talk to you when you are finished. Tony, more coffee for the young lady."

I finished quickly and headed up to the front of the diner to pay. George waved aside the young girl at the cash register and took my check and money himself.

"So you love the art," he said, clucking a little, like a mother hen. A mother hen with sharp claws tucked just out of sight.

"Yes, of course, it's my life," I answered.

"You buy too?" he asked, with an assessing glance, serious now.

"Not usually," I told him. "I don't have much money to spare right now. Supplies and studio rent are so expensive."

"But if I tell you about something very special?" he asked quietly, handing me my change and looking at me intently.

"What did you have in mind?" Did he know what would be special to me?

"Come, I walk you outside," he said, and we started through the doorway and out to the parking lot. Outside, the restaurant's aromas were momentarily lost to the heavy smell of gasoline as the next-door service station got a delivery from a tanker truck. In this mundane setting he told me that he knew where I could buy two pastel sketches done by the living hand of Edgar Degas.

"You're putting me on, right?" was all I could muster at first.

He came very close to me, held me by the elbow, and said "Look at me. I tell you the truth. I know you are a real artist. I see you for many years, now. I know you will see what these are."

"How did you get them?"

"It is not me. I do not have them. I know through a business acquaintance about this. He is in town several weeks, he comes here many times. He is going home soon. His daughter-in-law is giving him his first grandchild, and he will have to go back to France as soon as the call comes. He must be there for the birth," George said.

"Real Degas pastels? Can you be sure?" I thought of Jim and his maybe-Monet. *Wait a minute. Did this have something to do with the fact that Jim had seen me here?*

"Yes, yes, I have seen them. They are real and you can touch the paper and touch the chalks that the master himself once touched."

"I'm sure I couldn't afford anything like that," I said. "They're part of history."

"You will see. They are small, very small, but they are from the hand of the great artist. All the time you come in, summer when it's hot, winter when it's cold. I know that. I give you a break. He see you when you bring in your painting you are working on and he ask me about you. I say maybe you buy something like this."

George's face was full of innocence. It looked like he was being duped by someone trying to sell a forgery. I played along.

"When did you talk to him?" I asked.

"He ask me today, early. I tell him you always say how artists' life is hard. I tell him you are not rich."

"There've been Degas pastels that sold for millions."

"He said that. But these are not that. These are small, but for an artist it is a big thing, isn't it? He will sell them right now, before he goes back, and I will tell him to give you a good price."

This was beyond belief. It was just falling into my lap. "I guess I could meet with him," I said. "Can he bring them here?"

"No," he said, inhaling sharply, shaking his head, raising his hands as if to ward off my dumb idea, his whole body expressing shock. A car horn blared nearby, as if to emphasize his gestures. "This must be very quiet or he will have to pay the American taxes. He does this for a poor widow. She cannot afford the extra taxes."

"How did he get them?"

"He has them for a close friend. He is executor for her husband. My friend Pierre promised many times that he would take care of the widow when the time it came. They do not look for a fortune but they do not give them away, either."

"Why not sell them quietly in France?"

"It is asking for trouble. Here it will be far away and no one will ever know. No one will miss them because no one has seen them."

"Could he bring them to my studio?"

"You do not understand. This must be very, very quiet. You must meet him where no one is there to see or to hear."

"Well, I guess if you vouch for him…."

A chorus of car horns sounded as someone held everything up by trying to make a left turn in heavy traffic right in front of a large "No Left Turn" sign. George couldn't answer right away because of the noise, but he nodded. When the driver gave in and made a right, George said, "Good, good. Call me at 5 and I will tell you when and where."

"Okay, I guess I can't turn my back on an opportunity like this." I got into my car and headed for my studio, thinking about what Nick might say. Degas pastels, no matter how small…they couldn't be real. George seemed so innocent, but he didn't usually act so interested in art. Or in my struggles. And he had a temper. Was it some kind of prank? Had I sent back one too many charcoal-cremated burgers?

George couldn't be that good an actor. And I was a good customer.

I had to call Nick right away, and tell him I might have a forger for him.

Damn! I called his cell phone and got that frustrating clicking as it switched from ringing the line to ringing the voice mail. I heard him say the words but he wasn't there.

"This is Lieutenant Bellini. Please leave a message and I'll get back to you as soon as possible."

I sighed and did just that, and then I called the Detectives' Room at the station. "Sorry, ma'am," said the youngish voice on the other end. "Detective Bellini is testifying in court today in White Plains. I don't know when he'll back." *Damn*, I thought, *he* did *tell me about this. A big case with lots of complicated issues. Why did it have to be today?* I left a message with him, too, and hoped for the best.

At 5:00 I hadn't heard from Nick yet. I took a deep breath. I couldn't do this without backup from Nick. I called George.

"Ah, yes, Sweetheart, I wait for your call. You are lucky, Pierre can meet you right away."

"Could we make it tomorrow?" I asked. "I'm not feeling too well. I could do it early tomorrow."

"Tomorrow is no good. I tell you he will be called back to France at any moment. You will miss this chance." George sounded agitated. "You must go," he said.

I thought about all the pleasant, innocuous times I'd had at the diner. I couldn't picture George as a criminal. He wouldn't set a trap for me. Would he? What if I just went and talked to the guy? I could give Nick a description and a name. I could play dumb. How dangerous could it be?

"All right, all right," I said. "When and where? And how will I know him?"

We worked out the details and I left messages for Nick on his cell and at the station. I had an hour to kill but I had trouble concentrating on my painting, so I left my studio a little early and drove to the river, where I watched the geese and the waves until it was time to go.

CHAPTER THIRTY-TWO

The evening becomes night so fast in the winter. I headed out of Tarrytown as the sky began to darken. I made a right at the Horseman Diner, onto Bedford Road and soon passed an estate with a stable that was more attractive than most apartment buildings. It must belong to a Rockefeller; Kykuit was right down the road, and so was the farm created years before by David Rockefeller's wife. Cows grazed right next to the road, which I'd found strangely soothing until I remembered these storybook cows would eventually be dinner at the farm's elegant and pricey restaurant. One goal of the Rockefellers was to reconnect people to the knowledge of where food comes from. Not really so soothing, especially when you're not really sure you're at the top of the food chain.

I resisted the impulse to turn around, and made the left onto Old Sleepy Hollow Road, a favorite place for me to enjoy a quiet drive. Houses, some built with obvious wealth and others old farmsteads, were far apart and surrounded by acres of forest and creeks. Sometimes in winter I'd come there to enjoy driving alone in the freshness of new snow.

Tonight relaxation was far more remote than the road. I tried to convince myself that George's acquaintance

Pierre du Roncourt believed that I was on his side, truly interested in buying some Degas pastels on the quiet, no provenance requested. Let him think I was naive. I hadn't given George any reason to believe, I reassured myself repeatedly, that I suspected they had been done almost a century after the master's death.

I arrived at our rendezvous site just after sunset. At that time of year it gets completely dark very fast. Few cars were on the road now. The location he had chosen was an abandoned water pumping station, eerily quiet. The headless horseman would be very much at home there. I pulled my car as far into the driveway as I could. A chain, indicating that visitors were definitely not welcome, kept me from going any farther. I watched the road for the lights of his car, clutching my cell phone in one hand and tapping my pocket from time to time with the other to reassure myself that I had my can of Mace. There were no homes close by. The water station had a fair amount of land around it, and if any of the property in sight was privately owned, it wasn't inhabited.

The night grew darker and colder, but luckily it wasn't freezing. I kept the engine running and the heater on for a while. Every once in a while a car approached, but passed by without slowing down. After ten minutes or so, a green Ford van started to turn off the road in my direction, but turned away. My heart was pounding so loud they could probably hear it. As they pulled out I could see that it was just kids, two young couples, maybe looking for a place to have a little privacy. A Lexus slowed and came to a stop a few yards away, but the driver shouted into a cell phone for a while and left.

Finally I heard a car with a wheezing and sputtering engine, and this time the sound got louder and louder and didn't pass by. It was an old white Volvo with a ski rack.

He was here.

The Volvo turned into the driveway and pulled up next to me. I reached down surreptitiously and turned on the voice recorder I had placed under the seat, and turned off the car so engine noise wouldn't interfere with our voices. I took a deep breath and waited. Maybe if things went wrong I could start the car and take off.

When would Nick get my messages?

"*Aleeessa?*" he asked. This was it--unmistakably my Frenchman. I nodded, not finding it easy to speak. Could I carry off the performance? What would he do to me if he realized I wasn't on the level?

"Come in," I said, motioning for him to join me. "This is so exciting," I gushed. He got in and slammed the heavy door shut. He was slender, not very tall, dressed in dark clothing, and wearing a beret tilted slightly to one side. It was dark, but I could see that his skin sagged under his eyes and around his mouth. Like George, he must have been in his sixties. At least he wasn't physically intimidating.

What if he had a weapon?

His scent filled the car, flowery, maybe a little girly, I thought, but didn't some terrorists wear sweet colognes?

I couldn't assume he was a gentle soul, much as I wanted to. My mind replayed the image of Danny's body lying irretrievably broken in his studio. I was totally insane to be here. Why was I doing this alone? I tried briefly to remember, then forced my attention back to the package he was holding so carefully horizontal. I knew he was keeping the image side up.

"What did he tell you, *mon ami* George?" he asked.

"Just that you had some very exciting pastels that I could see. He knows I worship Degas, and he knows I'm not wealthy. He said you might be able to make a dream come true for me."

He slowly and gently unwrapped his package, revealing two small framed pictures, each about 11 x 14 inches. I reached for them.

"Take the care, please," he said in a fussy voice, sounding more like an artist than a dangerous crook. "The pastels, they are fragile, you know. The colors, they can shake off."

I reassured him. "Don't worry. I know how to handle art."

I had brought a small lantern with a bulb that mimicked daylight. I switched it on.

He looked around swiftly and nervously. "Too much of the light," he said. "We must not be seen. There will be the trouble." I asked him to hold the light for me and I raised my jacket to form a partial tent around the pictures. He looked around, appeared to satisfy himself that the darkness outside was undisturbed ebony, and began his sales pitch. "Here we have the *etudes*," he said, "the studies for the paintings in the big museums."

I looked carefully at the two small works. I had leaned them back against the steering wheel, nearly horizontal. I didn't recognize them as being made directly from any of Degas' major works, but they did have the typical subject matter. One was a woman brushing her hair and the other was a group of racehorses in a field. They were not fully developed scenes, but rather drawings with a minimum of details. The sensibility wasn't Degas. Unless they were from his childhood or his dotage, they were definitely not done by him. Since there was that tiny "unless," and even a bad work by a top master was worth a fortune just because his hand had created it, my opinion couldn't be the final word. We'd have tests done on the pigments and paper to see if they were nineteenth century and get an official verdict from Sotheby's or Christies.

"These are stunning," I said, "I can see the quality. Of course, I'd have to see them in daylight before I give you the money." I saw his subtle smirk. "But how much do you want? I probably can't afford them."

"Do not despair," he replied. "The seller she is a recluse. She wants no publicity, no fuss. It has been from the parents and grandparents this way. She will sell to people who must have the art and she will not ask for the stars. She will want it as if she finds a great home for a puppy who licks her face but she cannot keep him. She thinks only what is the best for the puppy." He sounded confident.

How stupid did he think I was?

"Are you sure she doesn't mind giving them up?" I asked.

"No, no, not the least bit. She is happy. She has the good life."

"Does she live in Paris?"

"No, no. She live in a small town, Argeles-Gazost, near to Lourdes. She does not go out from there ever, but to the mountains for the good air."

"Lourdes?" I asked. "Maybe a miracle came to me," I said, sounding sincere to myself, at least. "How much?"

"Ten thousand American dollars," he said, "for both," he added, in a tone that made it sound like it was an incredible bargain. I certainly didn't have that kind of cash, but if we went through with the sale, the money would be marked bills supplied by the police.

"I don't know," I said, trying to get the price down partly out of habit from trying to live on an artist's income, and partly because I thought he'd expect it. "I could go almost that high. How about eight?" We struck a deal at $9,250 and he prepared to get out. I handed the pictures back with a show of reluctance, saying "I hate to let go of the magic of Degas. I feel the energy right through the frames."

We would meet again the next day for the actual sale. Apparently his daughter-in-law was prepared to hold the baby in just long enough.

I felt a sense of elation. I'd pulled it off.

Who knew I could act?

"I'm so grateful, Pierre," I said. "I'm excited beyond words. How can I ever thank George?"

He smiled, looking very proud of himself, with more than a touch of arrogance mixed in. He got out, got into his own car and drove away.

As simple as that, I thought. I sat for a few minutes exulting in my success, and decided that I had to share it with Nick ASAP. I told my OnStar car phone to call the stored number for the Tarrytown P.D.

"Detectives' Room," said an unfamiliar voice, so deep and vibrant that it filled the car and bounced back off the windows.

"Hello, is Lieutenant Bellini in?" I felt my excitement bubbling into my words.

"No, Ma'am, I'm sorry, he's out. Is there something I can do for you?"

"Just tell him that Lissa called. Tell him I have big news. Please have him call me right away."

"Yes, Ma'am, as soon as he comes in."

Time to get moving, back to civilization.

Then I heard it. The rustling and the crunching of gravel. Pierre must be coming back!

What a fool I had been, thinking I was such a great actress!

He'd figured it out, parked down the road and he was coming back! He wanted to sneak up and catch me off guard so I didn't put up a fight!

Did he hear my call to Nick?

I reached for the mace and fumbled with it. It fell out of my cold, shaking hand, onto the floor, and rolled under the seat. I bent down to feel for it, and dared not look up. I saw, through the corner of my eye, the approach of the large dark figure. My heart thumped hard in my chest once and then pounded several more times as the figure came closer and closer, finally pressing against the car, trying to open the door. I wanted to scream, but who would hear? All the things I hadn't done yet were flashing through my mind, the trip to Venice I'd always wanted and the paintings I hadn't finished, the friends and family who'd be so shocked when my body was found...

I took a deep breath. I decided that I wasn't going out a coward. I might not be able to fight him off, but I'd look him straight in the eye. I sat up and stared out the window. Where *were* his eyes? It was so dark he was little more than a large shape. Larger than Pierre? I felt unsure. I saw his lips as the clouds parted a little to let the moonlight through. I silently cursed his wide grin. The sadistic bastard was enjoying this. Damn him for laughing so hard! The clouds parted a little more and I saw his face as clearly as I needed to. I felt the blood in my face. Not *on* my face, *in* my face. There was no smashing glass, no gunshot, no brass knuckles. I groaned and hit the button to open the window.

"Bogeyman!" he introduced himself cheerfully, almost singing the word. "You didn't think I'd let you be out here all alone with that scum, did you?" he said.

It was Nick.

CHAPTER THIRTY-THREE

"Damn you! Did you have to sneak up on me like that? You're just lucky I dropped my Mace," I said.

"Easy, girl. If you want to play detective you'd better learn to keep your cool," he said. "I got your messages about 15 minutes ago and I came right over. I didn't call you because I didn't know if there was anybody with you. It could've been bad for you."

After I started breathing again I told Nick what I could about the pastels. "I don't know exactly which paintings he copied," I said, "but I know that I've seen similar Degas figures somewhere, either in museums or in my art books."

"Do you have anything in books I could see now?" he asked.

"Right now?" I asked dubiously. I was more in the mood for a drink.

"The sooner the better," he said, "if you're going to remember exactly what he had."

He was right, of course, and I decided to soldier on. "Let's go," I said. "We can start with what I've got at my studio, but I'm not sure what's there and what's at home. And by the way, would you like his fingerprints?" I handed him the lamp, holding it by its front section where Pierre hadn't touched it. "And how about hearing the whole thing?" I pulled the voice recorder out from under the seat.

"Good work!" he said, beaming as brightly as the light had.

My elation returned full-force.

He smiled, more relaxed now. "Poor Lissa," he said. "Your first undercover. I hope I didn't spoil it for you," he said in a teasing voice.

"To the studio?" I asked. He nodded.

His car was tucked away a little down the road and I drove him there to pick it up. We went back to town in our two-car mini convoy. It was a quiet night and we arrived quickly at my studio. I opened the bottle of wine that had been sitting there for several months, waiting for a special event, and this seemed to fit the bill, though not in the way I'd expected. Nick settled into an armchair and I went to work looking through my bookcase.

"Here's one," I said, pulling out a catalogue from a show at the Met a few years before. I pulled a chair next to his and started flipping pages.

"These were typical Degas scenes?" Nick asked.

"They were recognizable, although the woman was too thin," I told him. "In nineteenth-century France women's curves were admired. At that time, starvation was not considered a good thing."

"I like a woman with curves," he said.

"Good," I said, since I was not one to starve myself.

"Was there anything else wrong about the pastels?" he asked.

"They weren't as complex as the real thing. Degas used a lot of layers, each allowing some of the under layers to show through. He sprayed fixative after each, except for the last one, which would be the surface layer. The fixative changes the look, and he didn't want that on the surface." I leaned towards him, bringing the book closer to him,

170

pointing out the places in the illustrations where the texture was most obvious. He put his glass of wine on top of a leaning stack of canvases as he took the book from me. I moved his glass to a safer spot, happy that I'd chosen white wine. I was just renting. It wasn't my carpet.

"Anything else?" he asked.

"The strokes are not the same and the grace is not there," I said. "Recognizing a master's work is like recognizing members of a family. Each is unique but they share some key similarities. Same as handwriting," I said, gesturing at his hands.

"I got it," he replied. "It's a major identifier."

"With traditional painting and drawing it's the same thing. Degas did it with hand and eye, and it expresses him directly. You'll still need to get it tested scientifically, of course. I'm not claiming infallibility."

"Anything here that du Roncourt may have copied?" Nick asked.

"Not yet. Let me see what else I have. This book is mostly landscapes. He wasn't known as well for those." I went back to the bookcase and pulled out a catalogue for an Impressionist show at the Met some years ago. I turned pages as I spoke, past Madame Monet in a green dress, past bunches of violets, Manet bullfighters, a naked woman in a forest having a picnic lunch with a couple of fully-dressed men.

"I like this one," Nick said playfully.

"I'll bet you do," I said, smiling. "It was quite scandalous at the time. It's a Manet, not a Degas."

"Where did he say the seller lives?" asked Nick.

"Near Lourdes. In France. He told me the name of the town but I don't remember it. I probably wouldn't be able to spell it anyway unless I saw it written down. He said she never travels farther than the local mountains--the Pyrenees."

"It's on the recording you gave me?" Nick asked.

I nodded.

"We'll check it out," Nick said. "It's probably just a bullshit story they use, but there's a small chance his little old lady is the real forger."

"I'll try to get him to talk more about it when we meet again. Maybe I can catch him in a lie.

"Good, but don't say anything to him that will put you in danger. Just tell him you're curious because you have an artist friend who's traveling to France for the coming year, to soak up the culture. Maybe say you might go with her. Ask what kind of place it is. Then let me handle it."

"Okay," I promised. "You'll be nearby when I see him?"

"Count on it. Me and at least three of my biggest guys. You'll be fine."

I looked into his eyes and felt reassured. Nick could be trusted. I could do this.

Of course, I had no inkling at the time that the second meeting with Pierre would run into an insurmountable obstacle.

CHAPTER THIRTY-FOUR

It was one of those brutally cold New York days that come less often than they used to, but when they did, some people with short memories went around saying, "Global warming? This is warm?" The air mass over Tarrytown had left the Arctic and come to us via Canada, lowering the overnight temperature to a stunning 6 degrees the night before. Polar bears could have frolicked happily on the Hudson's temporary icebergs, where waves had frozen in mid-roll. Most people didn't leave their homes except for work and school. Not surprisingly, there weren't too many takers for ice cream, and Bellini's had been deserted almost all day.

I had loaded on layers of jerseys and wool pullovers and cardigans under my coat and gone to work on the mural anyway. The shop was cold, but I was able to remove a few layers and press on with my depiction of the pond at Patriot's Park on a bright summer day. It was part of a composite of some of Nick's favorite Sleepy Hollow scenes. Art can transport you somewhere you'd rather be, and I was enjoying my "day at the park."

Gina was the only other person there. Since it was so quiet, she'd let the hired kids go home early. Around three o'clock she came to the back to check out my work.

173

"I wish I were there," she said, looking at the trees and flowers I'd created.

"You are," I said. "Just sit down and look."

"How about a cappuccino with the view?" she asked.

Milk carefully steamed and foamy, we sat down.

"This is good," she said. "I like what you've brought to us. And Nick likes you," she said, to my surprise.

"I like Nick," I replied. "I like all of you."

"You know what I mean, Lissa."

"I don't think about that," I lied. "Nancy's back. I know that."

"He told you?"

"No, I was here when she came to see you," I reminded Gina.

"You heard our conversation?" she asked, and took a long sip of her cappuccino. She looked around at the floor, the back door, the front counter. "Lissa, things change. You can't always go back."

I wasn't sure what to say. I didn't want to get involved with a man whose marriage was still going, even if it had hit a bump. Granted, it had been a huge bump. There were still times when I wasn't even sure I wanted to take another chance on any man, after what happened with my ex. I'd been so blind to his problems.

"Does Nick seem happy that she came back?" I asked. I could hear the wavering quality in my voice. I hoped Gina didn't notice.

She sighed and looked down into her cappuccino for what seemed to be a long time. "Maybe, in a way. I think he's happy that things didn't work out for Nancy. Only because he feels vindicated. Anyway, that's my take on it."

"You don't think he wants her back?"

"I don't know, but I don't want him to get hurt again. I don't know if I should tell him…"

When she didn't speak for an eternity, or so it seemed, I tried to prompt her. "Tell him what?"

Gina looked tired. "How much do you owe a friend?" She didn't seem to expect an answer.

"Nancy?" I asked.

"Would you like a cookie?" she asked.

She was stalling. There weren't any cookies on the table, so she'd have to get up and go to the front to get it. She might change her mind. "No, thanks," I said. "You know I care about Nick. What's worrying you?"

Gina stood up anyway. She walked to one of the windows in the back of the shop, looked out for a minute, and came back to the table.

"Look, Lissa, I know Nick trusts you. Can I trust you too? You won't tell anyone, especially Nick?"

"Yes, sure," I said. "I promise. Absolutely." What could this possibly be? Drugs? Other men before the English doctor?

"We were kids together, you know," she said hesitantly. "And they were married, and things seemed fine. Then Allan Bronson came do a research project at Manhattan Hospital."

"Allan Bronson? The famous one who claimed he was developing a cure for cancer?" I asked. "The handsome one who was in the society pages all the time?"

"Yes," Gina confirmed. "He was at Columbia University, on leave from Oxford for six months, and, life is so funny, if he hadn't known someone at the River Institute he probably never would have set foot in Westchester."

"And he met Nancy there?" I asked.

"Again, a fluke. She shouldn't have been there. She just went because her friend Peggy had to fill in for her sick boss by going to a fundraiser there, and she and Nancy had tickets for something afterward. So Nancy went with her."

"Sounds like it was fate," I suggested.

"You could say that. Nancy told me she got bored when people started to make speeches, and she stepped outside for some air. Allan had left some notes in his car and went out to get them. Their eyes met, and, you know. They should've been miles away from each other."

"A perfect storm?" I asked. "All those factors had to come together or the disaster wouldn't have happened? There must have been a problem with her marriage, though, or she wouldn't be interested in anyone else."

"As far as I knew, everything was fine between her and Nick," Gina said. "After that night, she started talking about feeling trapped. She said she'd missed out on opportunities and it wasn't fair."

"And when he went back to England, she went with him?"

"No, it wasn't that fast." Gina looked down at her cappuccino. "I've kept this to myself for years," she said. Her voice was soft. I could barely hear her. "I look at my little girl sometimes and I think about the cousin she should be playing with."

My throat felt tight.

"She was pregnant," Gina continued in a choked voice. "He doesn't know. He never knew."

"Nick's baby?" I whispered, my voice unable to function at full power.

"She'd already taken a pregnancy test, just before she met Allan," Gina confirmed. "She said she wasn't going to tell Nick yet, because the women in her family had a high rate of miscarriages."

"And that's what happened?" I asked. "She miscarried?"

"No," Gina said, blinking back tears. "She wanted to go to England."

I was stunned. All thoughts of my bad experiences with men faded from my mind. Nick seemed to be as good a guy as anyone could find.

How could she?

"She had an abortion?" I asked. "Without his knowledge?"

Gina nodded.

I took a deep breath and wondered what it felt like to be Nancy, and hoped I'd never really know.

CHAPTER THIRTY-FIVE

I was on a ladder in the back of the shop a few days later, painting some fair-weather clouds over Patriot's Park. The real weather had moderated and it seemed that everyone who'd stayed home during the icy blast had bounced back from cabin fever and come in to get ice cream.

At a nearby table a tiny, brightly-dressed Ecuadorean woman chirped cheerfully to her three tinier children. At another table squeals and screams issued every few moments from a group of teens who I'd seen a few times heading down the hill towards town, presumably from the college. A third table was occupied by a well-dressed middle-aged woman, who was with an elderly one who'd come in leaning heavily on a cane. One nice thing about Bellini's was that there was as much variety in the customers as there was in the ice-cream flavors.

A spicy perfume overrode the sugar cone aroma as Diana DeWitt, wearing a coat and dress ensemble that was vividly green and very chic, swept in as though coming onstage in a Broadway production. I recognized her glossy stiletto pumps and matching bag from an ad. They were Valentinos, worth about $3,000 total. Her blond hair must've been freshly trimmed, its bottom edges looking so sharp you'd imagine they could cut your hand.

Accompanying her was Brendan, an impeccably-groomed young man whose antique store in the Tarrytown Theatre was equally impeccable and quite unaffordable.

They bought coffee and small dishes of ice cream (he paid—she must've given him a large sale) and sat down at a table near me. They showed no signs of being aware that I was there. I went on painting. They were talking animatedly but I had to strain to hear over the loud rock music.

"I think it will look perfect in there, Brendan," she said.

"It will be a delight every day," he replied. "There's nothing more important than creating the proper ambience. With the Monet in the room it becomes critical. You have a responsibility."

"I appreciate that," she said. "The Monet has such lovely lilacs and blues. This will pick them up."

He nodded. "And it's comfortable, too." He sat back and folded his hands in front of his chest, almost in a gesture of prayer. "I have a surprise for you," he said. "I was saving it for when you were sitting down. I've just heard from a friend. It's something so special it deserves a champagne toast. Maybe I shouldn't even tell you here," he said, giggling. They both jumped as a particularly loud and shrill scream emanated from the college crowd's table, then both relaxed as it became clear that the disturbance was about a text from a very cute boy, nothing to do with Monet.

"Tell me, tell me, please," she said, tugging on his arm. "I know you, and if you're excited about it…."

"What would you say if I told you I had a painting that you'd kill to get?"

She sucked in her breath. "Brendan, tell me, tell me. Is it something so special that no one else in town will have anything like it?"

Apparently her money hadn't bought her the ability to feel anything other than vanity.

Brendan looked a little smug. "If you get this you'll have a truly museum-quality collection," he replied.

"I want it," she said, smacking the table with her right hand. "What is it?"

"I have a friend who has a friend who can get you a Renoir landscape. He knows a Frenchman who is here briefly, maybe for another day or two. He's got to rush back to Lyon when his daughter-in-law goes into labor."

I dropped my paintbrush, practically in Diana's lap, but they paid no attention to that or to my hasty recovery of it from the floor next to her.

"You must tell him we want to see it immediately."

"I'll try. It'll be quite a coup if you can get it. He's selling it on behalf of some old lady in France who doesn't want any publicity."

"Well done, Brendan. We're having a big party for Jim's birthday next week. I can see it now. I'll wear my red silk Valentino. We'll toast Jim, and then I'll unveil the painting. Can you call him right away?" she asked.

"Done," he said, pushing buttons on his cell phone.

"Will he bring it to the house?" she asked.

"Maybe for you," he replied as he waited for the call to go through. Bellini's didn't have the best cell phone reception. "These things have to be done quietly, but given who you are, I think he'll do it. You mustn't tell a soul about this," he said in a serious tone.

Diana smiled. Her position made a lot of things easier for her, I was quite sure. He tried his call again, and as he waited for a connection another scream and a whoop of laughter went up from the college table. Brendan's face showed his annoyance. "I don't think this is the moment to call, after all," he told Diana as he closed his phone. "I'll do it as soon as I get back to the shop," he said, and she nodded. They went back to chatting about furniture.

I called Nick as soon as they left.

"Did you hear from Pierre?" he asked, before I could tell him my news.

"No, I think he may be busy with bigger fish," I said, and told him what I'd heard.

"Jeez, they walked right in with this," he exclaimed. "Did you find out when and where they're going to meet?"

"No, no, the call didn't go through," I told him.

"Well, it's going to be sometime soon. This guy doesn't want people to have time to think," Nick said. "I'll get somebody to watch to the house. Call me if you hear anything."

"Sure. Maybe I'll take a walk up to Brendan's store and look around. If we're very lucky maybe I'll hear something there, too."

"Okay," said Nick. "But be careful. This is a big money deal. This is not a sketch, this is a painting. This has got to be something they won't want anyone to put the brakes on."

"I won't say a thing to him. I'll just tell him I need a chair for someone to sit in for a portrait."

"Let me know anything you hear, anything at all, even if you're not sure it's about this."

I agreed, wiped my brushes and stowed them temporarily in plastic wrap, and tried to make myself a little more presentable for a different sort of job.

CHAPTER THIRTY-SIX

I walked up the block swiftly, in fact too swiftly, because Brendan and Diana were still standing in front of his shop talking. He had the beautiful storefront at the corner of Main and Kaldenberg, with huge windows and a little mezzanine level inside. They showed no sign of seeing me, and I ducked into the Chinese restaurant on the opposite corner. I bought a cup of steaming tea and watched for Brendan to go into his shop.

A limo came by after five or six minutes, and stopped to pick up Diana. Brendan watched her get in and made the "I'll call you" gesture, mimicking a phone at his ear. He turned towards the door to his store. I dropped what was left of my tea in the garbage and headed after him.

I knew Brendan only slightly, and wasn't sure whether he knew exactly who I was. The phone was ringing as I walked in, and when he picked it up he launched into a long conversation with a client about a lawn sculpture.

"It *is* marble, Mrs. Goldfine," he said loudly. "Yes, it is. Come in and take a look. I *know* you can't be sure when you see it through the window. I had you in mind when I purchased it, in fact. It's very much the kind of thing that appeals to you." He listened for a minute and said, "Two feet wide and four feet tall, on a base that brings it up to six feet. Yes, around 1930's, maybe 40's." He listened again. "An estate sale," he said, "right near Kykuit. No, no, it didn't belong to the Rockefellers, but it's fine work nevertheless." I began looking around.

Brendan had an assortment of tables, lamps, chairs, paintings, jewelry, vases, and teapots, filling the space with little room to maneuver. I got around as best I could, feigning interest in lamps and earrings and chairs until Mrs. Goldfine was apparently convinced that it was worth her time to come get a close look at the marble sculpture. Brendan turned his attention to me as soon as he hung up.

"Can I help you with something?" he asked in a slightly frustrated tone.

"Just looking around," I said. "I need a chair for a portrait."

"A portrait?"

"I'm an artist. I have a studio across the street. I have someone coming in to pose and I just have plain chairs."

"Right across the street?" he asked with little interest. "You do look a little familiar. Any particular requirements for the chair?" Good, he wasn't showing any signs that he knew I'd overheard his conversation at Bellini's.

"I think something plush. Either pink or lime-green. Possibly a floral. I can't spend too much, though. Struggling artist and all that, you know," I said. Whatever glimmer of interest had been on his face disappeared.

"Well, look around, and let me know if you see something you like," he said, his hand making a sweeping gesture around the shop. I made a show of scrutinizing everything in the shop and after a few silent minutes he picked up the phone and dialed. "Sandy?" he asked into the phone. "Brendan here," he said. "I have a client who might be interested in the picture we discussed. Yes, yes, I know. As soon as possible. You have the address? That is correct. 7:00? I'll check with her and call you back."

I had a first name now to give Nick. Who was this Sandy? Was she the player or just someone's secretary?

He put the phone down, then picked it up again, looked at me, and put it down once more. I started trying on earrings. Just another hopelessly unfocussed female customer. He picked it up again and pressed a couple of keys. "Brendan here," he said again. "How would 7:00 be? Oh, he'll be home? This is a significant expenditure. You don't want to tell him? What time does he come in?" He listened. "Can you come here?" He looked anxious. "All right, I'll ask about Monday morning. But bear in mind that you may lose it. He may have to go back at any time." Another pause as he listened to the person on the other end, presumably Diana. "This may never happen again. It's a rare opportunity." He looked a little annoyed. "Yes, maybe he would come back if you pay for the ticket. Okay, that takes some of the pressure off, but someone else may snap it up. Okay, okay, I'll get back to you."

"How much are these?" I asked when he ended the call. I was holding up a pair of dangly earrings.

"Two hundred dollars," he said. "Twenty-four carat gold. They're a great value," he said in a mechanical voice. I looked around some more. He arranged and rearranged a stack of papers, then made a brief call, leaving a message for someone to please call him as soon as possible.

He turned back to me. "Have you found anything that interests you?" he asked.

Almost exactly what I wanted, I thought, but what I said, quite truthfully, was, "I do like this chair in the corner, but it's probably a lot more money than the earrings."

"A little," he said. "Nine hundred more, to be specific. Shall I wrap it up?" he asked with a slightly wicked grin.

"That's okay," I said. I'll have to think about it." I didn't want to push my luck. I decided that I had enough to tell Nick and made my exit.

CHAPTER THIRTY-SEVEN

I'd arranged previously to meet a prospective student at the Olive Tree Diner for coffee, and I decided to keep the appointment. It wouldn't take long to get back to Tarrytown afterwards. There were a lot people there, mostly older people looking for the early-bird special and parents with young children. One booth was unoccupied, but as I got closer I saw that it was full of dirty dishes. I sat down temporarily at the counter, facing the table, and looked for a waiter or busboy. The mingled aroma of coffee and fries gently tickled my appetite.

A deep voice on my right proclaimed "You can't get good help these days," and I nodded without really looking at him, until I heard "can you, Elizabeth?" I had sat down near Jim without even noticing.

"How's the art business?" he asked.

"Not too bad, how's collecting?" I replied.

"Nothing new, but I'm enjoying what I have," he said.

"That must be an understatement," I said. "If I had that Monet I would sit in front of it for hours at a time."

Jim swiveled his seat to face me. "You would, you really would," in a voice that sounded like it was a new discovery. "You really have a feeling for it, don't you?"

"I've only seen paintings of that quality in busy museums. It must be an incredible thing to be able to get into your jammies and sit in front of it with a glass of wine."

"I don't wear jammies, Elizabeth," he said with playful scorn. "What do you think I am, a Girl Scout?" His voice deepened to a good-natured growl. "I sleep like a man. In the nude."

I just nodded and looked towards the booth, which was finally being cleared.

"Would you like to see it again?" he asked.

"The Monet?" I just had to check what "it" was, given the context. I hoped he hadn't been so drunk the night of the fundraiser that he imagined we'd acted on his request to be painted in the nude.

"The Monet," he confirmed.

"When?" I asked, unsure of what I should do.

"Tonight?"

"Shouldn't you check with Diana?" I asked.

"Diana is not particularly interested in who I bring home. To see the collection. Anyway, she has a meeting tonight. She'll be home eventually, but she won't care."

I decided that I couldn't pass up the opportunity to see the painting up close. I thought of what Nick would say if I hesitated. *"You're a big girl, Lissa. If the guy gets fresh you knee him in the groin. You must know that."*

"I would love to see it," I said, "but I won't be able to stay very long. Maybe twenty minutes. I'm working on an ad for the classes I offer and it's due tomorrow."

"Ah, an artist who's also a businesswoman. Please do come, for however long. How about 7:30?"

"Thank you for the opportunity," I said with a nod. "I'll be there." I got up and moved to the newly cleaned

187

booth. My prospective student arrived soon after, and I got involved in a happy discussion of Impressionist color-mixing techniques.

My prospective student duly transformed into my new student, I asked for my check. The waiter informed me that it had been taken care of already. Oh no, not again, I thought. I tried to reassure myself that it was a good thing, but I couldn't stop worrying about not-yet-visible strings waiting to ensnare me.

CHAPTER THIRTY-EIGHT

Nick was having a busy day, Gina told me when I returned to Bellini's. A jewelry store had been robbed, and he and his partner had taken off down the highway after the teenage perps. They'd finally grabbed the kids inside a K-Mart, where they'd tried and failed to disappear into the crowd. Nick would be busy interviewing and processing them until late at night. I cleaned the brushes I'd stowed away earlier, left Nick a message and went home. It took me 15 minutes of pulling out all my clothes until I found an outfit that was attractive, professional, and not suggestive. A long gray skirt and a preppy sweater, in a soft green shade that went well with my eyes, seemed just right. I left the house with time to spare, and rang the doorbell a few minutes after the appointed time.

A voice was clearly audible from inside the house. "Coming, Elizabeth." The door opened, and to my relief Jim was fully dressed, in a camel and brown plaid sweater and tan pants. I'd half-expected a red silk dressing gown, parting ever so slightly when he moved.

"Welcome, welcome," he said. He was balancing a drink on the tips of the fingers of his left hand, and for a minute I thought he was offering it to me, but then I realized he was carrying it and looking at it lovingly, like a small pet he couldn't bear to put down even for a moment.

"Thank you for having me," I said. I was wearing a jacket, but he didn't say anything about a closet so I just kept it on. The better to give me freedom to dash out if necessary.

"It's my pleasure," he said. "You really *feel* the art. I think most people who come in are just calculating the price tags." He hiccupped.

I followed him to the room with the maybe-Monet, and he motioned to me to sit on the couch. I pretended not to notice, and backed into a chair while looking at the painting. He perched on the armrest of the couch, facing me.

"It's really something," I said, with no fear of misstating the truth. "I gather it's fairly new? To you, I mean?"

"It hasn't been here too long," Jim confirmed.

"How did you get it?" I asked.

"It's my trade secret," Jim answered. "Let's just say I got it at a distress sale. In my business I hear about people's financial problems and assets, and I was able to take this beauty off the hands of someone who needed money more than he needed the painting."

"So you bought it direct, not through an auction house?"

"These are tough times, Olivia." I looked around but apparently "Olivia" was me. He took another long drink. "People don't want their financial problems too well-publicized, so the big sales at Sotheby's or Christies are out. Where are my manners?" he asked suddenly. "Can I get you a drink?"

"No, thank you, I'm fine," I replied. "Art is enough of an intoxicant for me."

"Ah, intoxicants. Art is a good one, fine scotch is a better one, but love--love is the very best intoxicant known to man. Or beast, for that matter," he said, leaning towards me. "And if the conditions warrant it, man becomes beast."

"You seem to be lucky in love," I said, hoping it didn't sound like the lie it was. "Diana is quite a woman."

"Well said, Elizabeth. Well said in its total meaninglessness." I didn't like the way he was looking at me. Was he pathetic or a threat? Though admittedly still virile, Jim was over sixty. How feral could the sexual beast in him be? I was pretty sure that, at least while he was drunk, he was too needy to be dangerous. Alcoholism was a thorn in this beast's paw.

"Why are we talking about this? I came to see the Monet. I hope you got a good deal on it," I said.

"Can't complain. You don't want to let an opportunity go by. That's business. There'll be winners and losers and I'm going to be the winner every time," he said with a macho growl.

"So you knew the seller for a long time?" I asked.

"A while."

"Had you seen the painting in his home?" I asked.

"You do ask a lot of questions, Elizabeth," he said, taking another long sip.

"Did you know about the painting before you knew about its owner's financial problems?" I persisted.

"Who remembers these things?" he asked with a groan. "You sound like you're interviewing me. Remember I don't want publicity for this," he warned.

"No, no," I assured him. "It's not for an article. It's just so amazing to know someone who owns something like this. You can take it off the wall, hold it in your hands, touch it--although I don't recommend that. But there's no one to stop you if you did."

"Yes, you're right. Legally and physically I can do anything I want with it. Of course there is a stewardship role that the responsible art owner has to consider," he said with surprising sobriety.

"Have you looked at the back?" I asked.

"No, Elizabeth, it was my impression that the important part was on the front."

"Yes, of course, but sometimes there are interesting things on the back, too."

"Like what?" He sounded dubious.

"Like the name of the canvas-maker or the retailer who sold it to Monet," I explained. "And stickers from galleries where the painting was shown. That's exciting to me."

"You're okay, Elizabeth," he said, reaching for my hand. I accepted the invitation but withdrew my hand quickly and looked away from his puppy-dog expression.

"May I go up close to it?" I asked.

"Help yourself," he said, gesturing toward his maybe-Monet.

The painting was well-lit from above. I could see nice color variations and contrasts, but the energy wasn't there. This looked to me like a textbook example of copying. The lesser artist makes use of the mechanical aspects of the original, things like typical subjects or the use of warm-cool contrasts, but he or she misses completely on the "fine tuning" and the emotional substance.

"Lovely," I said, hoping I sounded sincere.

The front door opened with a click and closed with a bang.

"Hello, dear," Jim said, although I doubted Diana could hear him. He sat down in one of the armchairs and looked expectantly, but not happily, towards the hallway. Diana came into the room, her spicy perfume quickly filling the air.

"Hello," she said to me, more in the tone of a question than a greeting.

"You remember Elizabeth, don't you, darling?" Jim asked, taking another long sip.

"Lissa," I said, extending my hand to her. She took it for the briefest moment and turned back towards Jim.

"Elizabeth writes articles about art, darling," Jim said. "I've sworn her to confidence about us, but she's going to write a general article about paintings in the area."

His lie didn't make me feel any better about his interest in me. He'd said she wouldn't mind if I came, and now it seemed I needed an article to justify it.

"Remember her?" she asked, and she turned towards me. "Where would I remember you from?"

Apparently not from Bellini's or Main Street just a few hours ago, I thought with relief. "I was at the Artists' Guild fundraiser here."

"Oh, yes, of course," she said. "Wasn't that nice?"

"You have a wonderful home," I offered. "I'm so impressed with your Monet."

"I like to see my Jim happy," she said. "Art makes him happy."

"We have that in common," I told her as I started for the front door.

Jim walked me out, speaking in formal tones about public-minded collectors of the past. As we got to the door he stepped outside with me and said in a whisper, "You know, Elizabeth, there are no warning labels when people meet. The greatest love affairs can begin in the most mundane way. In time, the two people can't stop thinking about each other. You have to be open to it."

"I don't know how that will fit in my article, Jim, but I'll keep it in mind," I said in a loud professional voice. I walked to my car with the distinct impression that he was staring at me. I didn't turn around.

CHAPTER THIRTY-NINE

It was still early enough to look for Nick at Bellini's. It was that time of night, when the door had been locked but the staff was still inside, cleaning up and getting ready for the next day. The top of the door had several small glass panes, and I could see Nick up front near the coffee. I tapped gently on the glass and he came around the counter and let me in.

"I didn't think you'd be here," I said, slightly breathless, wanting to tell him everything in one long sentence.

"What a day I had," he said. "I couldn't just go home."

"Gina told me about the robbery. Great work, catching those kids."

"Just my job," he said. "They should know better than to pick Tarrytown, for God's sake."

"They know now," I said. "I had a busy day, too. I was at Jim's house just now."

"Jim's? Tonight?" He looked stricken. "I thought Diana put du Roncourt off," he said.

"Yes, it wasn't about that. Jim invited me to see the Monet again." I explained how we'd met at the diner. "I saw it up close, and again I felt it wasn't right," I told him.

"Did you say anything to him?" Nick asked.

"No way. He's so proud of owning it."

"You think he has any doubts at all?" Nick asked.

"I don't think so," I answered. "I think it's his baby. I wouldn't like to be there when he finds out it's a fake."

"*When?*" Nick asked.

"Okay, *if,*" I conceded. "But I think I'm right. Poor Jim."

"Poor Jim? Poor Jim is worth more than you and me combined with most of the other people in town," Nick pointed out.

"Still, I don't like to see anyone get hurt," I said. "He's got his obnoxious moments, but he really loves art. How could anyone who truly feels for a Monet be other than a decent guy at heart?"

"Listen, people get hurt worse than that," Nick said. "The damage would be to his ego and his bank account. I've seen much worse. What's he to you, anyway, that you're so worried about him?"

"He's not anything to me," I said, surprised at the turn in the conversation.

"Don't you worry about *me?*" Nick sounded petulant. "I flew down the highway after these kids. I was lucky the other cars got out of the way. The rule is, you're supposed to pull to the right to let a police car pass, but I was coming down the right lane. I was lucky they realized they should pull to the left. You know what could have happened to me?"

"Of course I know your work is dangerous," I said, feeling a little shaky. "It would be horrible if anything happened to you. It's just that I think you can take care of yourself." I didn't tell him that if I allowed myself to think about it I'd never be able to sleep.

"And Jim can't?"

"Why, Detective Bellini, I do believe you're jealous," I said, in my best Scarlett O'Hara voice. I put my hand on his. "I'm very, very happy that you're okay. And if I have any pull with the man upstairs, not the tenants in the apartments," I pointed to the ceiling and Nick smiled, "but the Big Guy, you'll stay that way for a long, long time."

He added his other hand on top of mine, sandwiching it in his warm and firm grip. I thought about Nancy and what she had done to him. There's more than one way a man can get hurt really badly. I hoped the Big Guy had his eye on that situation too. We just looked at each other for a little while, hands together. Eventually he said, "You're right, I can take care of myself. And so can the rest of the department. These damned kids better pick another town next time. All right, tell me, does Jim know about the Renoir?"

"I don't think so. I don't really know. He wouldn't tell me the details of how he got the Monet. I don't know whether it was a similar deal, but he didn't buy it at auction. He said that the owners of these works don't want their financial troubles publicized."

"Yeah, that could make sense," Nick agreed. "If it's real and legal there's nothing wrong with keeping it quiet. It looks like this next one isn't, so we're going to have a car at the house photographing anyone who comes to visit in the next several days. Am I going to see you in some of the shots?"

"He didn't say anything specific," I told him, "but if I get a chance I'd like to see the back of the so-called Monet. We were just starting to talk about it when Diana came home."

"Did she recognize you from here?" he asked.

"No, she didn't seem to have any idea she'd ever seen me before. But I didn't feel comfortable asking any more questions with her there, especially when Jim came up with a phony story that I was working on an article. It seemed like a good time to call it a night."

"You think you'll be asked back when she's not home?" Nick sounded cautious.

"I think it's possible," I told him, without going into detail. "I think he respects my knowledge about art. I think he likes me."

"Watch yourself, Lissa. He may not be the guy with the heart of gold you think he is," Nick said with a dark look on his face. "I've seen a lot of women get in trouble with men like that. They think the world was created just for them. Let me know right away if he calls or approaches you."

I promised that I would, patted him on his arm, and took off.

He phoned me the next morning. "I've got to take action even if the evidence isn't all there yet," he told me.

"You know who's behind it?" I asked.

"I have my suspicions," he said. "I can hold someone for a while. We have enough for that."

"Someone I know?" I asked.

"I wish I could tell you, Lissa. After the arrest, I'll see if I can get you in to hear what the person has to say."

"I understand," I said, though I wished he'd trust me a little more.

CHAPTER FORTY

And so it happened. Nick called and said he'd arranged for me to watch through one-way glass while he questioned Miles. They weren't sure about him and thought maybe I'd pick up on something. I went down to the Police Station, which occupied half of a new building on the street just before the river. As in old Venice, prisoners had a great view in their last moment of freedom.

"Okay, Miles, it's time to talk now," Nick was saying when I was escorted into the viewing room. I sat down in the hard wooden chair near the glass partition. The room smelled of sweat. Nick continued, "No more crap."

"What do you mean?" asked Miles, blinking rapidly. He looked in my direction, and even though I knew he couldn't see me I felt a twinge of guilt and maybe betrayal. My intuition told me he wasn't a killer, but I have to admit I have trouble picturing almost anyone as a murderer.

"You told me you worked at the Museum of Fine Arts when you were in college."

"Oh, in college. You asked about when I was in college?" Miles stammered.

"You think I can't check out what you tell me?" asked Nick. "The Gardner has you on the payroll for 1989 and part of 90."

Miles looked down at his hands. "It just wasn't a very good time," he said.

"You did night work?" asked Nick.

Miles looked like he would rather be suspended by small rubber bands off the Tappan Zee Bridge than answer Nick's question, but he did. "Yes," he said. "I gather you already know. I was a security guard."

Nick's eyes were steely but his behavior was restrained. Not swooping in on his prey, at least not yet.

"Why didn't you tell me?" Nick asked.

"Oh, I don't know," he said in a barely audible voice. "Who even remembers those days? It was just a lot of boring nights. Nothing happened when I was actually in the house." He looked like he knew this wasn't much of an explanation. So did Nick.

"A lot of people wouldn't forget working in a place with a major multi-million-dollar robbery," Nick said. "You were off that night?" He already knew that, too. He'd told me.

"I was lucky," mumbled Miles. "If you can call it that. I wasn't there when it happened. But the whole thing was still a nightmare. We were all questioned, interrogated really, over and over again."

"You'd been there for over a year?" Nick asked.

"I guess so. After it happened, I stayed just a month. It started out a fun gig. You were lucky to get it."

"How *did* you get it?" Nick asked.

"Through friends. I knew a couple of guys who worked there, music students. Not well. I met them and they seemed pretty cool."

"The robbers probably had a contact on the inside," Nick said.

"That's what the police said. In one night everyone became either a potential criminal or a colossal screw-up. I took it for about a month and then I left and waited tables at an Italian restaurant until I got my graduate degree."

"And then you went back to museum work?" Nick asked.

"Once I got my degree I could get a professional museum job. I didn't think anything would happen again. All the museums beefed up their security after it," Miles said.

"And now something happened and you're right in the middle of it again. I'm not big on coincidences," Nick said. "Did anything ever disappear from the Contemporary Arts Museum?" he asked. "And don't forget," he said in a hard voice, "I'm going to check out what you tell me. The best thing for you is to work with me."

Miles looked down at his hands, clutched in front of him. "No, nothing that I know of," he said.

"Did you ever work with Danny on an exhibition?" Nick demanded.

"No, he didn't have any work in the museum. And I didn't expect that he ever would. Danny was the stereotypical mad artist scrounging for fame. He was little more than a pornographer. He had no education. He'd never even heard of Damien Hearst or Jeff Koons."

I felt like saying that sometimes I wish I hadn't heard of them and their overrated work either, but of course there was no one with me to hear it. Or care.

Miles continued, "He was a small man with a small talent. There were no intellectual underpinnings to his work."

Nick's eyebrows rose. "I thought you were in the graphics department. Why do get so bothered about his work?"

Miles blinked hard, several times. "I wouldn't work in a museum if I didn't care about art. But I didn't care about Danny," he insisted. "I hardly ever saw him. I know he was bothering Juliana, though, trying to convince her to show his work. Until now she wouldn't hear of it."

"Did he ever ask you to help him get his work in the museum? As a fellow member of the Artists' Guild?" Nick asked.

"I think Danny knew quite well that I wasn't a fan of his work, or his personality for that matter. He was a mess," Miles said, adjusting his preppie sweater, which hadn't needed adjusting. "Forgive my cynicism, but I have a feeling that whatever they acquire of his work is going into storage as soon as his name is out of the news."

"Say it. You hated him didn't you?" Nick asked.

"Look, I didn't have to deal with him ninety-nine percent of the time. I only saw him a couple of times at the museum and every once in a while at Artists' Guild meetings. Why should I wish him any harm?"

Nick was staring intently at Miles as he said, "We'll find whoever is responsible. You know that."

Miles suddenly sat up straight. "If you ask me you should talk to Juliana. That bitch is capable of anything."

"Women like that can really get in your way," Nick said. His tone suggested that any red-blooded man would be justifiably enraged.

"No. Not *my* way. I just know what I saw. He was pushy. It pissed her off. Maybe sometime when they were alone, she snapped."

"Did you ever hear her say she was going to his studio?" Nick asked.

"I'm not sure, but I think he did ask her. My last day there she was in a really foul mood. I heard her assistant say Danny was on the phone and she refused to take the call. Maybe he called again."

"When was that?" Nick asked.

"Thursday," Miles answered.

Thursday night was when I walked into Danny's studio and found him so very dead.

CHAPTER FORTY-ONE

The Tarry Café, which was just a block from Bellini's, looked like it might have been opened by New York City hippies in search of peace in a small Vermont town. It was antiquey in a low-key, somewhat disinterested way. The wall color, which changed every year or two, was currently a pleasantly peachy crimson, dark and not too saturated, so it showed off the artwork well. Several of Ramón Baleras' large, colorful folk paintings were on the wall opposite the bar. The rest of the art had a faded look, from the yellowed map in the front of the room to the two oval portraits of soldiers underneath it, to the large somber canvas with the image of a large gray bird in a gray landscape. The tablecloths were florals in subdued colors; countertops displayed vases and glassware. It worked, in a homey way.

Ramón's paintings were bold, with large flat areas of primary colors. The compositions were graphic and symbolic rather than realistic. Birds with ribbons in their beaks flew across blue skies with big white clouds, brides in lacy wedding dresses cleansed themselves under waterfalls, groups of children danced with hands linked. It was pleasant to look at, and I felt the owner deserved credit for allowing Ramón to be so visibly more than a waiter. Some bosses would want their employees to focus on their jobs one-hundred percent of the time. I knew from previous visits that Ramón was allowed to spend some time discussing his work with those patrons who noticed it.

It was 1:30 and the café was quiet. Lunch ended at two, and then the café closed until dinnertime. Nick and I thought it was just the time to talk to Ramón.

"Buenas tardes," was the greeting we got at the entrance, as Ramón was the first to see us arrive. He ushered us to a table under a huge painting swirling with red birds in flight. "How are you today, Aleesa?" he asked politely. "And the Señor Bellini?" I hadn't realized that he knew Nick.

"Just fine, my man," Nick answered. "Qué pasa?"

"Mm, it smells good in here," I said. "Shrimp?"

"Sí, the special today is Shrimp à la Tarrytown. It has the extra-virgin olive oil, sun-dried tomatoes, and the fettuccine. Will you like that?"

I hesitated, but when I spotted the price on the blackboard, it wasn't too bad, so I ordered it. Nick ordered an open-faced roast beef sandwich with fries. We both opted for coffee. Ramón went to the kitchen to place the order.

"How do you know Ramón?" I asked.

"He volunteers for the annual shoreline cleanups," Nick explained. "I've worked alongside him a few times. He's a good observer. No gum wrappers get away from this guy."

"You're right," I said. "He's a sharp guy. I'll bet he doesn't miss much here."

"Exactly," Nick replied. "Let's hope the art crowd's been hanging around."

Nick's cell phone rang and he looked at the caller ID. He made an annoyed face but he took the call. "Yes," he gruffly answered the unheard other voice after a brief pause. "Again?" he said. "This is the second time this week." Then after another moment, he said, "Do what you want. It's not important."

He moved the phone away from his ear. In the instant before he pressed the off button, I saw the caller ID. It had been Nancy.

Ramón came back with our coffee and a basket of rolls. "Thanks, buddy," Nick said, "Isn't it terrible about Danny Bogart?"

"Oh, yes, so terrible. An artist! People should be good to artists," Ramón said, his eyes sad. "I never knew such things would happen here. When I was in my home country I read about America and I believe. I believe it to be a good place where *la gente*...the people...can make a good life. How could such a thing be here?"

"It's really bad, all right," Nick said. "I'm trying to find out exactly why and how this happened. Did Danny ever come in here?"

"Not much," Ramón said. "Maybe he would sit at the bar sometimes with a glass of wine. He was not a man who was talking to everyone. He sat alone most times, looking not happy."

"Do you ever see the other members of the Artists Guild here?" Nick asked.

"Sometimes. Miles, he comes in more than the others. Miles Armstrong, do you know?"

"Yes, we do. Does he come often?" Nick asked.

"Too often. He wants this and he wants that, and then he leaves just a little tip. Doesn't even look at my paintings, doesn't say anything about art to me at all."

"He's a bit of a snob, you think?" I asked.

"Sí, a snob. No es simpático. But I don't say anything."

"Does he come in with someone else?" Nick asked.

"He is here with some people one day, others another day. Mostly I don't know them." A bell rang in the kitchen, and since we were the only diners there it was a pretty good bet that it was our orders. "I check on your food now, okay?" Ramón said, and rushed away.

He reappeared shortly with two steaming platters, the aroma filling the air. He placed them on the table and started to walk away, but Nick stopped him.

"Sit down, sit down, man," Nick said. His tone was genial. "There's no one else here. Did you eat?"

"Yes, sure, they feed me here. It's very good. I don't worry about being hungry ever."

"That's the main thing. Starving artists don't really do good work, do they, Lissa?"

I concurred.

"So tell me, did Miles say anything about what happened to Danny?" Nick asked between bites of roast beef.

"He does not seem to care much. I am surprised. It's not right, the way he is, and he even had something he wanted from Danny."

"He told you that?" I asked.

"No, I hear things. I bring drinks, I hear something. I come back with food, I hear something. Little bits. I pass the table with food for someone else, I hear another little bit."

"What did you hear Miles say about Danny?" Nick asked.

"He came in the night before it happened," Ramón said, a disapproving look on his face. "He was alone that time. I remember because he was angry at someone. I know because he was on his cell phone with her."

"Her? Do you know who it was?" Nick asked.

"No, I don't know. He comes sometimes with a tall woman, black hair and sexy legs, but I don't know if she is the one on the phone with him that night. I heard the name, I think maybe Sally or Sara. No, no, I remember. Sandy. It sounded like she was his wife, the way he was angry with her. The way he talked, it was how you have arguing with your wife."

"I think I know what you mean," Nick said. "They sounded like they were stuck with each other and they fought all the time and never got anywhere?"

I winced at Nick's portrayal of marriage.

"Sí, sí," Ramón agreed, nodding rapidly. "You know well, Señor Bellini."

"Call me Nick. Did you hear anything else?"

"They wanted to talk to Danny. I know that. I don't know why, but they wanted something from him."

"Did Miles use Danny's last name, or did he just say 'Danny'?" I asked.

"He say just "Danny," but it was about paintings. I know because when I hear it I start listening a little. But it was a busy night. I don't listen all the time. And then two, three days later, we all know what happened to Danny, and he comes in and he doesn't say anything to me even then. He knows I'm in the Artists Guild and so was Danny. He doesn't say anything and he doesn't look unhappy."

"What a cold fish," Nick said. "Who needs people like that?"

When we left I tried and failed of think of a way to get him to talk about Nancy.

CHAPTER FORTY-TWO

With all the things that were happening, I'd gotten behind on my bills and invitations. Most came online, of course, but there were a few paper ones I had thrown into a box on my desk to go through the next day. Or maybe the day after that, or I'd get around to it sometime. I finally gave in. I had to get around to it now.

One envelope stood out. It had a bright blue fingerprint in paint that looked like an intentional design, but maybe...

I opened it and felt cold shock spread through my chest and into my stomach.

It was from Danny.

I checked the postmark. It was that Thursday, 5 P.M.

Just hours before his death.

I sat down hard in the big, comfortable chair near my easel. There were two things in the envelope, a handwritten letter, scrawled in big, childish letters, and a ragged piece of a map that had been printed on a computer. It was a map of somewhere in France, since the streets were "Rue d's" and Avenue des's." I read the note:

Hey Lissa,

I don't know what to do, and you've always been someone who looks like she does. I've got some people who keep bugging me to do things I don't want to do, and I'm afraid to say no to these people. I just want to be an artist, that's all.

They came to me. I didn't go to them. They want me to do something I can't do and they said they're coming back and I'm in trouble if I don't have what they want. Then they left and I saw this and I don't know if it's anything but I want you to have it in case it is. One of them dropped it when he pulled something out of his pocket. I wasn't about to tell him because I didn't owe him any favors. I hoped it was something important and the hell with him. I'll tell you all about it tonight. You have to believe me. Someone has to stop them. I don't know if this is anything to do with the rest, but in case you don't come, I want to make sure you have it.

That was it. It was signed simply, "Danny." I sat for a while just staring at the map. I would give it Nick. Nick would have to connect the visitors to the paper.

I studied the map as though staring at it could make the names of the streets mean more. Maybe I could find something, anything, before I gave it to Nick. I crossed the room, sat down in front of my computer, and went to Google Maps. Okay, France. What now? I hesitated, then picked a street name from my fragment, typed "Rue D'Antin" into the "search nearby" field and hit "enter." Of course it wasn't enough. It gave me a list of places with similar names but not that one. What if it wasn't even France? Could it be Belgium, or some former French colony?

I thought of my meeting with Pierre du Roncourt. *Where had he said the woman who was selling the pastel lived?* I couldn't check the recording of our conversation, since the police had it. I wanted to know right now. *Damn.* The name Argenteuil popped into my mind, but I knew that was wrong, because that was a familiar name to anyone who'd ever studied Impressionism. I wouldn't forget it. It was "Ar…" something, though. I zoomed in on the France map in the areas around Paris, but after a few seconds I realized this was wrong. He hadn't said it was near there. In fact, I had the impression that it was well away from the crowds. Then I remembered. *Oh, yes, yes, yes, somewhere in the Pyrenees.* I looked north and then south on the map. I clicked to get more and more detailed maps. *Lourdes! How could I have forgotten?* He'd told me it was near there and I had told him that it was a miracle that I was touching a "real" Degas. I scrolled around the area and saw it: Argeles-Gazoust. That sounded right. I zoomed in and started looking around. It took a while, but I found them: all the names on the paper: Rue d'Antin, Avenue Besques, Impasse de Catibere, Chemin De L'Herbe. Success! I could tell Nick I really had something for him.

How interesting they sounded, I thought. I wondered if they were quaint and bucolic village thoroughfares that hadn't changed for centuries, as I was picturing, or just ordinary streets with apartment buildings and strip malls. If I were there, would I see small villages full of half-timbered homes or steel and glass buildings interspersed with squat, garishly colored Le Hut de Pizza's and Le Roi des Burgers? Google Street Views solved that question, and the next ten minutes were spent imagining talking Nick into funding a trip to these delightful streets, many as old and gorgeous as I could hope, some with the mountains as a backdrop. I'd go to look for the old lady, of course. *Dream on,* I told myself. I sighed and clicked myself out of France.

Suddenly I shivered and sat up very straight as I heard someone at the street door downstairs rattling the handle. Was it the policeman on the beat? He tries every door each night around nine or ten p.m., to make sure all are secure. *But was it that late?* I looked at the bottom of the computer screen and saw that it was only eight. *Who was down there? What should I do?* I picked up my cellphone and got the police number onscreen from the directory in case I had to call, but no more sounds came.

This situation was so unsettling. It was serious.

I carefully placed the map in a plastic bag to give to Nick. Whatever the streets looked like, the important thing was that it really couldn't be a coincidence. Nick would still have to find corroborating evidence, but I was already sure.

Whether it was part of a totally made-up scam or there was a real woman quietly selling her art forgeries long-distance from one of these streets, the people who'd approached me about the "Degas" had to be the same people who approached Danny just before he died.

CHAPTER FORTY-THREE

Looking back, I have to admit that I shouldn't have done it. It wasn't like me, and Nick certainly wouldn't have approved, and it got me in big trouble. But I'd probably do it again.

I hadn't planned it at all. I was visiting the museum's professional library to get information for my latest article. And it certainly wasn't *my* fault that I saw Juliana near the entrance, and heard her greeting a small group of academic types.

"I'm Professor Kimura," a small man with salt-and-pepper hair announced. The other three bowed and introduced themselves as well.

"How was your trip from Tokyo?" Juliana asked, and they chatted briefly about airline security and pilots recently in the news for various heroic or distracted acts. Then she got down to business. "We'll be meeting in the conference room downstairs," she said. "My husband is already waiting for us there."

The group was murmuring excitedly as they walked away. I heard one woman say, "It's so much an honor to meet you. Your contributions are respected in my country. We see your exhibitions on your web site and we read your husband's articles in *Contemporary Arts Worldwide...*" By the time she said that, they were getting on the elevator, and as the doors closed behind them the idea popped into my head. Was it insane? Yes, of course, but that wasn't going to stop me. I looked around for security cameras. There was one at the entrance, I knew. I walked back as though going to the checkroom, looking through my pockets to mime what I would do if I thought I had forgotten something, and stopped near the security desk. I glanced briefly at the monitors, looked away and mimed my pocket search again, glanced quickly at the monitors, over and over until I'd checked out all four screens. They showed the main entrance, the restaurant entrance, the rooftop garden, and the entrance to the first floor galleries.

I didn't see a monitor showing the set of galleries that led to Juliana's office.

And so I went.

How had we gotten there last time? It was an unobtrusive little door in a shadowy alcove off the farthest corner of a gallery three away from the one with Paul's installation. I didn't want to attract attention by asking where that was, so I tried entering a set of rooms to my left, wandered around past purple and green clay fish and carburetors, through a gallery with nothing but dangling strings, and eventually found the one with Paul's work. *Where now?* I walked through the open archway to the left, but the exhibit in that gallery looked unfamiliar. The only way out was to backtrack. The opposite archway led to a gallery hung with photographs and collages. Maybe, just maybe, we'd been through there that day. It took a few tries, but I found myself facing a soft blue recessed hallway with the white door I believed was my target. The only problem, and not a small one, was the guard who was standing in the middle of the room. I decided to wait for an opportunity. I sat on the bench and tried to look busy by writing in a small notebook I kept in my purse.

There were few visitors, so disappearing into a crowd was not an option. *My luck may have come to an end*, I thought, but I hung out for a while. At the Met the guards used to rotate every so often, and there hadn't been guards in every room at all times. After about 15 minutes, I got my chance, as my obstacle walked into the next room, leaving me alone with Juliana's door. I looked around for cameras that might be monitoring the space. There were probably security posts in the building other than the one I'd checked near the entrance. Who knew how many monitors there might be. But this gallery wasn't full of blockbuster art, and I didn't see any cameras. I decided to take a chance. Maybe I could claim that I thought it was a restroom if I got caught.

I walked to the door and tried the knob. It opened easily and I went in and closed it softly behind me. It was the same cluttered little room, just as I remembered it, and I had no idea where to start or what to look for. Juliana had a normal collection of art books, from Vermeer, Rubens, and the Impressionists to today's less luminous (to me, anyway) artstars. *What a journey art has taken*, I thought. But that was not the point today.

I didn't have any idea where to look or exactly what I was looking for. Notes on suspect paintings? With names of the forgers? Was I acting like a fool?

I think the idea to look for the calendar was more to settle my nerves than anything else. Breaking and entering had never been my style. Even if I was on the side of the angels, would they be around to rescue me if I got caught? So I looked for the Monet calendar she'd tucked away during our visit. I'd allow Monet's positive, beautiful images to inspire my next move.

It was where she had put it that day, behind a stack of books. I pulled it out and looked at the cover illustration. Standard Monet, a water lilies painting. It was a 1997 calendar, so I figured there must be something important about it if she kept it so long. I flipped through the pages and didn't see any entries in the spaces, so presumably she hadn't kept it as a diary. What made this such an important collection of Monet reproductions?

With an ear cocked for sounds, I looked through each month. The color wasn't that great. Digital printing had come farther than this now. I recognized two more water lily paintings, the blackbird in his snowy landscape, various Madame Monet paintings: indoors in a long gown, looking in the window from outside in winter, on a garden bench in summer. A field of flowers. I knew the works for all but November. That one was from a private collection, it said, showing a country road. The colors were less inflected, more straight-out-of-the-tube than his usual. The hand seemed less sure, less sophisticated than the usual Monet. Interesting. I would have thought it suspect, but here it was in a calendar from a highly reputable publisher. It must be one of those master-having-a-bad-day paintings you need to watch out for when authenticating paintings.

I looked around and saw nothing particularly unusual. Exhibition schedules, loan requests and confirmations from other museums, copies of the magazine her husband wrote for, hair spray, a spare pair of pantyhose. I started to slide open a drawer of the file cabinet and felt a shock of fear radiate in all directions from the middle of my chest up to my throat and down through my stomach to my legs.

Voices. Right outside the door. Would they come in and find me?

I slid the door shut as quietly as possible and looked around for a coat rack to hide behind, or maybe a closet. Nothing. It sounded like two guards, discussing a visitor who'd been a problem. What would I say if they came in? My looking-for-a-restroom excuse might be barely believable if I'd just walked in, but not workable at all if they realized I'd been in here for a while.

I started imagining the news articles about the artist caught breaking into a curator's office.

Why hadn't I let Nick handle it?

The voices got a little farther away, and hope returned. I stood completely still for what seemed like an hour, but was probably more like three minutes. Then silence.

Was I in the clear—or were they waiting outside the door?

I went back to the Monet calendar, which I'd left open to the painting I didn't recognize, took out my cell phone, and snapped a photo of it. I'd have to look at it sometime when my heart wasn't pounding and my stomach wasn't threatening to spill its contents back from where they'd come. I placed the calendar back where I'd found it, behind the stack of books.

Time to go. I opened the door a crack. The gallery was empty but I could see one of the guards just beyond the open arched doorway, in the next room. Luckily his back was to me. I opened the door wider—*would it creak?* I stepped out into the public space, pulling the mercifully silent door behind me. As I entered the next gallery, the guard looked startled. Did he realize that the gallery from which I was coming had been empty a moment before? I smiled and looked as innocent as I possibly could.

I thought that was the end of it.

I was very wrong.

CHAPTER FORTY-FOUR

It was late. The streetlight in front of my studio was out, so the night was darker than usual. There were people around, though, so I told Nick to go ahead and drop me off there. I could see lights on in the law office next door anyway, which meant that I wouldn't be the only one in the building, and it was a good chance to get some extra work done.

Nick was in a much better mood than I was, and I decided not to share my doubts with him. *After all*, I thought, *he might be right*. There was time to work it out. I jumped out of the car, punched my code into the building's front door lock and its red light changed to green. I pulled the door open and turned to wave at Nick, who honked the horn in reply. Funny how much emotion you can get out of a one-note horn; his three short beeps were clearly a celebratory message.

The only problem was that I wasn't so sure they'd arrested the right guy.

Miles just seemed too refined to be a criminal, I thought, as I headed up to the second floor and let myself into my studio. Maybe I was naive. As I turned on the light

I was surrounded by color. My river scenes, town paintings, park images, all comforted me with light and warmth. I'd recently hung a lot more paintings, almost side-by-side and stacked one above the other. It was the old salon way of hanging, and it might not be fashionable, but it kept everything off the floor and safe in my small space. I enjoyed the complex multiplicity of designs they created on the walls.

The light on the answering machine was blinking rapidly, indicating that I'd let too many messages accumulate again, and there was no room left. I played three or four messages that were pretty ordinary. Did I give classes for children? Did I have a print of my Tarrytown Theatre painting? Wouldn't I love to switch to Verizon?

The last one was different. The voice was a near-whisper. It sounded gruff and maybe even angry. He, whoever it was, said that we'd met on the street the week before, while I was carrying a large painting of the river at Dobbs Ferry. He'd asked where the scene was and I'd told him, he said. I talk to so many people. I didn't really remember it but it sounded like something that could have happened. He'd seen me going into my studio, too, he said.

It could have been another routine message, since a lot of people saw me working, but something told me that something was wrong with this man and this call.

I waited for him to get to the point, but just as he finished his introduction the machine beeped and a mechanical voice said, "End of message. Remaining recording time zero minutes and zero seconds. Memory full." I didn't know whether to be relieved or frustrated. What could he want? I checked the caller ID: "Private Caller". Of course. Only five minutes ago. Would he call back? I cleared some messages, hoping that he wouldn't be the one to fill up the new space.

I'd come in to work and I wasn't going to let a little uncertainty stop me. I sat down at my easel and started to squeeze out little bits of pigment onto the palette. I'd gotten to the earth tones when the phone rang. I jumped and smeared red paint all over my hands. The phone rang again and then a third time as I scrambled for hand wipes. I could see the caller ID; again it was "Private Caller." Did I want to answer? It could be someone else.

The answering machine clicked and there was silence. I knew my outgoing message was being played. A voice came on. Damn. It was him. I heard the door to the office next to me close and saw the cleaning woman pass by. So that's who'd been there. I heard her go down the stairs and out the door. Now I probably was all alone.

"Miss Franklin, I have something to discuss with you. Please pick up. I am nearby and I can see your lights. I know you're there."

What should I do now? I wasn't in the mood for trouble. I'd had enough today. I picked up the phone slowly. For a moment I considered answering in a phony voice and insisting I was the cleaning woman, but what if he'd seen me come in just now? Anyway, it might be nothing. I picked up the receiver.

"What can I do for you?" I asked, trying not to let my voice go squeaky. Before he had a chance to answer I added, "I'm afraid I can't stay on too long. I'm in the middle of something."

"You certainly are," he said. I breathed in sharply but didn't say anything. "I left a partial message earlier tonight," he continued.

I said, "I got an incomplete message. That was you? We've met?"

"Just briefly, but I've heard a lot about you. You're a friend of Miles Armstrong, I believe?"

"I don't know him too well," I said, "but I guess you could say that." I didn't say anything about the arrest. Maybe he didn't know.

"I need to talk to you. About the museum," he said. "May I come up?"

"I'm afraid that won't be possible," I said. "I have some important clients coming any minute," I lied. "They're very fussy and I can't be distracted."

"Soon, then," he said, insistently.

"I can meet you at Bellini's tomorrow," I offered.

"Not there," he said.

Did he know about Nick?

"I'll meet you at the bar in the Mexican restaurant at noon."

"No, no, that's too early. You'll have to call me tomorrow," I said quickly, and hung up. I gave it a few seconds to disconnect, and took the receiver off the hook.

I pulled out my cell phone and pushed the speed-dial button for Nick.

"What are you worrying about?" he responded when I told him. "It's probably just some guy who wants something a little shady, like a nude painting. The case is over. We've got the guy."

"No, he mentioned Miles," I said.

"He didn't say it was about the case, did he? Miles worked at the museum. He did other, ordinary things in addition to killing Danny."

"How can you be so sure?"

"We've got him, Lissa. There's a very good chance he worked alone. It's just a matter of finishing up the details. He was at the Gardner and he lied about that. He was at the museum here on false pretenses. He's got a record, for God's sake."

"Not a really violent one," I said. "He was a kid who got into a fight and knocked a guy out. That doesn't make him a forger and a killer."

"Lissa, it's going to be okay. We've got all kinds of record searches going on and he'll be tied to everything. I'll let you know tomorrow night what we find out."

"Fine, fine, if I'm still alive."

"Okay, just in case, I'm going to have the patrol cars pass your studio as often as possible. I'll have one park at the bus stop on the corner, alongside the jewelry store, whenever possible. No one will follow you home."

Nick's reassurances didn't work all that well. I painted for only about a half-hour. I checked the street from the window before I left the building and breathed a sigh of relief when I got home, but not a very deep one.

I dreaded the follow-up phone call every minute of the next day.

It never came.

Another one did.

CHAPTER FORTY-FIVE

Anne's voice was barely recognizable. She was screaming incoherently. I had to hold the phone a little away from my ear.

"Anne, calm down," I said, three times before she settled down a few decibels. "What is it?" I asked. "What happened?"

"You've got to come, Lissa," she begged. "You've got to come to my house."

"What's the matter?" I asked, in a tone I hoped was soothing. I was in my studio, working on my portrait. Whatever it was, I'd like it to just go away.

"Now," she said, sounding near hysteria again.

"OK, now," I said agreeably, though I wasn't so sure I'd follow through. "Just tell me what it's about."

"He's dead," she said.

"Who is?" My stomach felt queasy.

"I don't know. He's just there. Outside my house."

"Did you call the police?" I asked.

"Yes, of course," she said. "I just came outside, from my studio, and he was there. On the ground. I need you to come here. Please."

"I will," I agreed, though it was the last thing I wanted to do. "Are you sure he's dead?" I asked.

"Oh, ye-e-es," she said, "his eyes...."

Oh God, those horrible blank eyes. I didn't want to see that again. Even in a movie, when I knew it wasn't for real, that empty stare was deeply shocking to me. "Don't go near him again," I said, remembering the toxic fumes from Danny's horrible death. "It's really important. Wait for the police inside. I'll be there soon."

Anne wasn't someone who usually lost her cool, but this situation was nothing we'd encountered before. I couldn't blame her. My friendship with her, though we'd lost contact at one time, had begun in childhood. Images of her being there for me at various minor life crises kept popping into my head. After taking a few minutes to collect myself, shaking more than a little, I got my car keys and headed outside.

The streets outside my studio were alive with urgency. Sirens pounded my ears as two cruisers sped up Main Street, lights flashing, and turned onto North Broadway; a van marked "Police Supervisor," also with siren whooping and lights flashing, came down Neperan from the direction of the lakes; and then, very fast, another loud cruiser came from South Broadway, followed by a screaming ambulance. All headed towards the residential area east of Broadway where Anne lived.

Before I could start out, I sat in my car and took several deep breaths. I turned the ignition. I'd promised her.

When I arrived at the house on Beech Lane the police wouldn't let me in. I should've expected that. I still hoped, against the evidence, that Anne had been wrong and the man was still alive.

An officer I knew slightly agreed to get word to her that I was there, and I'd be waiting until they let me in. Soon after that, Nick arrived.

"What are you doing here?" he asked me. He didn't look happy.

"She called me," I said.

"OK," he said. "Maybe you'll be useful later. Just hang out until we talk to Anne and document the scene."

I sat on a small bench just inside the front gate, absolutely freezing. I shivered for that, and for the rest of it, too. The police all hurried to the backyard. A van marked "Medical Examiner" pulled up and a man in a surgeon's mask and jumpsuit made his way past me to the path along the side of the house. People came in and out, doing their various assigned tasks, and finally, just as my icy fingers were losing their last bits of sensation, Nick came over and asked if I would look at the body.

"How bad is it?" I asked, flinching. I thought about the glassy stare of eyes disconnected from any life force.

"He got hit on the back of the head," Nick replied. "His face isn't too bad. Your friend says she has no idea who he is and none of us know him."

"What makes you think I do?"

"Give it a shot, Lissa. Just in case. There must be some connection with Danny. This is Tarrytown, after all. We don't usually find bodies on every corner."

"All right, I'll give it a try." I hadn't really thought this out before I told Anne I would come. Now I was stuck with acting like an adult. I walked with Nick to the backyard, legs shaking but still getting me from place to place.

The body was in a large, dark plastic bag. That made it temporarily easier. I could pretend for however brief a time that I was approaching a bag of mulch. I got close to it and Nick took my arm and looked into my eyes.

"Can you do this, Lissa?" he asked, in the most serious tone I'd ever heard him use.

"I can do it," I said, in the shakiest voice I'd ever heard come out of me.

He pulled the bag back from the man's face. My first response was relief that he wasn't someone I knew, but of course it was still horrifying. He was still a human being who was newly dead.

I'd never seen this bright orange hair on anyone. It was obviously dyed, right down to the eyebrows and beard. He looked like an actor. I shook my head.

"Maybe you should check with the Tarrytown Theatre," I said. "Maybe he was doing some kind of show there."

I took a deep breath, looked again, and felt a little dizzy. There was something, though. I tried to think of the face as a visual puzzle rather than part of a person. I looked at the cheekbones, the shape of the eyebrows, the color of the irises, the shape of the mouth. I bent down slightly, on a hunch, to get a profile and then a three-quarter view. I stood up and looked at Nick.

"You have something?" he asked. Now he was studying *my* face.

I struggled briefly to speak, and then I choked a little as I said, "I think so, yes."

"Who is he?" Nick asked.

"He didn't look young then, but if he's an actor,...I think...I think it's Pierre du Roncourt!"

CHAPTER FORTY-SIX

"Du Roncourt?" asked Nick in surprise. He studied the dead face and whistled softly. "Maybe I let you get *too* involved, Lissa," he said. "Jeez, I didn't see this coming. Damn, I never should have let you meet with him."

"You didn't *let* me," I reminded him. "You didn't know about it until I was already there. Anyway, I'll be okay." I'm sure it sounded as unconvincing to him as it did to me.

Nick looked at me with a tenderness I haven't seen in many faces. It moved me despite the horrible circumstances. Could he actually be someone I could count on? A man who would give as well as take?

"Stay close to me for now," he said.

I had no problem with that.

"Well, if you insist," I agreed, making my voice sound reluctant.

"We didn't get a hit yet on the fingerprints from the flashlight you gave me the night you met du Roncourt," he said, "but I'm going to widen the search. This guy does look like an actor. If he's the same guy, the 'du Roncourt' and for that matter all the Frenchie stuff was probably a total sham."

"It's possible," I admitted. "Why didn't I pick up on it?"

"It's okay. You've already done much more than I expected. We'll find out who he was. If he's got a record or served in the military, we'll know. If not, there are other ways."

"What about the map?" I asked. "The one that's supposed to show where the old lady lives in France?"

"Probably just a prop," Nick said. "They used it to show people where the paintings supposedly came from. We'll find out for sure."

Anne came around to the front of the house and Nick signaled to the ambulance attendants nearby to take the body. He turned to Anne and asked if we could come in the house.

"Yes, of course," she said.

"Are your kids home?" Nick asked her. "Kids shouldn't be involved with this."

"Luckily they're at friends' houses for now," she said. "But they'll hear about it. It's going to be on the news, isn't it?"

"Channel 7 is already asking for an interview," Nick affirmed. "They've got a camera crew nearby, but we're keeping them at a distance. The chief called me to prepare a statement."

"How am I going to explain this to the kids?"

"There's no easy way. Can they spend a few days with relatives or friends?"

Anne nodded, looking very pale, and when we got in the house she made the calls to arrange it. We sat in her living room and waited for her to finish. Several of her sculptures stood on tables and pedestals around the room. The dark hardwood floors and the cool white marble artworks were offset by a yellow silk couch and two matching armchairs. A giant, sea-green vase in the corner reminded me of one in a John Singer Sargent portrait of three young sisters. It was an elegant room, recently redone in the currently fashionable open floor plan that united the kitchen and dining room with the living room. I hadn't spent much time in it; usually when I came over we were in the studio.

"Nice place," Nick said while we were waiting. "They must have put a lot of money into it."

"Anne's husband is doing well," I told him. "He's a banker."

"Is Anne's work selling?" he asked.

"Some, but I think on a modest scale."

Anne came in and sat in one of the yellow chairs. In spite of the situation I couldn't help but visualize her as a portrait, her tawny skin, golden blond hair, blue eyes and blue clothing all fitting perfectly into an elegant composition.

"Where's your husband?" Nick asked in a low-key, conversational tone.

"He's on his way home," she said. "He was in Philadelphia on business. I called him right away and he'll be here in a couple of hours."

"He has some sort of finance job?" Nick asked.

"He's with the Bank of Mid-Westchester, in Corporate Investment Strategies," she told him.

"Sounds important," Nick said.

"It is. He works long hours," Anne replied.

"That must be hard on you," Nick said. "Leaves you lonely?"

"Not at all. I have my kids and my art," she said. "They keep me very busy whether he's around or not." She sounded defensive.

"What was he doing in Philadelphia?" Nick asked.

"There was a regional meeting. Times are tough. His bank is okay, but of course you know that some others in the area aren't."

"Your husband is happy with his work?" Nick asked. "Despite the difficulties?"

"He's fine," Anne replied coolly. "This has nothing to do with him, I'm sure."

I had mixed feelings about where Nick was taking this. I couldn't even begin to imagine Anne or her husband being involved in anything criminal, but I knew that Nick had a job to do. I didn't say anything. This was not a dinner party; this was serious business.

"Do you think the dead man might have known your husband?" Nick asked.

"I have no idea," Anne said. "I've never seen him before. I told you that. I have no idea what he was doing here. You can't think my husband or I had anything to do with this."

I spoke up gently. "Nick," I said, "You know that Anne is an almost life-long friend of mine, don't you?"

"Relax, Lissa," Nick said. "It's routine. I'm not asking her to come to the station. I'm just looking for a reason for this guy to be here."

"Go ahead," Anne said, "I've got nothing to hide," but I noticed that her arms were crossed in defensive position.

"You and your husband were both friendly with Paul McGill?" Nick asked.

Anne looked surprised and none too happy. She looked at me questioningly. I shook my head to signal that I hadn't said anything to Nick.

"Paul is someone who meant something to me a long time ago," she answered. "It was long before I met Ben. It's ancient history," she said.

"It didn't look all that ancient at the memorial," he said.

Now I was surprised. I hadn't realized he'd seen them.

"That didn't mean a thing," she said, looking at the couch and picking off several invisible bits of lint. "Sometimes you see an old friend and you feel something. Especially at a memorial, when you're thinking about the terrible fragility of life. But then you walk out into the sunlight and back into your everyday life, and the feeling is gone."

"How long have you been married?" Nick asked.

"Almost twelve years," Anne said.

"It gets to be old after a while, doesn't it?" Nick commented, with a trace of bitterness in his voice. "I had to get out of a stale marriage myself."

He may have been telling the truth, but I figured the reason he brought it up was to open the door for her to admit to a bad marriage. And maybe a lover.

"Neither one of us feels the need to get out." Anne sounded annoyed. "This man had nothing to do with us, I told you."

"I'm sure Nick knows that," I said. "What was he hit with?" I asked him.

"We don't know yet. Nothing was found and I had several men comb the yard and the house."

"Maybe it really didn't happen here?" I asked. "Maybe he was brought here afterward?"

"We're looking into everything," he answered.

Anne's face brightened a little.

"That wouldn't be nearly as bad," she said. "If he was killed somewhere else…"

"That would be better," I agreed.

"We haven't found the murder weapon yet," Nick said. We're still looking. But a lot of the time they take it with them, and dump it. Especially now that we can get DNA off the smallest deposit. At this point we don't know if we're looking for a rock, a hammer, or even a folded portable easel."

"An easel? You don't really think…" I asked.

"No," Nick said, "Just saying. Anything is possible and anyone may have been involved. We don't know yet."

I didn't like the thought of that. None of the local artists I knew could do anything so violent. I hoped.

"Will they be able to tell from the wound what hit him?" Anne asked.

"Probably," Nick said. "We have the best experts in the area. We'll find out what happened." He seemed so strong and capable at that moment that I had no doubt that he would.

Nick asked Anne if anything was missing from the house. She turned pale again, and looked around.

"You think someone was in the house?" she asked.

"We can't rule it out," Nick said. "How long were you in your studio before you found him?"

"About an hour. Oh God, they could have been in here?" she asked again, more upset now.

"We don't know yet. Do you keep the doors and ground-floor windows locked?" Nick asked.

"I do now," she said. "Please come upstairs with me while I check there," she said.

Everything seemed to be as she had left it in the bedrooms, she told us. I was glad that Nick was acting concerned about her welfare. She couldn't be a suspect. I knew that. I hoped that.

"Lock up tight," he told Anne. "I've got a car across the street that's staying all night, but from now on, no open doors."

She nodded. "Ben will be home soon. I'll be okay." She looked a little more confident, almost back to her usual self now that the focus was off her supposed dalliances. At least for now.

"He knows what he's doing, Lissa?" Anne whispered as were leaving.

"He's good at what he does, Anne. Don't worry. I know he's not going to throw around accusations," I said.

231

"You're lucky he's the one who's handling this. It'll be okay."

"I hope you're right," Anne replied.

Nick walked me to my car. I thought again of the orange-haired man with the bashed-in head, and I found myself looking around, as though I half-expected a raging lunatic to come out of nowhere and start swinging at us too.

"Relax," he said. "We've got a car across the street and another car patrolling the area. We're ok."

"It's unbelievable. These things happen on TV, not right here," I said.

"Unfortunately, they did happen here, and they happened in real life long before there was such a thing as TV. We'll get the guy."

We'd reached my car. I used my remote to unlock the door and Nick reached out to open it for me. I stepped in and Nick closed the door, and then motioned for me to open the window.

"You went to school with Anne?" he asked. His face was very close. I could see every bit of razor stubble.

"Yes, our mothers met when we were five, while they were waiting for us outside the school. Our families were very close for several years, until they had to move away because her father got a much better job in another city."

"I'm just wondering, if Anne's been married for twelve years and you're the same age...?"

"Why am I not married?" I filled in the blank reluctantly.

Nick nodded.

"I spent several years with the wrong guy, and had to get out," I said.

"Are you looking?" he asked.

"I might be," I said. "But I need to find someone who'll let me be my own person as well as his wife. Do you think that's possible?"

"Anything's possible, if you try hard enough," he said. He tapped on the car door three or four times in a "get going" gesture and walked away. Just before he turned to go I saw a hint of a smile on his face.

CHAPTER FORTY-SEVEN

Nick downed the cup of coffee in what seemed to be one giant gulp. This time we were at the Olive Tree Diner, not Bellini's. I'd told Nick their coffee was really great, but of course that wasn't why we were there.

He'd called ahead and arranged to meet George, who arrived at our table at the same time as our burgers. I introduced Nick as a friend, leaving it to him to explain that he was a cop if he wanted to. He asked George in a conversational tone if he would look at a photo and see if he knew the man in it.

"Where I have my glasses?" George fumbled in his pockets for a couple of minutes and then picked up the small photo Nick had brought. "Okay, okay, we see what we have here." He frowned as he looked at the picture. Nick had it made in black and white, so the freaky orange hair wasn't too distracting.

"Do you think he's been here?" Nick asked.

"No, no. I don't know this man. You know I'm not here every minute. He could come when I'm not," George replied.

"Keep looking. Maybe you'll remember something," Nick encouraged him.

"This is all the picture you have?" George asked. "The eyes, they're not even open. This guy, he looks like he's dead."

Nick and I looked at each other. George looked at each of us and whistled softly.

"What you have a dead man's picture for?" he asked.

"For my job," Nick said. "I'm working on finding out who he was."

"You're the police?" George asked.

Nick nodded. George stared at the photo.

I jumped in. "He may have looked a little different," I said. "See if there's anything about him at all that looks familiar." Nick gave me a look that I interpreted as "leave it to me," so I put my mouth to another use, chewing my burger.

"Maybe something," George told us.

"What are you seeing?" Nick asked.

"Maybe he could be the family of somebody I know," George said slowly. "He looks like him but young."

"Who?" Nick asked.

"Maybe this could be a son or grandson of my friend Pierre. He said nothing like this, that he had family here. But maybe he has," George mused. "But why he not come in ever with Pierre?"

"A very good question, my friend," said Nick. "Have you seen Pierre lately?"

"No, he must have gone back in France," George said.

"Do you know where he was staying while he was here?" Nick asked.

Loud voices and a clattering noise from the kitchen made George jump up from the table, and soon his angry voice came through the door as well. I looked hard at Nick, trying to read his expression. It looked like satisfaction to me.

"There were keys in his pocket?" I asked.

"Yes, but no local address. We're running his prints but this could get us in his door that much faster."

George came back and handed Nick a piece of paper.

"His phone number?" Nick asked.

"His phone, yes," said George. "I think it is cell phone. Maybe he is in France and it's no good, but is what I have. I hope is not his tragedy. Such a nice man. To lose someone so young..." George shook his head and sighed deeply.

"Thanks," Nick said, pocketing the piece of paper. "I hope not, too. While we're at it, how about this man?" Nick showed him a picture of Danny that he'd taken from the studio.

"Yes, he comes sometimes. Sits at the counter and doesn't eat much," George said.

"Did you ever see these two together?" Nick asked.

George shook his slowly, as though trying to remember. "Not together, I think. I have a lot of people, but I think not these two together."

Another burst of agitated voices took him away again, head back and eyes raised as if imploring the heavens to send him a new cook. One who'd work cheap, of course, really cheap.

"You can't find his identity from his cellphone?" I asked Nick.

"Maybe. If we can't get his name, if it's a throwaway, we can try to find out where he spent his time while it was on. We'll get there."

CHAPTER FORTY-EIGHT

The polar air mass in retreat, Bellini's was bustling the next day. There was plenty of sun coming from a deep blue winter sky, and it looked like half the town had the craving for home-made ice cream. I was in the back, painting a white building on the mural, deeply involved in mixing in just enough yellow ochre to the shadow tone to keep it purple but not too purple. People often stood behind me watching me work, and I'd never get anything done if I didn't ignore them sometimes. When it became clear to me, via the scent of his aftershave, that the eyes watching my hands belonged to Nick, I turned around.

"I have news," he said. It sounded important.

I put my brush in a deep container of water. "Tell me," I said.

The place was buzzing with conversations, punctuated by the occasional high-pitched happy shriek or a momentary burst of sibling rivalry crying. Add to that the music just under ear-splitting level, and it was one of those times Nick and I could have a perfectly private conversation in the midst of the crowd.

"Someone delivered a package to Jim and Diana's last night. It was a large, flat, wooden crate that would be just the right depth for a framed painting."

"Really!" I said. "I thought with Miles in prison, it wasn't going to happen."

"We came to believe he wasn't working alone, so we kept the surveillance on the house," Nick said. "There's a lot of money at stake. They should lay low, but criminals aren't the smartest people around. If they were, we'd be in trouble."

"They'd have to be really arrogant to think you won't be able to catch them," I said, hoping he was really that good.

Nick smiled. "Thanks for your faith in me. I'll try. It *is* what I do," he said.

"I wish I could see what's in that package," I said.

Nick nodded. "We don't know it's the painting she discussed with Brendan. She could have bought something else."

"Is there any way *you* can see it?" I asked. Better if it were me, but Nick was a sharp enough observer to tell me the basics of what he saw, even if he couldn't tell whether it was a real Renoir.

"Not right now. We can't be direct. If it's a fake and they know it, they'll be tipped off, and if it's a legit purchase, my chief will have my head for causing them problems."

"Who brought the crate?"

"Two men, big guys. Here, take a look at the photo and see if you recognize them."

We sat down at one of the tables. Nick hadn't changed into his Bellini's t-shirt. He looked polished and very attractive in his dark suit.

I looked at the photo and shook my head. "I don't think I've ever seen them."

"Keep it," he said, when I tried to give it back. "It's just a copy. Maybe you'll spot them somewhere. But just call me, okay? Don't get involved."

"Don't worry. They didn't deliver it in a truck with a company name, I presume?"

"No, they came in a rental car. They used French ID's, which we're trying to check out."

"Can you check Jim and Diana's credit cards?" I asked. "Maybe she bought something through one of the galleries in Peekskill."

"We have to sit on it for now," Nick said. "They aren't suspects, and the chief doesn't want me to pull their financials. We have no evidence that they're knowingly involved in fraud. Diana could have bought something in Peekskill or from any gallery in the city," he said.

"That's true. There are art dealers all over Manhattan. Not to mention the auction houses, Sotheby's or Christies. And several smaller ones."

"There's more. A few minutes later, our old friends Juliana and Alexander Leighton visited her."

"Really?" I asked. "You're sure?"

"I saw them myself."

"Maybe she asked them to check out her purchase," I said.

Nick nodded. "But why? Was she showing off or was she not satisfied with the seller's authentication?"

"She seemed to trust Brendan without hesitation," I reminded him.

"We need another fundraiser in their house," he said, "so you can get a good look at whatever it is."

"If I hear of one," I said, "you'll be the first to know. I'll see if I can find an excuse for contacting Jim. Maybe hit him up for a donation to the Artists' Guild."

"If it *is* a Renoir fake, do you think you'd know?"

"I could give my educated opinion. Nobody can swear absolutely, just by looking at a painting. You have to be really careful these days. Especially since it wouldn't be an academic examination, with the worst that could happen being a polite challenged by another expert. These days people are being sued, even threatened with violence, for giving professional opinions that paintings are fakes. The collectors can lose a fortune."

"What does a real Renoir go for?" Nick asked.

"I was wondering that myself, so I looked at Sotheby's web site. We don't know what size it really was, inside the crate. Even for a little one, say nine by twelve inches, it would have to be well into six figures."

"What about a bigger painting? Say maybe twenty by twenty-four?"

"Gotta be over a million," I said.

"Unbelievable," Nick said, his eyebrows raised. "I can't imagine wanting a painting enough to spend that kind of money on it."

"It's the fact that they can do it that makes them feel so important. Some of these one-percenters, the superrich, want to impress everyone, to have something that no one else in town will have. And they want to make a profit by selling it a couple of years later. A lot of them go for contemporary art, of course, and they manipulate the prices. It's all they understand. I don't think Jim's like that. Diana, maybe."

"What would they do if they found out they'd been ripped off?" Nick muttered, not expecting an answer.

And I didn't give one.

CHAPTER FORTY-NINE

Having arrived outside the diner for lunch the next day, I was standing next to my car, bending over at the passenger-side door to find today's newspaper. It had slipped down into a jumbled mass of two weeks' worth of papers I was intending to throw out any day now. Hearing footsteps behind me didn't usually make me nervous, but this time I looked up a little too quickly and hit my head on the car.

"Lissa, Lissa," the deep voice sounded slightly mocking but concerned too. I was more embarrassed than hurt, but there might soon be a little bump on my forehead. Damn, did it have to be in front of Jim? I didn't want to look vulnerable or incompetent in front of him. Too late. "Come into the diner," he said. "We'll put some ice on it."

"No, no, really," I insisted. "I'm fine. I'm going in, but there's no need to make a fuss."

"Let me escort you in, anyway," he said, extending his arm. "It's probably my fault. I didn't mean to sneak up on you."

"No, really, it's nothing," I said, patting his arm instead of taking it. A gentle rejection of the physical, I hoped. "I can go in under my own power."

"At least let me buy your lunch," he said.

"You've already done that twice," I said. "Oh, I've never thanked you for those. Thank you."

"You're very welcome, Lissa," he said. "Three's a charm. Maybe it'll bring you good luck. At least your lunch today won't deplete the coffers any further. I hear artists have it pretty tough."

"That's certainly true," I agreed, and couldn't find any reason to say no. Jim was looking good, well-dressed in a dark suit with a crisp white shirt and red tie. There were no visible signs of his fondness for alcohol. If I hadn't seen him drunk and needy, I'd never know he had a problem. He was hiding it well—but for how long?

I suddenly realized that he was calling me by my correct name. Was it because he was sober?

We went into the diner and sat down in the third booth. The place was pleasantly noisy. My coffee arrived promptly as usual, and Jim ordered one for himself.

"How's the head?" he asked.

"I'm not losing it yet," I said.

He smiled. "I'll bet you'd lose it pretty quickly if the young Claude Monet walked in the door."

I laughed at the incongruous image. "I'd like to meet him, yes, but to be swept off my feet, I don't think so. I wouldn't like to live at Giverny," I told him. "Too quiet, too isolated. Of course, by the time he bought Giverny he wasn't all that young."

"How about Renoir?" he asked. "Would you like to meet Pierre-Auguste?"

Here it is, I thought, my heart thumping. *It was the Renoir—the maybe Renoir- that maybe was delivered to his house and he's going to tell me about it.* I did my best to act casual.

"I suppose that would be exciting," I said. I made myself relax by thinking about Renoir paintings rather than forgery and murder. "There's a great little landscape of his at the Met. *Road to Louveciennes*. The depth, the light and shadow, the variety in the foliage..."

"Yes, I know the one you mean," he said with obvious excitement. "It's a little thing, but it's a work of genius. A small, perfect gem."

"There's a still life at the Met, too, that I really love. Fruit in a blue-and-white bowl. Peaches, I think, with the leaves still on," I told him.

"You do know your stuff, Lissa," he said.

"I almost miss being called Elizabeth," I said. "It was growing on me."

He laughed. "I apologize for my error," he said. "After our last meeting I looked at your website. Your name is now firmly fixed in my mind."

"I'm honored. I hope you liked my paintings."

"I certainly did. And your articles as well," he said. "You should go ahead and write the one we were talking about last time. About the collections in the area. I could introduce you to two or three other collectors. But remember--no names, no locations."

It wasn't clear whether he remembered that the article was something that he'd invented to explain my presence to Diana, but I wasn't about to turn down the offer.

"Yes, wonderful, thank you," I said. Usually when people say they've looked at my website I feel disappointed if they don't talk about buying a painting, but under the circumstances this was much better. Anyway, maybe in time...

"We can start with getting you back to my house sometime soon," he said, exactly as I had hoped. "I have a new addition since you've been there. I'm not going to tell you what it is, but you'll find that it's definitely worth a trip."

"I'd love to see it," I said. "Just tell me when."

I was going to see the "new" Renoir—or the newest fake.

CHAPTER FIFTY

"We've got the ID on your friend 'Pierre'," Nick told me that evening. We were sitting in his car looking at the river sunset from the parking lot behind the train station. Berthed near us was the police boat, the HEAT. The acronym was cleverly decoded on the side of the boat as "Hudson Enforcement Assistance Team." I'd been admiring it briefly until Nick's announcement got my full attention.

"That was fast," I said with surprise. I'd thought it would take at least a day or two.

"The cellphone wasn't registered to him. It was a throwaway. We used tower records to get his most frequent late night/early morning location," Nick answered. "Then we showed his photo to a few store workers in that neighborhood and got a name and address from a dry-cleaner."

"Was he really French?" I asked.

"Nope. From New Jersey. His real name was Anthony Becker," Nick told me. "He was some kind of performance artist."

"I knew it," I said triumphantly, although I hadn't known it very long. "When I saw that orange hair it just clicked. Did you get in his apartment?" I asked.

"Yep. Turns out he was staying with a friend. Friend didn't notice he was missing because he's busy at County Jail."

"A lawyer?" I asked. I should have known better but I wasn't used to being in these circles.

"A criminal," Nick replied. "Newly imprisoned. Wanna guess?"

"Miles?" I asked, astonished. Who else would I know in County Jail?

"Miles," Nick confirmed. "Your 'innocent' friend."

"You know I don't know him that well," I said, "And it's just an association between them, so far." I knew I sounded defensive. I don't like to be that wrong about people. "You don't know if Miles knew what Pierre—Anthony—was up to."

"We'll get him to talk. I can smell these things, Lissa. Trust me."

"I'm sure you know what you're doing," I acknowledged.

"We'd gone through the apartment before, looking for forgeries or anything relating to them. Now we went back looking for things to tell us more about this Becker, and we found a large box of theatrical makeup."

"Which looks more interesting under the circumstances," I said.

"Absolutely. One of the things we found was a wig of white hair. And the type of makeup a skilled person could use to give the illusion of lines and wrinkles. The old man was Becker. Or Pierre. One and the same. I'm sure of that. And here's another thing you'll be surprised to hear: the call you were so worried about to your studio after we arrested Miles came from that cellphone," Nick told me, his voice gruff and scratchy.

"That was Pierre?" I asked, shocked again. This meant that making that call was one of the last things he did before he was killed. And that I had been close to danger.

"Anthony," Nick said. "He was no more a 'Pierre' than I am."

"What do you think he wanted from me?" I asked.

"You said he wanted to talk about Miles." Nick reminded me. "Someone saw to it that he didn't."

"So there's someone else out there still," I said.

"Yes. Miles was already in jail."

"What was Pierre doing at Anne's?" I asked.

"We don't know yet. We will."

"Someone dangerous knows that we're getting close," I said with a long look into Nick's eyes. I didn't see the denial I was hoping for, however irrationally. "It's hard to reconcile this with all the beauty out there," I said, turning to the landscape as I often did to calm myself. The Tappan Zee Bridge lights had come on, jewels on twisted steel strings. Behind the bridge the sky was luminous crimsons and yellows; high above the towers the sky was deep turquoise. It was hard to combine alizarins, cadmiums, pthalo to get the colors exactly this way. Nature did everything figurative and abstract artists do, and she did it first and mostly better. We humans just play catch-up.

Everything was reflected in the water. In this cold weather the only boats in the water were the moored police and fire boats, close to us, their mirror images broken by the movement of the currents. All of the other boats had either been towed away by their owners to stay at home until spring, or were among the hulking dark shapes a little farther away at the marina's dry dock, across a narrow channel of water from where we sat, between two popular restaurants. Visible through the big windows of the one closer to us, waiters and waitresses were rushing back and forth in the most ordinary way in the brightly-lit dining room, serving drinks and setting up for dinner. "All those people in the restaurant look so safe," I said, a touch of jealousy in my voice.

"It *is* a dangerous situation, Lissa," Nick replied in a reluctant, serious voice. "When I got you involved it was just forgery. I never expected anyone would be murdered. Maybe you should go away for a while."

"I'm not afraid," I lied. "I need to be here. Anyway, if I am already in danger, they could follow me."

"Isn't there someone who could go with you? Just until I wind up the case."

"No. I want to stay," I said. "All right, maybe I am a *little* scared, but I want to see it through."

He gave me a long, assessing look. "Okay," he said finally. "I think you're strong enough. And you're smart enough, too. I'll do everything I can to keep to keep you safe," Nick said, moving close, his hand cupping my chin, his serious eyes looking deep into mine, "but you know that I can't be with you every minute."

"I know," I said. "But you're right. I *can* handle it."

"If you change your mind…"

"I'll let you know. Don't worry."

And then he kissed me. A long, slow, tender kiss. I rested my head on his muscular shoulder. He smelled of leather and spice. "We'll get to the bottom of this," he said, his arm around me. "We'll get these people. Tarrytown will be safe for you, too."

"Nick, please be careful," I said, moving away a little bit so I could look at him. "You're important to me."

I wanted to tell him that the criminals weren't his only problem. I wanted to say that Nancy was no damned good for him. I wanted to tell him what she'd done to him, to his child.

I didn't.

He leaned towards me, his hand caressing my cheek and then my lips. He kissed me again.

The hell with the danger. I just wanted to be with Nick.

"Stay out of this as much as you can, Lissa. Just go ahead with your art," he said. "And don't get any ideas about getting involved with these people on your own. Promise me that."

"It's a deal," I said.

I meant it. At the time.

His cell phone rang. *Damn! Was it Nancy?*

When he answered it was clear that it was his work that would take him away. "Where?" he said into the phone. "Do you have the driver? Jesus, I've got a murderer out there. All right, okay, I'll be there in three minutes. He put the phone away and turned to me. "I have to go to work," he said. "I'll drive you up the hill."

He started the car and we moved towards the railroad overpass. "My girl," he sang. It was barely audible. I wondered if he even realized he was singing out loud. "Ba ba da da da, ba ba da da da, talkin' 'bout my girl."

I leaned back and enjoyed the concert. This time I got to hear almost the whole song.

CHAPTER FIFTY-ONE

Diana wasn't my favorite person, but no way was she was a former nude model, and I wasn't about to make a fool of myself by asking. And of course Nick had told me to back off. But it couldn't do any harm to visit my alma mater, could it? Just to catch up on old friendships and memories. I hadn't been to Central Park in so long, and it was just around the corner, and stunning even in the dead of winter. Bare branches looked like dancers' limbs, and the park's small bridges and buildings were just as beautiful as in the summer.

The Art School of New York had owned and occupied a graceful four-story Beaux Arts building on West Fifty-Seventh Street since the end of the nineteenth century. Big display windows featured works by the current crop of students and teachers. Small figure paintings filled one window, different versions of a pose done from various angles by several students. The model was a young woman with dark brown hair, and the better artists had captured some of her spirit. Many of the models were aspiring performers, in search of a flexible job they could drop for a while if they got a role, and come back if it didn't pan out as their big break. Most never got that break and eventually left for other jobs, but a few who couldn't give up the hope of stardom just stayed at the school forever. To the model booker, aging was just a difference, not a disqualification, since this was about the human anatomy, not fashion or glamour. Of course, the most popular models were still the pretty, young ones.

I made my way slowly up the outside staircase, weaving through the crowd of people who'd just finished the morning session. The students, like the models, were of all ages, so there were youthful shouts and darting figures interspersed with more sedate walkers and a few who made their way slowly and painfully with the help of a cane. Aspiring artists often have to take breaks of years or even decades to raise a family or earn a paycheck at something more practical. Then they come back, hoping for another chance.

The huge wrought-iron gates at the top of the steps were open, and I went in and turned right to go in the office. It was simply and sparsely furnished, with paintings hanging everywhere "salon-style," like my studio, so they too could fit as many as possible on each wall.

A sad-looking young man stood behind the counter where I used to stand. I asked for Rob, the school's director and my former boss. The clerk mumbled something inaudible and went towards the back. Given his apparent disinterest, I could only hope that his departure had something to do with my request. I was afraid he'd just decided it was his lunchtime.

"Alissa, what a surprise." Rob came towards me with long strides, and extended his hand over the counter. He was tall and slim, with longish dark hair now mixed with a little silver. His intense gaze radiated intelligence. He'd come there several years ago as a student, taken a part-time job in the office, and ended up running the place. He'd been one of the best artists I'd met there, and probably didn't have much time for that anymore. Still, he looked like a person who was satisfied with his life.

We sat down in his office, a small space partitioned off inside the main room, and caught up on the people we both knew, and the current school activities.

"What brings you here today?" he asked.

What was I going to say? I hadn't worked out a story, but I knew I couldn't tell Rob what was really going on. I was counting on some last-minute inspiration, and suddenly it came. "I'm doing an article about how different artists capture different aspects of the same model," I told him, remembering the school's display windows. "I thought it might be fun to include some of my own works. I have a photo of a painting I did here, with a model I can't identify. I was wondering if she still works here, or if you can show me anyone else's paintings of her."

Rob held out his hand for the photo of my painting. "Oh sure," he said, "Easy one. That's Ramona."

"Ramona?" I asked. The name didn't ring any bells. "Are you sure?"

"Absolutely. She was with us for a couple of years."

"Is it really a good likeness of her?"

"You knew what you were doing," Rob said. "Yes, it's good."

"I don't remember her at all. I don't think I did any other paintings of her."

"Maybe she came just before you left," he said. "I may have one other painting of her," Rob said, "because I think someone won the Ledderer Prize with it. He got to travel to Europe with the prize money, and he was so grateful, he donated the painting to us."

He motioned me to follow him, and led me to a small storage area filled with racks of paintings. He pulled a few out and quickly shoved them back into their spaces. He held one out to me and said, "This isn't the one I was looking for, but I think it's her." It was a female nude, reclining on a vivid red couch.

"Nice," I said. "It does resemble her." Maybe Diana, maybe not.

He continued looking and pulled out another. "This one too. I guess we have more than I thought," he said. "They must be ones people left at the end of a session, and we thought they were too good to throw away." He was displaying an eighteen-by-twenty-four canvas panel depicting a bare-breasted woman with a flower in her hair. There was a strong resemblance.

"Oh, here," he said, "this is the one that won the prize." It was a six-foot-tall stretched canvas, with a full-length standing nude done in a coldly photographic style. Now the likeness to Diana was unmistakable.

"Most of the time she posed nude," he said. "Your painting may be the only portrait pose she did. You remember, I'm sure, they want the extra money for posing nude."

"Yes, sure," I said. "This is great. If you find any more, would you let me know?"

Rob nodded. "I'll ask around. A lot of students who painted during those years are still here."

"Thanks," I said. "You're the best. Is there any chance I could contact the student artists and the model for permission to use photos of these in my article?"

"I can give you the names. The model is Ramona Katorsky from Co-op City. She hasn't worked here for several years, but I'll give you whatever information we have."

Ramona Katorsky. Co-op City.

It looked like Diana was not only capable of being involved with forgers, but was herself a walking human forgery.

"Listen, I wouldn't tell you this if I didn't trust you to keep it to yourself," Rob said. "Be careful. We had to let her go. I take care of my people, but something happened that I couldn't shove under the rug."

"What was it?" I asked, excited, but trying not to show it.

"I can't give you details. Let's just say she got caught between a rock and a hard place, and she made a really bad move."

I tried to get him to tell me but he wouldn't budge. I thanked him when he gave me the contact information, and decided to take my walk through the park and think it through.

What could she have done? I thought about Diana all the way from Fifty-seventh Street into Central Park, where I walked my favorite route past the carousel, up the Mall and then to Bethesda Terrace. This had been a favorite place to paint when I'd finished taking classes and struck out on my own. Now a sketchbook would have come in handy, but since I didn't have one, I settled for the pleasure of seeing the park's beauty. I loved the elaborate Victorian double staircase near Bethesda fountain and the lake, but it was too cold to linger. In a space that was lively three seasons of the year, only a few hearty souls were around now. I made my way a short distance to the Boathouse Café, deep inside the park around 74th Street. I sat there with a hot chocolate, a view of the lake, and a lot of questions.

Was Diana just a social-climbing fashionista, or had she really dipped her toes into criminal behavior as well as Manolos?

CHAPTER FIFTY-TWO

Was Jim involved too? My instincts said no. Despite his sometimes threatening or vulgar behavior, I felt that he wasn't really a destructive person. More talk than action. He'd made a bad choice when he married Diana, and was having trouble living with the consequences.

I called Nick. After he scolded me for getting more involved, he sounded excited too. "I knew it!" he said about Rob's ID. "I'll check out this Katorsky woman and see if she disappeared when Diana appeared."

"Maybe she's even got a record," I said, almost numb with shock at realizing how deep into it I was. I had never liked her, but I had never doubted her entire identity. Even when Nick had insisted that the model in the painting had been Diana, I'd imagined a youthful rebellion that had put her in a modeling job. I never thought she was lying about her whole past.

"Listen, go carefully," Nick said. "There's something you should know. The chief is a friend of Jim and Diana's. They're not just wealthy, they're connected. Keep this to yourself. Understood?"

"Of course I understand. I knew from the beginning that it's risky to go up against the rich and powerful. But we've gotten this far. We can't stop now."

Nick made a sound halfway between a laugh and a snort that was a lot like what my father used to do when he was proud of me. "Good for you," he said. "That's my girl."

Would the chief cover for his friends if they were guilty of a serious felony? If so, what would happen to Nick and me?

CHAPTER FIFTY-THREE

My back was *not* to the wall. Quite literally. On the contrary. And in this case, that was a bad thing. I felt completely exposed as I sat outdoors painting. Actually, I was wearing a winter coat, hat and gloves. The relatively mild weather was totally unexpected at this time of year, and I hadn't been able to resist the pleasures of being outdoors. I'd go back to working on the mural the next day, when the cold weather was expected to return with full intensity.

I couldn't wait for spring and I couldn't wait for Nick to solve the case.

We were getting close, I was sure, to finding out who'd killed Danny and Pierre/Anthony, and the phone call after Miles had been arrested showed that my role in the investigation was becoming well known. Maybe too well known.

The bright sunlight made the colors of the buildings glow again, after several weeks of drabness. I began to feel safe sitting in the middle of busy Main Street in such crystal clarity. I had chosen my spot on my usual side of the street, facing north, with the afternoon sun lighting everything from my left. Across the street were Bellini's and the four buildings I'd first seen in the Historical Society book. In front of me was a short span between two driveways, just big enough for one car to park, but parking wasn't allowed there. This was one reason it was a good spot—my view was unrestricted a lot of the time. Still, there was a steady stream of cars pulling in for just a one-minute dash to the liquor store. The occupants of the cars spilled out and many greeted me as they dashed by.

"Lissa, hi," said one young mother I recognized from Bellini's.

"Hey, there's the artist," said many people as they rushed by. "Where've you been?" It was hard to imagine any kind of crime happening in this town, much less murder. Poor Danny's studio was right around the corner. I forced my mind back to my canvas.

A brown car came by, nice-looking but with several dents, and slowed down but didn't stop. It might not have caught my eye except that it was making a slightly odd noise, a little clickety-clack instead of the usual steady motor sound. There were two men in the front seat, and the second time I saw them, they were looking my way. Probably needed directions, I thought, and I went on sketching my underdrawing on the canvas. The third time I saw them I began to feel a little uneasy, especially when I got a better look at the face of the one in the passenger seat. Something about his expression didn't look right. He looked like he was really focused on me. Of course, people always watched me work, but this felt different. I forced myself to concentrate on my painting for a while, but sooner than I wanted to, I folded my easel and went into Bellini's.

Nothing really happened. As Nick pointed out when I told him.

So why did it feel so unnerving?

CHAPTER FIFTY-FOUR

I went back to working on the mural the next day, in safe and cozy Bellini's, my visit to Juliana's office on my mind. I hadn't told Nick about it, and I decided to keep it to myself for the moment, at least until I'd printed and studied the photo I'd taken. I was afraid he'd be angry. After all, it was a private space, even if it was inside a public one. I'd deal with it, but today would be for the mural.

I worked for several hours, until it was getting late. Nick had come in, and he liked what I'd accomplished. The customers were few and far between now, the sound of the wind rattling the shop windows explaining that. I looked up from my work. "Oh, damn," I said to Nick, "the forecast was right. More snow, any minute. I'd better start for home." I began to pack my art supplies and load them into the closet. I emptied my brush-soaking water and gave the brushes a thorough cleaning, squeezed them and patted the bristles into place so they would dry properly. I closed the closet doors and walked to the front of the store.

"It's pretty raw out there," said Nick. "How about a coffee for the road?"

"Sounds good." I wasn't really eager to leave. I preferred to stay a while after I finished, looking at what I'd done and thinking about what needed to be done the next day. I took a couple of digital photos of sections of the mural, figuring that I'd look at them at home. Along with the ones from Juliana's office.

"I'm going to nuke it for you," said Nick, holding up my cup of coffee, "so be careful. Don't try to drink it while you're driving, you might burn yourself."

"OK, don't worry," I said with gratitude, and a minute later took the coffee, in a doubled cup wrapped in several napkins, with my umbrella tucked in the crook of my arm.

I walked out onto a nearly deserted street and headed up the block to my car, freezing from head to toe except for my fingers, which were burning from the coffee. I had to pass the cup from hand to hand as I walked. In front of the third antique shop the shadows began to move. I could barely see him for the darkness. He was dressed in dark clothing and he came out of the doorway. I kept walking, faster. Then he was right behind me, and I felt an icy hard something poke my neck.

"You shoulda kept your nose outta other people's business," the gruff voice said right in my ear. "You made a big mistake."

The anger in his voice and body language were chilling. This was for real. I had to act and act fast. The heat of the coffee broke through the coldness of my fear and I decided to take the plunge. I let the umbrella drop and ripped the lid off the coffee and quickly flung the burning liquid back over my shoulder where I thought his face would be. I turned and ran as fast as I could back to Nick when the scalding coffee met its mark.

The man's cursing followed me down the block.
But he didn't.

CHAPTER FIFTY-FIVE

Bellini's door was locked. As I banged on it, I could see Nick through the glass panels. His face was concerned as he rushed to let me in.

"What happened?" he asked, his voice hard.

"A man grabbed me," I told him. "I think he had a gun."

"The bastard!" he said. "Are you okay?" He gave me a quick glancing inspection from head to toe, and seemed relieved. "How did you get away?"

I told him about the coffee.

"Wow, Lissa, great!" he said, squeezing my arm. "We'll get him. Wait 'til he finds out how the Tarrytown P.D. handles scum." He rushed to the door. I followed him, and we both looked up the street. No one was visible.

"Stay here," he said, and ran out into the icy air, still dressed in his Bellini's t-shirt and cotton slacks.

"Be careful," I yelled after him, "Nick, please." I felt sick at the memory of the cold hard object against my neck.

Was Nick running into a gun battle?

It seemed like forever as I waited inside the door, peeking out from time to time and then slamming the door shut and locking it again. Finally, to my great relief, he came back. He put his arm around me and got out his phone. "Look for someone with possible facial burns," he said into it. "Check Walgreen's and CVS. He could be buying salve. Or try the hospitals. I'll have more for you in a few minutes."

"Tell me about him, Lissa," he said, sitting down with me in the front of the shop, next to the mural.

"I didn't see him. He came up behind me."

"Did he say anything?" Nick asked.

"Yes, he said I should have minded my own business."

"What did he sound like?" Nick prompted.

"Rough. Like a thug."

"What do you mean? His words or his voice?" Nick asked.

I hesitated, trying to make sense of an experience that had lasted for just a few seconds. "He spoke like a movie gangster, I think, a little dumb," I said, a thought forming in my mind that Nick would express before I got the chance.

"A movie character?" he asked. "Like he was playing a role? Another fake, like Pierre?"

"I'm not sure," I said, thinking hard. "It was only one sentence. But I think as he spoke it was like an actor in a scene who can't sustain an accent in every word."

"How?" he asked.

"The way he said 'other people's business' was more mainstream, more educated. The rest was pure Brooklynese."

"It's a start," he said. "How tall was he?"

"His voice came from above my head," I said. "He must be six feet at least."

"Good. What else? Any smells, any texture of his clothing?" Nick asked.

"His sleeve was soft, I think. A soft wool. It wasn't a scarf. His whole arm was in it. If it was a cashmere coat, he spent a lot of money on it."

"How sure are you?"

"I think so," I said, again trying to relive the moment. "Yes," I said, with more certainty. "For a second I was surprised, because the cloth felt good against my face, but then he started choking me. It was incongruous, I remember."

"You make a good detective, Lissa," he said, leaning across the small table. He picked up his phone and called in the information.

The phone rang as soon as he put it on the table. "Keep looking," he said into it. "Turn over every god-damned rock. We've got to get this guy."

I had to ask, although I knew the answer. "Do you think he'll try again?"

Nick didn't say anything. The look in his eyes was enough.

I shuddered. He stood up. I felt his closeness, his physical warmth and emotional strength.

"We'll get him," he said. "We'll get him good."

CHAPTER FIFTY-SIX

I would've liked to be at Bellini's, working on the mural, the next day, but a client who'd been away called to say she was eager to get the painting I was doing for her. It was an interior of her house, with her dog sitting in the middle of the couch in a regal pose, staring intently at the viewer. In some hands it would be kitsch, but I'd worked hard to make it elegant and serious, like one of my favorite Van Dycks at the Met, a duke with a golden-haired dog at his side. There were just a few touches left to do, and I needed the money she still owed on it. I gave myself an extra couple of hours to sleep and went to work around noon.

Nick had reassured me that there would be police cars on the street, some marked and some not, and I was happy to see a patrol car on the corner of my block. I was happy to have a normal day.

Or so it seemed.

I set out my colors on the palette and tried to focus on the painting on my easel, but I couldn't. I placed it aside and put the Diana painting there instead. I sat a little distance from it, my back to the door. I could hear people coming and going in the hall outside my open door, to and from the offices of the attorneys and therapists who were my neighbors, but I paid little attention to them as I studied the portrait. Background noise and movement made me feel comfortable and energized.

"Okay, then," a deep masculine voice in the distance penetrated my reverie, but only barely. "We'll pick this up at the meeting tomorrow," he continued.

Didn't I know that voice? I wondered vaguely. *Who is that?* I thought with no sense of urgency. When it boomed out right behind my shoulder, I nearly fell off my chair. Now I realized whose voice it was.

"Well, hello, Elizabeth," Jim said. "So this is where you do what you do."

So I was Elizabeth again. "Jim, how nice to see you," I croaked, my throat bone dry from anxiety. *What was I going to say when he noticed the painting?* I was too far away from it to throw a cover-up on it, and it was too late anyway.

"Nice work, nice work," he said as he looked around the room. He was studying the local landscapes and street scenes on the wall. He appeared hale and hearty, as he had at the beginning of the fundraiser and at the diner, but when we were face-to-face I could smell liquor on his breath.

He spotted the painting. He stared at it silently, and then at me. "Did I ruin a surprise?" he asked.

"What do you mean?" Dumb was the way to go, I decided. Use that good old primitive defense, denial.

"Is this for me?" he asked in a booming voice. "Did Diana hire you to paint her portrait for me?"

"Diana?" I stalled. What was my story?

"Yes, Elizabeth, Diana." He sounded like he was patiently explaining the obvious to an idiot. "You've got a painting of my wife on your easel. It looks like it's finished. It must be a surprise gift, right?"

I pretended to study the painting. "Why Jim," I said, "I do believe there is a definite resemblance. I hadn't noticed. Maybe I'd seen her just before I painted it and her face was on my mind. But it's not her. I wish she *had* commissioned me, but she hasn't."

"Oh, you're putting me on," he said. "That's Diana. Okay, I see. You're trying to pretend the secret's not out. I'll go along with it. How I indulge you, Elizabeth. I hope you're grateful."

He'd probably forget about it in a day or two anyway, I told myself. With the collection he had, how excited could he be about a painting by an unknown?

"You won't tell Diana you saw it, will you?" I asked. "I'll be in so much trouble," I said. *More than you know*, I thought.

"Shake," he said, and held out his hand. I held out mine, and he kept it a little longer than necessary. His eyes radiating irony, he bowed in an old-fashioned gesture and left.

CHAPTER FIFTY-SEVEN

Nick had to work late that evening. Around 6 P.M. he called to ask me to meet him for a drink. There was a bar next door to Bellini's, and I agreed to a glass of wine around 8 o'clock.

The first person I saw when I walked into the Settle Inn was none other than Jim. He was at a table about halfway back, and I saw him looking at me and saying something I couldn't hear over the music. His gesture to the seat next to him was unmistakable, though, and I slid in.

"I didn't expect to see you here," I said. This was an understatement. The Settle Inn was more blue-collar than 24-carat-gold necklace.

"It has its attractions," Jim said. "I used to come here when I was a kid. Maybe I got sentimental. And maybe I thought that, since it's right next door to Bellini's, I might see you."

I was shocked. It was one thing to sit with Jim when I happened to run into him, but the thought that he had come with a premeditated intention made me temporarily speechless. When I found my cool I said, "How nice. I'm meeting Nick here, but I'm happy to keep you company for a few minutes."

Jim put his hand on mine and looked at me for a long time without saying anything. I didn't pull back. He had an empty glass in front of him, and he signaled the server to give him another, and a glass of wine for me.

"We have to make a time for you to see my new treasure, Lissa," he said. "I haven't forgotten. I want your professional opinion on it." He didn't look concerned, so I doubted whether its authenticity was on his mind at all.

"I'd love to see it, of course," I replied. "It would be an honor. Sometime this week?" I hoped I didn't sound over-eager.

"I have to check my calendar, but maybe Thursday night?" he asked.

"Yes, that works for me."

Nick was late, as usual when he was coming from work. I decided to plunge in and try for a sense of whether Jim knew that Diana was not who she claimed to be. To my relief he seemed perfectly happy to talk about their relationship, at least for a while.

"How did you meet Diana?" I asked.

"It was at a Sotheby's exhibition, before an auction," he said. "I'd stopped by to take a look only because I was early for an appointment in the building next door. I smelled her perfume next to me, turned to look at her, and that was that."

"So quickly?" I asked with a smile. "I'd think you would be harder to hook."

"Oh, Elizabeth, how kind you are," he said, with his usual tinge of irony. His eyes went from me to somewhere in the distance. "I can still picture her as she was that day. So beautiful, so elegant. Wearing a sapphire blue dress."

"She has lovely clothes now too," I said. "Was she knowledgeable about the artwork?"

"She knew what she was looking at," Jim said. "She told me she'd come in from San Francisco to see a Seurat her father thought he might buy."

"How exciting. Did her father come as well?"

"No, apparently he trusted her judgment. Which impressed me. Along with her good looks. After the exhibition I kept thinking about her, and two or three days later I went to the auction just to look for her and ask her out."

"That's so romantic. From a chance encounter," I said. He nodded. "Amazing how life can change completely just because you've gone somewhere at the right time."

"Or the wrong one," he said, but he didn't actually say that applied to this situation. His face suggested, however, that it might.

"Did she buy the painting?" I asked. *Fat chance. Not with the salary of a nude model from Co-op City,* I thought.

"No, she didn't. Bid once, but she wouldn't go beyond the minimum. Told me later it was inferior in some way."

It was daring of her to bid at all, but she'd been at the exhibition and maybe she'd heard people talking about their intention to go after it. Or a staff member telling someone there was a lot of interest in it.

"Did it sell?" I asked.

"Oh, yes, yes," Jim said. "There was quite a lively bidding war. Of course, we spent most of it looking at each other."

"How long did you have together before she went back to San Francisco?" I asked.

"We went out four or five times. Then she was called home because her father had taken sick. He'd had a stroke and was in bad shape."

"Oh, how awful for her. It's terrible to be away from home when a parent is ill."

"Yes, it is. She and I had already clicked, though, and after a few days I called her and she said she wanted to come back to New York."

"Did you have any trouble convincing her parents to let her go?" I asked. I hoped it sounded like small talk, but I was trying to find out if she'd introduced him to a real family in San Francisco.

"She'd lived in New York for a few years, working for some designer, and she'd just moved back to San Francisco a few months before," he told me. "I'm sure her parents were disappointed when she told them she was coming back here. I let her handle all that. Her father was sick, she'd already been on her own for a long time, so I just called her on her cell. Who needs the aggravation of in-laws if you can avoid it?" He looked a little uncomfortable.

"Did you get married here?"

Jim sat back and gave me a long look. "Why Elizabeth, you ask so many questions."

"I'm just curious what it's like to marry a man as successful as you," I said. *Oh, God*, I thought, *I hope he doesn't mind a little fawning.*

"Oh, Elizabeth, it'll happen for you. Who's this gentleman you're waiting for tonight?"

"Nick Bellini. His family owns the building next door, and they run the ice-cream shop."

"I think I've seen him around. Big guy, dark hair?" Jim asked. I confirmed. "What does he do?" Jim asked. "He's not a professional scooper, I take it? I can't picture you with a man whose primary mission in life is to dish out ice cream all day." His expression was somewhere between a smirk and a condescending, avuncular smile. "No matter how big his muscles might be."

"There's nothing wrong with being a businessman," I said. "I'm sure your bank is happy to have money from successful shops in town." It was evasive, of course, but I didn't want to say more.

"Is it serious?" he asked. "The two of you?"

"No, no," I said. "We're just friends."

Jim's hand landed on my knee with more of a thud than I would imagine he'd intended. The drinks were affecting his coordination. Still, his hand managed to start working its way up my thigh. I removed it firmly.

"An artist needs a different kind of man," he said, leaning towards me and talking right into my face. "You need freedom. You don't want to get up at 5 A.M. to make breakfast for him, and spend your day doing things for him. You need a man who comes to you every once in a while, gives you the financial backing you need, makes you comfortable, you make him comfortable, and then he goes home to the old ball-and chain. You get the best of the deal."

"Like a banker?" I asked.

"Yes, what a splendid choice," he said, leering.

"I'd have to be sure that I wouldn't lose my freedom that way, too," I said. "Powerful men like to control their women, don't they?" I could never live like that.

"Powerful men can and do control the women they want, Elizabeth," Jim said in a low tone. "It's the way of nature. The weak are protected by the strong but they have to submit. Otherwise all kinds of nasty things can happen."

The look in Jim's eyes didn't reassure me that he was talking about other, distant people. To my relief I heard my name and looked up to see Nick. I felt a rush of pleasure as I studied his tall, substantial frame and his kind and intelligent face.

"Hey, Nick," I said, with obvious pleasure.

Jim looked annoyed.

"Do you know Nick?" I asked him. He shook his head and then Nick's hand.

Much as I was looking forward to time alone with Nick, I didn't want to leave Jim, because I was on track to find out what he knew about Diana's past. I made no move to get up.

"Sit down, old man," Jim said, and Nick took the chair on my left.

"Jim was just telling me about his wedding," I said.

"Was I?" he asked, looking slightly unfocused.

"Yes," I said, then turned away from Jim, towards Nick. "Jim met Diana at Sotheby's," I told Nick. "It was love at first sight. Isn't that terribly romantic?"

"Sure, sure, that's great," Nick said. "When was that?" he asked.

"I don't know," Jim said. "The women know that sort of thing, don't they?" he asked.

"Yeah, sure, that's for the girls," Nick said with a shrug of his shoulders and a big smile.

"Tell me about the wedding, oh please," I gushed. "It must have been beautiful."

Jim answered after a long pause. "We got married here, in Tarrytown, very simply. A few friends at Abigail Kirsch, that's all."

"Didn't she want a big white wedding?" I asked. "With her family?"

"We weren't kids, you know," Jim replied. "I'd let my first wife have a big wedding and that didn't make our marriage any better."

"Smart man," Nick said. "You spend so much money on a party. It doesn't make sense."

"My good man, we weren't hurting. We could have thrown the best, but we didn't need it," Jim told him. "You're not in that position, I know."

I looked at Nick, but if he felt belittled he didn't betray it.

"Didn't her family come here, though?" I asked Jim. "Or do you visit them?"

"Oh, Elizabeth, it's a busy life," he answered. "I didn't marry her family, I married her. We didn't need her family at the wedding and I don't need to run out to California to see their big house. So it's a nice mansion, but I'm not exactly living in a hovel myself. And it's just her brother and sister there, now, anyway. What are all these questions, Elizabeth? Are you hoping to sell them a painting? I'm afraid you'll have to talk to Diana about that."

Nick had looked startled when Jim called me Elizabeth. "Alissa," he said, enunciating in an exaggerated way, "doesn't work that way. If she likes you, she wants to hear about your life. That's all. Right, babe?" he said, turning to me.

"Right," I said. "I'm just interested. You're such a great couple. Tarrytown is lucky to have you. So her parents passed away?" I asked.

"Well, they're gone. Her father died a few months after we married, and her mother took ill and went into a nursing home not long after that. Diana goes to see her every once in a while for a few days, but I don't go with her. The old lady's not all there, Diana says, so what's the point?"

"How sad," I said, expressing sympathy far beyond anything I felt. "Is she close with her brother and sister?" I asked.

"I suppose so. They talk on the phone like any family. Her sister, what's her name, Mary or something, comes to us for a couple of days every few months. The brother stays with us a couple of times a year. I'm busy. I don't pay much attention. They have a good time and I go my own way."

"You've gotta keep your life from interfering with your work," Nick said.

"It keeps things peaceful," Jim agreed.

"But aren't you the least bit curious about the family history?" I asked.

Even in the dim light, Jim's face was unmistakably red. "What the hell does that matter?" he asked. "I don't have time to be curious. Not about them, anyway. Where's my drink, for God's sake?"

"Next round's on me," Nick said. Both he and I could see that I'd pushed a button Jim couldn't bear to have pushed.

All of Jim's wealth and power couldn't help him stand up after the next drink. Nick had to call a cab for him, and convince him to get in it. Jim kept insisting he was fine, that he lived only a few blocks away, but he couldn't do a thing without Nick's help. After Jim was packed into the cab, Nick came back and sat down next to me.

"Not bad at all for an amateur," he said. "You got right to the heart of it."

"Glad to help," I said. "He knows something, I'm sure. But do you think he knows everything?"

"I think he drinks so that he doesn't have to know everything," Nick said. "If he weren't so pathetic I'd want to give him a good hard punch in the face, the way he acts so smug. And the way he looks at you."

"If he ever stopped drinking, he might be an interesting guy," I said. "He invited me over on Thursday night to see his new 'treasure'." I hope he remembers when he sobers up."

Nick's expression turned dark. "Lissa, watch yourself. Don't get too involved. He may be *too* interested in you. He could be trouble."

"I can take care of myself, Nick," I said, not particularly liking the way the conversation had turned. "Come on, relax," I said, touching his hand. "I'm happy that it's just us now. You know, don't you, that I'm only interested in Jim because of the forgeries." I thought of the sweet kiss at the river, and the way Nick's powerful arms had felt around me the night before. I also remembered very well what Gina had told me about Nancy. Would Nick be able to have a real relationship? Once burned…But I'd been burned, too, and maybe I was ready, so maybe he was, too?

"Yeah, yeah, I know," he said, his expression returning to normal. "All right, you go and see what he's got. I'll be outside. If he tries anything, just scream. I can smash a window and get him in 10 seconds."

"Don't worry. I'm not a child. I don't think Jim's knowingly involved. I can handle him."

The rest of the evening was what I'd hoped it would be. Nick and I connected, we understood each other. It was a meeting of the minds without any no-that's-not-what-I-meant's or awkward silences. And when it was time to drop me off at home, he came in for a nightcap. And stayed for the night. And I woke up happier than I'd been in years.

CHAPTER FIFTY-EIGHT

I hadn't mentioned when I made an appointment with Alexander Leighton that I'd been to his office before. I reasoned that he'd probably been focused on Nick when we'd come, but just in case, I wore a curly brown wig and uncorrected sample glasses I'd borrowed from the optician in my building. Sure enough Leighton was showing no signs that he remembered me. I was hoping to sound him out on the subject of forgery, and used my connection with the local news website to give it a try.

He greeted me from behind a newspaper when his secretary ushered me into his office. I couldn't see much more than one eye and a sliver of cheek.

"Pardon me if I just finish reading this review," he said. "I've got to write a response immediately."

Leighton walked to the window and sat down in front of it. The sun was right behind him. I had to squint to see him, but it was too painful even then. I focused on my notebook.

"So you're from InTarrytown.com?" he asked.

"Yes, I'm a freelancer, doing an article on contemporary art."

"They're interested in that sort of thing in Tarrytown?" he asked. "I don't think I've seen a truly contemporary gallery there."

"Have you been there often?" I asked.

"My wife and I go to the Tarrytown Theatre from time to time," Leighton replied. "And we like the restaurant across the street. It's a charming little town."

"I love it," I said. "Do you know any of the local artists?"

"A few. It's been a while since Tarrytown has produced a big name, though."

"Yes, not since Paul McGill," I agreed. "But maybe there'll be more sometime. It's an inspiring place."

"I suppose so," Leighton said, with little enthusiasm.

"He came back recently for a memorial," I said, not mentioning that I knew very well that both Leighton and his wife had attended. "A friend of his. David, David....what was that poor guy's name?"

"Danny Bogart. You don't know that?" Leighton asked. He looked suspicious. "There aren't that many artists in Tarrytown. Certainly not many who came to such a lurid end."

Maybe I'd gone too far. My stomach cramped up.

"Yes, sure, I know the story from the news," I said, "but I couldn't think of his name. He wasn't well-known before his death. If our paths crossed, I guess I didn't pay much attention."

Leighton sounded more relaxed. "I guess that makes sense. You are a journalist, though?"

"Strictly part-time freelance," I said, looking in his direction as long as the glaring light allowed, wearing what I hoped was a charmingly self-deprecating smile. "I'm an artist who writes. This article is about quality in art. Who better to ask about that than a well-respected critic?"

"Very well," he said. "Ask away. I don't have too much time, but I'll try to help you out."

"Do you think there's any place in contemporary art for the qualities that made traditional artists stand out from their contemporaries?"

"Well, of course there's no need for rendering these days," he said. "We have photos and computers to make our images. The important work now deals with the conceptual, the political, and the psychological."

"Is there any merit to the idea that the artist should be the one who sees his concept through to the final production?" I asked. "In other words, is there any validity to the views of those who fault an artist like Jeff Koons for having their work made by others?"

"Not at all. Many artists have assistants to do the grunt work. But that's not new. Rubens had that, and so did Rembrandt. Many works came out of their ateliers with other hands involved."

"Didn't the assistants of the past do the less important sections, for example the backgrounds of a portrait?" I asked in a tone that suggested confusion rather than challenge.

"Yes, but now the goal is to provoke the viewer. It's no longer about the hand that pushes the brush. It's about the act of smashing our preconceptions of what we should spend our time viewing and considering."

"So the mastery lies in the idea and not the execution?" I asked.

"The execution is supervised by the master artist, of course," he said.

"Wouldn't this affect the value of forgeries? After all, if it looks like a Renoir, (*was that a little choking sound in his throat?*) and the hand of the master is no longer important, shouldn't it be worth the same as a real Renoir?"

He laughed. "Perhaps you've got something there. I'm all for it." His voice sounded steady. "All one has to do is find an artist who can paint as well as Renoir, in his style." Now he sounded just a little more emotional.

"Pretty hard to do, don't you think?" I asked.

"Anything's possible. Anyway, most people don't know to look for the fine distinctions. But who's to say? And most experts don't want to call a fake a fake these days because the money lost by the duped owner can be the basis for a very nasty lawsuit. It's so subjective." His tone was professorial again.

"That sounds ideal for forgers," I said.

"Aren't we getting off the track here?" he asked. "Didn't you come to ask about contemporary art?"

"Yes, of course," I said. His reaction to the subject of forgery was interesting but not conclusive. There certainly hadn't been a passionate defense of authentication. I could tell that much to Nick. "Where do you see the next important trends coming from?" I asked, and let him expound for a while. I thanked him for his time and left.

As I put on my coat in the outer room, I heard him on the phone. "Can we meet early tonight?" he asked the person on the other line. Again there was nothing blatant, but he did sound a little rattled. I wished I knew who it was and what the subject of their conversation tonight would be.

I put my hands in the pockets of my coat and realized that I'd left my beloved leather gloves in his office. When I went back in, he was facing the door, away from the window, and for the first time I saw the ugly red patch on his face. Some horrible skin disease, I figured. No wonder he'd positioned himself so I couldn't see it before. I mumbled an apology, grabbed my gloves and left, hoping he didn't have something contagious.

CHAPTER FIFTY-NINE

The summons from Jim came the next day, in the form of a message on my studio answering machine. I picked it up remotely, while taking a break from painting the mural at Bellini's. Jim had made no mention of the circumstances of his exit from the Settle Inn. I suppose that people who drink that much expect others to take it in stride and spare them the burden of reflecting on it.

"Lissa," his recorded voice said, "I'm expecting you tonight. Don't forget." That was all. I couldn't read any emotion or calculation into his tone. Still, it seemed clear that he must have an interest in me beyond what I could do for him as a little-known artist and writer. I'd have to be as friendly as possible without leading him on.

Nick was full of instructions when I told him. We were sitting together in Bellini's over steaming cappuccinos. "Don't bring up Diana's past," he said. "This guy might be ready to blow."

"I won't," I promised.

"And don't mention how he was at the Settle Inn," he cautioned.

"I won't," I said.

"And don't mention me at all," he insisted. "Not as a detective."

"I wouldn't," I replied.

"And mess up your hair a little." He made vigorous gestures around his head to illustrate. Apparently he thought I should look like Albert Einstein.

"I can't do that," I pointed out sensibly. I don't think he heard me.

"Don't wear anything too nice. Wear the glasses you wore at Leighton's."

"He's not going to let me in the door if I'm a total mess. At least I haven't caught Leighton's awful skin disease."

"He had something wrong with his skin?" Nick asked.

"Ugh, a big red splotch down one side of his face. Maybe a blister or two. Don't worry, I'll stay away from you until I'm sure I didn't catch it."

"Jeez, Lissa, I have to worry. About more than skin. Be careful with Jim. You don't know what you're doing."

This was going too far. "I know what I'm doing as an artist, all right," I told him. "I know why I'm going there. If you had someone in the department to do it, maybe I'd let them. But you don't."

"All right, all right. I just can't stand the thought of him slobbering all over you."

"He's not that bad. And he's sixty years old. I don't think I'll need brass knuckles."

"It's not a joke. Jim's no weakling. I've seen what out-of-control men can do to women. If he tries anything, tell him I'll break his head into three bloody parts."

"He probably wouldn't expect more than two. Anyway, I thought I'm not supposed to mention you."

"Lissa, be serious. If you get in trouble, don't say I'm a cop. Say I'm your boyfriend."

This was getting interesting.

I arrived at Jim's a few minutes after seven. Under my bulky winter coat was a simple black wool knit dress, not clingy so it didn't accentuate my curves. But it didn't make me look frumpy, either. My eyes were not hidden behind glasses and my hair was not sticking out in all directions, no matter how sage Nick might have felt his advice to be.

Jim answered the door himself again, wearing a gray and white tracksuit. His hair and skin looked warm and youthful by contrast, and he did seem quite fit for his age. There was no liquor in sight, a situation that wouldn't last very long.

"I'm so glad you could make it," he said, ushering me in with a broad sweeping gesture. There was no sign of Diana or anyone else. He stood close to help me off with my coat and I quickly twirled out of it, stepping away from him so quickly that I was lucky he didn't drop the coat on the floor.

"I can't wait to see what you want to show me," I said, though as soon as I heard my own words, my mind unhappily returned once again to his desire to be painted in the nude. I kept my tone professional, in the hope that he would also. "You are so lucky to be living with such treasures."

"First let me offer you a little wine," he said, walking to a table that had two waiting glasses. We were in the wood-paneled entry hall, which was large enough to have four graceful chairs and two small, elegant tables.

"No, thank you," I replied quickly. I wanted all my faculties. "I'm fine."

"This is not just any wine," he said, his voice velvety. "It's Chateau Margeaux, 1995. A delightful sensory experience. Do you know anything about wine, my dear?"

"Not too much," I said. "My father had a small collection some years ago, but I don't know much about it."

"Did you ever taste a wine that costs $500 per bottle?" he asked.

"Wow, no, never," I said, "but I don't know if I'd be able to appreciate it."

"Oh, my dear, I'm sure you would. Come, let me give you just a sip."

I approached him at the table with the wine glasses. I didn't see anything in either glass yet. I figured that if they were empty and he'd be pouring both drinks from the same bottle, he couldn't slip in anything that didn't belong there. I hoped. Still, I tried to stall and think of a gracious way to decline.

"I have to go back to my studio after this to answer my e-mail," I said. It didn't sound all that strong and he didn't buy it.

"Miss Franklin, I'm offering you a look at a great work of art that few people will see in such agreeable circumstances. In return, you must give me the pleasure of sharing a small amount of a very fine wine. Is that too much to ask?"

How could I say no? I accepted the gold-flecked stemmed glass. He filled it almost to the top, did the same for his own glass, and then lifted his for a toast. I obliged. "To new friends," he said.

I sipped slowly. It *was* unusually pleasant. As I relaxed, I noticed a photo of Diana on the table. She was standing next to a handsome young man I didn't recognize. "What a lovely photo," I said. "Who's this with Diana?" I asked. "I don't think I've seen him around here."

"That's her brother," Jim said. "The last time he visited. It does make her happy when he comes, so I put up with him. You're really getting to know all about us, aren't you? Now come see my new love. One of them, anyway."

I was relieved that I'd be getting to work. I followed him into the room where most of the fundraiser had taken place, and then into the next one, where I'd seen the Monet.

When we got inside, I saw that the Guardi and the Hogarth had been moved higher on their wall, making room at eye level for a small country landscape.

Renoir had a graceful, delicate touch. He'd been a decorator of porcelain when he was very young, and the prettiness carried over into his mature works on canvas. When Renoir was great, he made scenes of tremendous appeal and convincing psychological presence. Of course, his lesser works, like Degas, or any other master, were still worth a fortune because they came from the hand that created masterpieces. Renoir had created spectacular works such as *The Luncheon of the Boating Party*, *A Waitress at Duval's Restaurant*, and *By the Seashore*. I loved those, but I'd seen others that he supposedly painted which were of far less interest to me. Some outed forgers claim they've gotten away with placing work in museums, so you can't count on every "ironclad" authentication. Maybe the ones I didn't like weren't really Renoirs at all. I wasn't instantly sure one way or the other about Jim's painting, but I certainly had doubts.

I announced in an awestruck tone, "This is amazing, Jim. I can't believe what I'm seeing here." Non-committal, really. "Maybe I should've gone into banking, too," I told him, "if bankers can live so well."

"You can have a banker in your life," he said. "You don't have to be one. Of course, my own job didn't buy me all of these. The core of my collection was acquired by my grandmother, many years ago."

"You're very lucky," I said. "It's thrilling for me just to look at it for a while."

"My pleasure, my dear. Sit down," he said, indicating the plush white couch in front of the new painting. Jim sat near me, but not right on top of me, which I hoped meant that there was a chance he'd behave himself this time. Maybe he only lost control when he was drunk.

He angled his body so that he was facing me. I looked at the painting and Jim looked at me.

The landscape was composed in a way that Renoir might have chosen, but as I studied it I found the edges a little hard and the strokes too careful. Renoir's oils looked like pastels, in some sections, anyway. This one made me think of Gerald Parker's Botoxed face: once-removed from the real thing. In Parker's case, the missing element was true youthfulness, and in the painting it was the Renoir sensitivity and mastery of hand. But each was in the ballpark.

"It's really something, isn't it? Diana got it for me, for my birthday. Do you like it?"

"It's incredible. I'd think it would be in a museum."

"It was being sold by a private collector. Paintings are often held quietly and privately until the owner is forced to sell. Or someone inherits the work and doesn't share the passion."

"It's lucky that great works like this don't stay hidden away forever."

"That part of my life is lucky," Jim said, taking a long sip of wine. "Other things aren't so good."

"That's hard for me to believe," I said. "You seem to have everything a person could want. I have to struggle just to keep painting. I don't dare hope to have a home and an art collection like this. Ever."

"You have a good life, Lissa," Jim said in a soft tone. "You create a beauty that other people can only observe."

"I love being an artist. I do. I love the creation and also the sense that I can feel something of what was in the artist's mind when I look at something like this." Maybe the mind in question wasn't really Renoir's, but there was no need to mention that.

"When I was young I wanted to be an artist," Jim told me.

I was surprised. "I thought you were a totally committed businessman," I said. "The kind who's worn three-piece suits since the age of eight."

"I'm not wearing a three-piece suit now, Lissa. There's a lot you don't know about me." He leaned towards me and stroked my hair.

Oh, damn, I thought, *I can't get up and leave now. I'm not finished looking at the painting.*

He didn't look predatory. He had a gentle, pensive look that was not unappealing, but of course he was married. And there was Nick. It was so wrong. I moved his hand away gently.

"Let's enjoy the painting," I said, in a futile attempt to keep things on the intellectual plane. Suddenly, he grabbed my legs and swiveled me into a reclining position, then plunged on top of me.

His physical abilities hadn't yet been affected by his drinking. I put my hands flat against his chest and tried to push him away. I couldn't budge him. "Jim, no," I said. "What if Diana comes in?" *Why did I pick that to say? It implied that we could go somewhere else.* "Jim, this is wrong."

"Diana goes to her …her....whatever the hell it is, every Tuesday night. She never misses it. She won't be home until ten or eleven. Lissa, I need you," he said while I wrestled with his hands as well as his conscience. "You're so fresh, so passionate about your art. You're so free. I envy you. I want to be part of it. I can do things for you."

"No, Jim, no," I said as best I could when I could get my mouth away from his. "You have a beautiful wife. Men envy *you*."

"Diana was a mistake," he said, caressing my ear. "She doesn't care about anyone but herself. We barely talk."

I said in the firmest voice I could muster, "I'm seeing Nick. He'd kill us both. You don't want to mess

with Nick. He's a possessive guy. A big, possessive guy."
Jim backed off and sat up. He turned away from me.

"Nick. Who the hell cares about Nick?" Jim turned
back towards me and I could see that his face was beet red
and contorted with anger.

I stood up to rush out but I stopped when I heard the
faintest sound of a key in the front door. It hit me with one
of those intestine-melting pangs of fear. "Diana comes
home late on Tuesdays?" I said. "Jim, today is
Wednesday." *Damn! How could I deal with her now? One
look and she'd know something had been going on. And
blame me.*

"Where's the back door?" I asked, my vivid
imagination briefly inflicting on me the image of Jim
leading me instead to some hidden room where I'd live out
my days servicing his needs in return for an occasional
bowl of porridge. Nick would come and look for me
eventually, of course. But would he find me?

Why had I insisted I could handle this?

Jim led me to the door at the back of the room and
then through a narrow hallway and into the kitchen, which
was surprisingly old and dowdy. They must have a maid, I
thought. I couldn't picture Diana in this room, even to
make a cup of coffee. No shiny granite counters, no freshly
painted cabinets with glass doors. Just beyond the kitchen
was a most beautiful sight: a door to the outside.

"I know I can count on you to keep your mouth
shut," he said, all traces of the needy little boy gone.

He wasn't exactly the most stable guy in town, I
thought, but I'd been right after all. He wasn't totally out of
control.

I'd just gotten past the kitchen windows when I
realized my coat was still inside, in the front closet. Good
thing I compulsively carried my purse around. I heard Jim
saying, "In the kitchen, dear" in a sullen voice, and I had no

choice but to let my coat spend the night with my dear friends the DeWitts.

I took off down the street.

Should I tell Nick the whole story?

CHAPTER SIXTY

I didn't have long to decide. He was leaning on my car.

Usually I'd be thrilled to see him, but this time I would have preferred to be alone for a while to compose myself. As it was, he could see right away that something had happened.

"He made a move?" Nick asked. His eyes looked hard. I hadn't seen him like this before, and I didn't like it.

"I told you I could handle it. And I saw the painting."

"What the hell was I thinking, letting you go there alone?" he said.

"We had to see the painting. It was important," I said.

"What kind of woman goes to a man's house all alone when she knows he's going to try something?"

"Are you blaming me?" I asked, stunned. "We discussed this before I came." Not only was Nick forgetting that I was there to help him, he was being unreasonably critical.

"I don't like the look on your face," he said. "It's all soft and I don't feel you're really with me. You're thinking

about him, aren't you? Are you attracted to him?" All this
was in a tone worthy of the interrogation room.

"I'm not Nancy," I said. At another time I might
have taken offense but at that moment he seemed a little
pathetically insecure. If he went on with it, well, it had been
nice while it lasted.

He looked shocked. "What do you know about
her?" he asked.

"A little," I said. "I know she made you unhappy."

He looked even angrier. Maybe I shouldn't have
said anything.

"Jim means nothing to me," I said, although I had to
silently acknowledge that Jim had stirred some feelings that
weren't completely bad. "It was for the investigation."

"I didn't pimp you out," he said.

"Nick! What's the matter with you? Nothing
happened."

He looked a little relieved.

Then some idiot with my mouth said "Nothing
much. Jim's not that bad. He's emotionally wounded, not
evil. I handled it. It was nothing that doesn't happen on first
dates all the time."

"So now you're saying it was a date?"

"No! I'm just saying nothing out of the ordinary
happened. Drop it."

"We'll see. Tell me about the painting. Is it a fake?"
he asked.

"It's possible, though I didn't have a chance to
study it. It looked slick, almost a little plastic. Maybe
literally—it could be an acrylic, although you really can't
tell that by just looking, usually. I was just about to ask to
see the back when he…I had to leave."

"Exactly what happened? Did you let him…?"

"Nick, I told you to drop it. I'm not like that. He
tried and I pushed him away. I did have to tell him you're
my boyfriend, and he backed off. Take my word for it,

Jim's not violent. And I don't think he'd get involved with forgers. My guess is that, if it's a fake, he doesn't know. He may be married to Diana, but she goes her own way. I have good instincts about people."

"What are you going on?"

"He told me they're having problems."

"His wife doesn't understand him? What are you, twelve years old?"

He was starting to get on my nerves. "It's not just that," I said. "I can see that Jim feels art. When he looks at it, he doesn't just think of how much people will be impressed that they own it, like Diana does."

"Did he know she might come in and find the two of you?" Nick asked.

"No, I don't think so. He got the day wrong. He thought she was at a meeting until ten o'clock."

"What happened when she came in?"

"You saw her?" I asked.

He nodded. "Of course I didn't think you were doing it in there with her husband. Not that I could have warned you...if I'd wanted to."

This was getting annoying. "Nick, stop it. I told you, nothing happened with Jim. Anyway, I went out the back door just before she came in."

Nick grunted. "Coincidence, right? You were completely in control of your emotions, just an innocent visitor. You could have chatted with the wife if you'd wanted to. So where's your coat?"

I had no ready answer.

His face softened. "Lissa, get in the car. You're right, you're not Nancy. You're not hard. You don't understand how dangerous this could be. Life isn't all about picking which shade of green to use."

"I know what I'm doing," I insisted, but I was glad when he told me he'd call to make sure I got home safely.

"I want to see you drive away," Nick said. "I'll try to get your coat back tomorrow when she's not home. And stay away from Leighton too. Come in to the shop and get that mural done."

CHAPTER SIXTY-ONE

On my way home I got another call from my impatient client, just as I was passing North Broadway at Central Avenue, right near my studio.

"Alissa," she said, drawing it out into three long syllables. "Haven't I waited long enough? What is this, the ceiling of the Sistine Chapel or a 24 by 36 inch canvas?"

"I know, Francesca, it's been a while. You've been just great," I said. I couldn't tell her what had been going on.

"I need it now. Tomorrow. My in-laws are coming in from Colorado, and I want it hanging in the living room when they arrive."

"Couldn't I..." She didn't give me time to finish my sentence.

"Give it to me tomorrow or keep it," she said, and slammed down her phone.

This wasn't my night. She'd given me a deposit, but there was a big balance left that I couldn't afford to lose. I'd have to put the last touches on it immediately.

Tonight. Even though Nick had told me to go home.

They wouldn't dare try anything now, would they? Everything looked so normal on the street. If it was really late when I finished, I'd call Nick and ask him to follow me home.

I went upstairs to my studio, pulled out my tubes of color and somehow managed to zip through the difficult passages I'd left to the end. It was a frenzied effort. My brushes were full of paint, even on the handles. I'd laid them flat on the palette as I switched from brush to brush, instead of placing them carefully on the side, away from the paint. And there were more brushes than usual, so it was a big clean-up job. I'd never stayed so late. Just before midnight, I wiped down the wooden brush handles with a paper towel, dipped the business ends in a small bottle of turpentine to get out the excess paint, and headed down the hall to the Women's Room.

I always closed my door, even late at night when no one seemed to be around, because you never knew. It wasn't easy to manage with my keys in one hand and the six brushes and a plastic basin with a bar of soap in the other, paint-covered hand. I juggled enough to get the bathroom door open, and placed the brushes in the sink. For the next several minutes I lathered and rinsed until the brushes looked almost new. This wasn't my favorite part of the day, and I was happy to be done with it. I had to leave the wet plastic container on the sink while I opened the door. It was a task which required both hands, one to hold open the spring lock, and the other to pull the heavy door towards me. I could then prop it open with my left foot and lean back into the room to get my brushes.

I got halfway down the hall when the lights went out. *Damn!* It was so creepy when this happened. Hadn't I checked the timer downstairs on my way in? Sometimes other tenants came in very early in the morning and turned the dial to make the timer think it was later so the lights would come on, instead of using the override switch, or setting them to come on earlier every day. If they turned too far the lights would go off too early at night. By the dim red light of the EXIT sign near the stairs, I could just barely make out my studio doorway. I felt for the lock with the side of the hand that was holding the keys. My brushes and their washbasin occupied the other hand.

I managed to get the key into the lock, and was relieved at the thought that light was about to shine from the open door. As I began to turn the key, a tingling sensation at the back of my neck made me turn around.

Had there been a movement in the dark hall?

An instant later I got my answer.

Hands grabbed me from both sides. Strong, determined hands. As I was pulled back, the keys dropped on the floor, the door unopened. I screamed and let go of the washbasin, still tightly gripping the six paintbrushes. I tried to lunge at the man on my right with the hard, pointy ends of the brushes, but he was holding my wrist. He shook the brushes out of my hand.

He said, "You won't need those anymore."

I felt sick.

It sounded so final.

"Your brushes aren't going to help you out of this," he said in a tone that made it easy to picture the smirk on his face. "You're coming with us."

The other one said, "You can't leave 'em on the floor here. People will think it's funny."

"Hilarious," said the other one. "Open the door," he ordered me.

I didn't move.

"Which key is it?" he asked, shaking the key ring close to my face.

I didn't answer.

He made a noise that presumably expressed his disappointment in me, then tried three or four keys until he found the right one. With the door open, he threw in the keys, the washbasin, and the brushes. He slammed the door shut.

The light coming out of the studio had given me my first good look at them. It didn't tell me much. I couldn't say I'd seen them before, but I couldn't say I hadn't either. My throat was constricted but I managed to croak, "Who are you? What do you want?"

They didn't answer.

They pulled me along the short stretch of hallway to the top of the staircase. I tried to wriggle free, but they were too strong. We were right in front of the EXIT sign and its red light was enough to allow me to aim one good hard kick at the man on my left. After a most satisfying yelp from him, I saw a fist coming at my face from the right. I yelled, "Okay, you win." The hand went down.

One of them said, "Either you walk down the stairs with us or we throw you down right now." The stairway was steep and hard. I wouldn't want to ride it headfirst. My legs were barely working, but I offered little resistance and they escorted me down the stairs, one on either side of me, lifting me between them just a little so my feet alternately touched and dragged along the steps.

I'd be able to get away later.

Wouldn't I?

When we got outside, the cold air revived me a little. I looked around for someone to help me, but it was late and cold, and there was no one on my street. The police patrol was probably keeping an eye my house. *Damn!* I should've told Nick about the change in my plans. I saw three people in the distance, deep in conversation in front of the 7-Eleven store, but a fire engine was heading down Main Street, siren blaring. I screamed anyway, a short, loud burst. "Help!"

No one heard me. No one turned my way. No one came. One of the men put his hand over my mouth and they pulled me toward a car waiting at the curb.

I tried again to kick them but as my leg rose, the fist came back towards my face. There was no way I could pull off an escape here. My spirits rose a little as I spotted my car, with its cheerful Bellini's bumper sticker, in the nearly empty parking lot across the street. How many times had Nick told me he'd seen my car this place or that? He'd spot it sooner or later, or the night police patrol would tell him it was there after hours. They'd know something was wrong. Emboldened, I said, "You won't get away with this. I have a friend who's a cop."

"Yeah, yeah, I'm peeing my pants," one of them said. "You're crapping yours, right?" he asked the other one.

"Shut up now," the other one said to me. His voice was higher-pitched than I'd imagine for such a powerfully-built man. "We're calling the shots here," he said.

The door opened and I was shoved in.

I had no choice but to settle into the back seat. There were people in both of the front seats, wrapped in dark winter clothing, facing forward. I couldn't see who they were. Neither spoke. The two men who'd brought me out of the building got in the car on either side of me, and each one leaned hard against one of my arms.

We drove north on Broadway for several blocks in total silence. There was nothing I could do. Even if my hands had been free, there was no cell phone in my pocket whose buttons I could push surreptitiously. I had no pockets. My cell was neatly tucked away in my purse, sitting next to my easel in my studio, getting farther and farther away.

Suddenly I noticed it: a spicy, flowery scent I'd smelled before. I knew who was in the front seat. Then I heard the voice. "Didn't you forget something, dear?" The sugary tone was clearly sarcastic. A piece of heavy cloth flew at me from the front passenger seat. "I believe you left this in my closet," the cold female voice announced as my coat hit me in the face. "When you came poking around my *private* art collection." She stretched out the word "private" for emphasis. "Not to mention my husband. What bad manners, darling."

Diana.

CHAPTER SIXTY-TWO

Several minutes later, as we waited at a long red light in Ossining, Diana and the driver started kissing and laughing softly. Just as it looked like he was going to stick his hand into Diana's coat, one of my back-seat companions said, "Okay, Romeo, the lights green."

The driver turned around and snapped, "Just do your damned job. I'm in charge up here." I saw his face well enough to recognize him as the man in the photo on the table in Jim and Diana's house. Her brother, she'd told Jim. The man she visited a few times a year. A *very* close family, obviously.

We arrived, after about twenty minutes, at a dark, four-story building. It was pretty large and there was a parking lot, but we went past the lined spaces to the back. I could smell the garbage as they opened the door.

Diana ordered the men to bring me in the back door. "We'll meet you upstairs," she said. "We can't leave the car here. We'll go in the front."

They ushered me into what seemed to be a loading dock, with crates clustered around the perimeter. I didn't recognize the company names on them.

They led me through a series of long, drab gray and green hallways, with exposed pipes hanging off the ceiling. We passed many doors, but none offered an escape. A man was waiting for us in a freight elevator, the open cage kind that would give me chills even under the most innocent of circumstances. I couldn't quite feel my legs, but somehow they were moving.

The elevator took us up two floors and we got off in a dark hallway, with just a little light along the ceiling and another one way off in the distance. The two men with me seemed to know their way, and I allowed them to lead me along. Given that they had a tight, inescapable hold on me, I didn't really have many options.

The lighter room, distant when we began our walk, became a little clearer as we walked, but I couldn't yet make sense of the shapes I was seeing.

"Where are we?" I asked the man on my right.

"You'll see soon enough," he replied gruffly.

He was right. A minute later I saw all I needed to see.

We were in the Contemporary Arts Museum.

We walked through two more galleries and we were at Juliana's office.

It was Diana who was waiting for us at the door.

CHAPTER SIXTY-THREE

"Here she is," the tall one said as he pushed me towards her.

"Bring her in the office, quickly," she replied.

Diana and her boyfriend/phony brother were already there. One of the thugs pushed me into a chair as far from the door as you could get. They tied me to the chair's polished wood arms. I wiggled my hands a little, and was relieved that the bonds weren't too tight. The knots looked pretty fancy though, and I didn't see any way I could release myself and get past everyone.

"Don't move from there," he told me. "We're going to be right outside the door. You won't get away," he added, as though I hadn't realized my predicament.

My chest was tight. Breathing was the only thing I could handle at the moment.

He went on, this time talking to Diana. "Don't take things into your own hands, now. We're the pros."

"I understand," she said coolly. "I just need to discuss things with Miss Franklin. As you know."

"All right then," the thug said. "Keep it that way. You're not going to involve us in some clumsy amateur hit."

Diana looked angry but spoke coolly. "Who do you think hired you?" she asked.

"Yeah, sure," the thug replied. "Just don't forget why. You get carried away, you do something stupid, you mess it up. We're all in hot water then. Our beautiful friendship would end ugly cause we'll have to keep you from talking, if you know what I mean," he said in a menacing tone, with a chilling stare. His hand brushed his jacket near his armpit, presumably reminding us of his gun.

"Oh my God," said Juliana, looking and sounding near hysteria. She turned towards Diana. "What the hell did you get me into? It was just supposed to be about money. We just needed some money."

Diana looked like she was about to slap Juliana but she didn't. "You're not a child," she said. "You knew what could happen." She turned towards the tall thug. "Leave us alone for a few minutes, please," she said.

"Girls, girls, girls," he said with a smirk. "Just because you're crooks doesn't mean you can't be ladies. Keep it under control and call us when you're done. We've got to finish the job tonight. We don't get paid by the hour, you know." He and his accomplice went out into the gallery.

Diana turned towards Juliana. "You had to know that people don't walk away quietly when they find out they've been duped out millions of dollars," she said. "And now two men are dead. We can't let them find out." She walked up to Juliana and screeched right into the curator's frightened and angry face, "We can't let them find out!"

"It's not my fault, it's hers," Juliana said, pointing at me. She sounded scared, almost as scared as me. "What did you see when you came in here the other day?" she asked me.

"Nothing," I replied. "I got lost looking for the restroom, that's all," I said. It sounded as pathetically flimsy to me as it must have to them.

"Bullshit," Diana's phony brother said.

"Let me handle this," Juliana told him. She turned back to me. "What did you do with the photo?"

"What photo?" I asked, unwilling to speed up what could be my last conversation.

"Let me give her a taste of what happens when a bitch won't talk," the phony brother said eagerly.

"Shut up, Carey," Diana said. "You heard what the man said. Everything has to be just right. Otherwise it won't look like an accident. They know how to do it so everything fits."

What the hell do I do? I wondered with increasing desperation. *It can't end tonight. I have paintings to do. Where was Nick? Nick will come. Won't he?*

"Where's the photo of the calendar?" Juliana asked.

"I don't have it," I said truthfully. "It was a cellphone picture. I don't have my phone."

"Did you show it to Bellini?" Diana asked.

I hadn't, but I didn't want to tell her that. "I didn't print it yet," I said. "I didn't think it was that important. So Juliana likes Monet, that's embarrassing for her, maybe, in contemporary art circles, but..."

Now I knew what the calendar really meant.

Juliana hadn't tried to remove it from our sight to conceal a fondness for Monet.

She was afraid we'd see that she owned a calendar with a fake Monet.

CHAPTER SIXTY-FOUR

It was probably Miles who'd used his graphic design skills to replace whatever real Monet had been in that spot in the calendar when it shipped from the publisher. They must have the painting, and when they try to sell it, she'll be able to authenticate it by "finding" it in this calendar.

"You shouldn't have brought her here," Juliana told Diana. "I don't think she even knew."

"If she didn't, it was only a matter of time. She'd have figured it out," Diana said. "She knows about provenance. She'd realize the calendar had a planted image. What the hell is the matter with you, Juliana? You didn't look weak before. I have no use for weak people."

"We'd better get rid of her too," Diana's fake brother said.

Juliana looked stunned. She gulped. "I can handle it," she insisted. "Sandy's almost here. I'm fine. I'll leave with Sandy and that'll be it. We'll go away. We'll go to Europe."

"Sure," Diana replied. "If Sandy's bringing your backbone, everything will be fine."

Juliana looked at the floor.

Who was this Sandy? Why was she so important? All we knew about her was that Ramón had overheard

Miles arguing with her on the phone. He'd said it sounded like the kind of argument someone had with his wife, but Miles wasn't married. He didn't live with a woman. Maybe she was an ex-girlfriend. Maybe he had a Nancy.

We sat and waited. I was glad for every second of the delay. More time for Nick to figure it out. How he'd track me was none too clear, but he would. He had to.

While we waited, Diana and Carey nuzzled each other and Juliana shuffled some papers. After about five minutes, I heard loud footsteps. Heavy footsteps, not a woman's clattering heels.

The door opened. Alexander Leighton stood there, white salve covering the red skin on his face. Juliana greeted her husband. She sounded relieved.

I looked behind him, to see if he'd brought Sandy. Then I realized. How could I have missed it?

Alexander, of course. Not anybody's wife. Just someone's old chum and ally.

Sandy had arrived.

CHAPTER SIXTY-FIVE

Alexander/Sandy Leighton strode into the room and his wife rushed to his side.

"Sandy, take me home. Right now," she said.

"Just a minute," Leighton said. "Let's get all the provenance papers together and get the hell out of here before they get rid of her," he said, with a nod in my direction.

Juliana continued going through her files.

"I think you've all been very clever," I said. "No one had any idea you were involved."

"Do you know how little money they pay us to teach civilization to their children?" Leighton asked. "That's the real crime. We put up with their lateness and their dense essays and their adolescent moodiness and what the hell do we get for our troubles?"

"Yes, sure," I said. "You've got to get something for your knowledge. How many people know what you know? You absolutely deserve those designer shirts and all."

"You noticed!" Leighton said, running his hand over the smooth fabric on his chest. "Unfortunately, it's too late," he said. "I'm afraid there won't be any time for us to form a beautiful friendship."

"I could help you," I insisted, ignoring his sarcasm. "You're right if you think I wouldn't have gone along with it, absolutely right. But now that you explain it, it makes a lot of sense, really."

They didn't buy it for a minute.

"Sure, sure," Leighton said. "You want in. We're not falling for a childish ruse like that. And thanks for this" he said, indicating the raw-looking part of his face.

"I didn't give you that," I said. "You had it when I came to your office. You didn't catch it from me."

Suddenly, the expression on his face, the contempt at my confusion, cleared it up for me.

It was no skin disease. It was a burn from the super-hot coffee I'd flung at him.

"That was you on the street?" I asked, not quite believing it, but somewhere in my mind knowing it was true. "You were the one who grabbed me?"

"Some things should be left to the pros," he said. "I know that now."

"Sandy, I want to go," Juliana said again.

"You whining little bitch," Diana said. "We have to get rid of her. You're in big trouble too, if we don't. You screwed this whole thing up."

"Hey," Juliana said, standing taller than she had since we came in. "At least I've never been caught in the Men's Room of the Hard Rock Café turning tricks," Juliana said.

Diana's face was turning purple.

"And I didn't have to dress up in a stolen designer outfit to catch *my* husband," she went on.

"Shut up, you bitch," screamed Diana. Her fake brother grabbed her arm to keep her from lunging at Juliana but the strength summoned by her rage was beyond stopping.

The two women started tearing at each other's hair and scratching each other's faces and hands. Leighton and Carey tried to separate them and everyone was flying around the room. Lucky for me I was in the far corner, working on the ties that were holding me to the chair. Diana pushed Juliana and she went flying into the closed door. Two seconds later the men who'd brought me there came in.

"Break it the hell up," one of them said. "Break it up or we'll shoot the lot of you." His commanding voice obviously penetrated the rage, because slowly the combatants retreated to different corners.

CHAPTER SIXTY-SIX

"All right," Diana said to the men. "You know what you have to do. She knows way too much."

Juliana shuddered but said nothing

"So this is it?" thug #1 asks. "You want me to get rid of her permanently? Just so there's no mistake."

"Get rid of her," Diana said, almost spitting. "That's what we discussed, that's what I hired you to do. She'll have a fall. She didn't know where she was going because she wasn't supposed to be there. We have her on video, full face to the camera, breaking into this office."

Damn, I thought I'd been clear of the security camera. Where the hell was it?

Diana continued, "We'll say she broke in again, and didn't see where she was in the dark."

"Yeah," said the thug, "a terrible tragedy for an artist who broke in trying to....? To do what?"

"Just leave that to us," said Diana. "Are you pros or not? Do it right now, and keep us clean, or we'll find someone to take care of *you*."

"That sounds like the boss lady to me," he said, looking at me. He pulled me out of my seat. "Can't say no to the boss."

"My cop friend is probably out there right now," I said, acting as brave as I could. It's possible the effect was undermined by my high-pitched Minnie Mouse voice, but I did my best.

"Lady, we're going now. Say your goodbyes to the nice people."

"Wait a minute," a voice said, with a tentative tone. It was Juliana. "I don't know if we have to do this," she whined.

"What the hell, you idiot," Diana spat.

"We're not like you, Sandy and I. Right, darling?" she asked, but she sounded uncertain of his response.

It would have been an interesting conversation for someone who was free to go whenever she got bored, but my circumstances were wearing on me. The others were interested enough to give me a little wiggle room, and wiggle I did until my bonds were loose. I didn't get up, but I knew time was running out.

"You're in this as much as I am, you bitch, the hell with your knowledge of civilization," Diana said, mimicking a British accent as she drew out the word: "civ-il-eye-zay-tion." She added, "You think they're going to care about that if they get you into court?"

"They're not going to put me in the same category as a cheap whore like you," Juliana answered, leaning into Diana's face. Unfortunately for her, that also put her own face close enough for Diana to grab, and everyone started going at it again.

This was my only opportunity. I lifted my arms out of the bonds and made it out the door.

CHAPTER SIXTY-SEVEN

Which way?

The galleries were dark. The only things I could see were the red EXIT signs at the doorways. I hadn't been there enough to have a mental map. The times I'd come, I'd used the exhibits as landmarks. Lucky for me there was still plenty of noise coming from Juliana's office, but they'd be noticing I was gone soon enough. I took a chance and went to the right, into the next gallery.

I felt light-headed, and not in a good way. *What would Nick tell me to do?*

I stayed close to a wall, as if its solidity would keep me upright. They'd turn the lights on when they realized I'd gotten away. If only I could slip inside the wall, I thought, and then I remembered all the damsel-in-distress novels I'd read as a teenager, where the first wife, or some man who'd try to cheat with the wife had been walled up forever. But crawling into the wall wasn't a real option anyway, so I moved on from that gallery to the next, and then the next.

Now I heard them. "Miss Franklin, give it up. You can't get away."

Very polite thugs, I thought. I kept going.

"Where the hell are the lights?" I heard one of them say.

Thank God they'd apparently left Juliana without asking her that question.

"Miss Franklin, you're only going to make it worse," one of them said. Despite the formal term of address, his voice sounded angry, but not too close. I still had a chance.

I pushed on. I went about ten more feet, and a wave of nausea hit me. I'd walked right into one of them, his jacket against my face.

I waited for his arms to grab me.

Nothing happened. The arms didn't move. He wasn't attacking me but he wasn't offering any support, either. I put my hand out very tentatively. "Who are you?" I whispered softly. No one answered, because when my hand met the hand that stuck out from the jacket, it was smooth and hard.

As plaster always is.

I'd bumped into an exhibit, dressed in a suit.

Under other circumstances I'd straighten his tie, but this time I passed.

I could see the red EXIT sign, and I made my way to the wall more cautiously, afraid that I'd bump into something that would fall over and make a loud noise. When I got into the next gallery I couldn't follow the wall anymore, because there were exhibits on stands right against it. I took my time. I reached out a few times to touch whatever was there, and the third time I felt a stack of jars. *Aha!* I thought. This must be Paul McGill's installation, which likely meant that I was going towards the exit. I continued on, and as I approached the next gallery I felt a mixture of hope and anxiety. There was a little more light coming through the doorway.

I found myself on a balcony, overlooking a courtyard with several large blocky sculptures. On one of the lower ones, a uniformed guard sat with a newspaper, writing something on it. I saw his lips move and I strained to hear him.

"Look at this," he said, "Filly with a Pearl Earring in the fifth race, odds are 10:1."

Another voice answered, "I'm in on that. How much you putting down?"

I hesitated about whether to yell for help. They weren't exactly the knight in shining armor type. Not to be picky at a time like this, but I was sure they weren't supposed to be doing this on the job. What did I have to lose, though? How long could I stay ahead of the men who were after me?

I opened my mouth and took a breath and began to form the word. Just as I did that, the one who was sitting took off his cap and turned just enough in my direction to give me a look at his face.

I shut my mouth.

Fast.

It was the man who was driving the van that had come to Jim and Diana's house that night.

The man who'd brought the Renoir.

The package that was most likely a delivery from the forger.

I turned and made my way back into the other gallery as quietly as I could. I didn't hear any voices but I was shaking. Maybe they'd seen me and were calling Juliana's office right now to let them know where I was. I was starting to panic.

A dimly lit stairway came into view and I headed down. One flight, was that enough? What if I ended up in that awful basement? I tried the exit door. It opened with a slight groan. Where was I? In another dark room, that was all I knew. Looking left and right, I couldn't see anything but darkness and deeper darkness. I took a few steps forward, and then I heard him.

"Stop!"

It was the voice of the tall thug. I put out my other foot to take the next step.

"Stop! I'm telling you, stop right now, you must! Where the hell are the lights?"

Just as I began to put the weight on my left foot the place was flooded with tiny dazzling LED lights.

I looked down. My foot, the one I'd been about to put all my weight on, was dangling in mid-air over a ten-foot deep "negative art" installation the size of a swimming pool.

I started to get dizzy. I felt myself sway toward the pit.

The thug grabbed me.

I waited for the hard push into the void.

It didn't come.

Instead he pulled me back from the edge.

A moment later his partner came in, slightly out of breath. "You got her!" he observed, looking relieved.

"Okay, careful what you say now," the tall one said. "We gotta know if the boss can see us." He scanned the room. I figured he was looking for video cameras.

The short one said, "I hear you." Then he turned to me and said, "You just can't stay out of trouble, can you? You don't know what the hell you're doin'."

"We'll take her to the basement," the tall one said, now in a loud voice. "We'll do her there. She's got to disappear. We can't chance it that she crawls out of the hole."

"Yeah, yeah, you never know," the short one said. "She could get lucky. Fall just right so she doesn't die right away. Yeah, we gotta take her downstairs."

I was shaking. They were so businesslike. All in a day's work. I felt dizzy again. The tall one's arms gripped me tighter.

There was no escape.

"It's all falling into place, if you'll pardon the expression," he said. "It's a job well done. Tonight we have the best steak and whisky in town. I feel so good, I gotta sing."

How cold could he be? He was going to enjoy killing me?

And sing he did. "I've got sunshine, on a cloudy day..."

It was "My Girl."

The song Nick sang when he was happy.

Was he telling me something? Something he couldn't say directly?

I stared into his eyes, trying to pick up clues the same way I would if he were a painted portrait.

Who was he? Was that a smile on his face? Or a smirk?

The face itself showed no evil. I hung on to my new glimmer of hope.

They took me back to the freight elevator. There was no operator this time. One of them worked it himself.

The door opened in that dingy, endless basement.

"Okay," the tall one said to me. "Get out. The end." His voice was cold and rough again.

Damn! It can't happen. I'll never see Nick again? Never do another painting on Main Street?

I'd been a fool to hope. I braced for the blow.

It wasn't quite over yet. We walked down one grim hallway with grey paint and brown doors, turned right into another that looked exactly the same, then another. How did they know their way through all this sameness?

I looked up as I heard a door open at the end of the third long corridor.

A man stepped out.

My heart pounded.

I saw a green jacket.

I smelled an expensive men's cologne.

I saw his face.
I laughed. I cried.
Nick!

CHAPTER SIXTY-EIGHT

Nick's powerful arms enveloped me. "Good work, Lissa," he said as my tears wet that familiar, beautiful green jacket. I luxuriated in the feel of his hard muscles against my cheek and the smell of his man sweat, mixed with the cologne Nancy had given him.

"You *are* made of strong stuff," he said.

"These are your men?" I asked.

"Pardon me," he said with mock formality. "You haven't been properly introduced. These are my very best undercovers. Sorry we couldn't let you know."

I backed away from him and smacked him on the beloved chest. "Sorry?" I said. "You're 'sorry'? I was nearly scared to death."

Nick grinned and held my hand. Away from his chest. "I asked you if you wanted out," he said. "That night at the river. Do you remember?" he asked.

"Yeah, I guess you did," I had to admit. "But why couldn't you tell me?"

"I didn't know how good an actress you might be. You could've been in trouble if you gave yourself away in a lie," Nick said. "Maybe I sold you short there. Anyway, you were in good hands. You just didn't know it."

I'd thought when I'd gotten into this it would be an exercise in connoisseurship, a test of skill in spotting fakes. The worst I'd feared was a lawsuit. I never imagined this.

I took some deep breaths. My heart wasn't pounding anymore.

I had a sudden thought. "Were they the men in the old brown car who circled the block several times while I was painting on Main Street?"

"They sure were. You could've kept your eyes on your painting."

"You should've told me that much when I came to the shop so creeped out," I said.

"I'll tell you everything now," Nick promised. "Right now let's finish tonight's business. We've got empty prison cells all ready for company."

"Where are Diana and the others?" I asked Nick.

"On their way out of the front door of the building in handcuffs. I've got to get out there. Lissa, for an amateur detective, you did a great job. My friends here didn't hurt you, did they?"

"What do you mean, hurt *her*?" one of them said. "I'm gonna be limping for a week from where she kicked me."

Nick laughed. "Better watch your step, my girl, or I'll get you for assaulting an officer."

I said, "Then I have nothing to lose if I make it two." I pressed my fist against his belly, looking for a soft spot and not finding one. I didn't mind.

He laughed and took my hand and kissed it.

CHAPTER SIXTY-NINE

I woke up the next morning momentarily confused, opening my eyes to see an unfamiliar room. Damn, where was I now? I turned to my left and my anxiety was replaced by a flood of pleasure as I recognized Nick's thick dark hair on the pillow. The night's events came back to me and I smiled, even though he was fast asleep and couldn't see it. I reached out and he woke up and turned towards me. He put his arms out and I moved into them.

Independence isn't everything, after all.

A half-hour later, Nick told me, between bites of the waffle I'd made for him, "The whole thing started to fall apart when they approached Danny to do some forgeries."

"Wasn't that fairly recent?" I asked. "Didn't you hear about forgeries before that?"

"Yes, Leighton was the one who did the "Monet" and the "Renoir" they sold to Jim, and he admits to several others they placed around the county. He was feeling the pressure of all his other work, and wanted to delegate the painting to someone else. When Danny started pushing to have his work shown at the museum, he tried to validate it by showing them what a good education he'd had, and how good he'd been at copying the masters. Big mistake. At that time, he apparently was in better shape. He started drinking heavily and doing drugs after they started pressuring him to do fakes."

"Miles knew? He was at the meeting that time when Danny wanted to show us something."

"Yes, he knew, and that was the reason he had the blow-up with Juliana. He told her it was trouble. They let him leave his museum job, but they had enough on him to keep him quiet."

"What had he done for them?" I asked. The aroma of coffee was so delicious that it called me despite my curiosity. I went to the coffeemaker and poured us each a cup.

"You were right enough about Miles. He was crooked, but no murderer. It had been impressed on him early on, from his experience at the Gardner, that there are ways to make money from art other than the legit ones. He handled the fake provenances, photographing the forged paintings and skillfully planting those photos in books from the museum's library, and in the calendar in Juliana's office. Then he got caught up in more than he bargained for."

"How did you find this out?" I asked.

"I got some of it out of Miles," he said, "and some from Leighton. We cut a deal with both of them. We had them and they knew it."

"The chief must be happy with you," I said.

"He's happy with you, too," Nick said.

"Me?" I feigned surprise, but I was proud of my work.

"In fact," Nick continued, "he may commission a painting for his house. He says you must really know your stuff. And it turns out the reason Becker played the old man in the diner was *you*."

"Me?" I managed to croak. This was interesting news. That meant I'd been involved in a completely different way than I'd thought.

"He'd seen you there before, and hatched a plan to lure you into meeting him about buying a fake. He'd had only a small role in the sales of the forged paintings, making brief appearances as the Frenchman to suggest to the marks that the paintings were coming from Europe. Leighton handled the real business of the deals, with Juliana doing the authentications. Becker got carried away with his own importance and thought he could play a bigger role. He'd seen Danny refusing the good money they were offering for painting forgeries, and he wanted to try his hand at it. They'd turned him down but he wasn't about to give up. He'd been painting every chance he got, trying to get better at it."

"But why bring *me* into it?" I asked.

"He was testing his work on you. He'd seen you working outdoors, and he'd read your articles. Then one day he saw you at the diner. The waitress mentioned that you were a regular there. Becker couldn't trust you, so he couldn't just say, 'Hey, is this a good forgery?'"

I laughed. "I guess that wouldn't have been a great idea," I agreed.

"So he came up with a plan. He got out his theatrical makeup and started going to the diner done up as the old Frenchman. He cultivated a friendship with George. Eventually he convinced George that he had great works to sell very quietly and cheaply. And when you agreed to meet him, he got out the makeup again and became Pierre."

""He thought he could fool me?" I asked, my curiosity mixing with indignation. "That's not so flattering. He was a pretty good actor. He should've stuck with that."

"It wasn't paying the bills. He had to find other ways. He didn't expect you to buy the artwork. It was about whether it was good enough to deceive you," Nick told me.

"Wow," I said. "I never imagined that meeting on Old Sleepy Hollow Road as a teaching gig. But why did he call me after Miles was arrested?" I asked.

"He got scared. First Leighton had found out about the charade and was livid. Becker wanted you to get me on his side, to give him a deal if he turned himself in. At that point, he didn't know everything. Still, they were concerned that he might talk and the rest would come out."

"What was he doing at Anne's house?" I asked.

"It looks like Becker had followed Paul McGill there. Leighton had just told him everything, hoping to cement their tie by letting him know just how deep in it he was. Leighton told Becker that he'd been the one who switched the tubes of black paint at Danny's, leaving the lethal one for Danny, and that it was the day Becker had been there with him. Becker said he'd keep his mouth shut, but he couldn't handle it. We think he figured McGill was rich and powerful, and maybe could help him somehow. Leighton was watching him, trying to figure out a way to keep him calm and quiet, but he could see Becker's desperation that day. He had to act, and fast. We have a witness who saw someone with that wild orange hair trying to wave down McGill as he got in his car on Main Street, but McGill either didn't see him or didn't acknowledge that he did. Becker followed the car, but on his bike, so he took longer to get there. By the time he did, your friend Anne must've been letting Paul in. We think he was trying to wait for him to come out."

"He didn't make it much of a challenge for Leighton to follow him, with that orange hair," I said.

"The perils of being a performance artist," Nick said. "I'm sure he didn't know Leighton was on his tail. They knew he was cracking and if they didn't stop him it would've been the end of them. So he stopped him for good, right there outside Anne's house. We found a lug wrench in a dumpster near his office at the university. It's something that could've come out of the trunk of almost any car, only this one has a little bit of blood on it. They're checking it for DNA."

"He almost killed me on the street that night," I said, thinking back about the hard thing pressed into the back of my neck.

"He says he was just trying to scare you," Nick said. "He hadn't done direct violence to anyone before, and he says he didn't want to. Of course, he'd been completely responsible for Danny's death, but he knew he wouldn't be there when it happened. He says it was different from Becker, given everything he knew. But you were great, doing what you did to get away from him. We're charging him for the attempt on you, no matter what he says."

"Did Paul know about the forgeries?" I asked.

"We don't think so. The guy was just trying to help his old pal Danny by introducing him around, and we think he was really broken up about the way it all went down," Nick replied.

"I certainly thought so, that day we went to Danny's studio with him," I said.

"It seemed like the real thing to me, too. He didn't look dirty. I'm still not impressed with his olive jars, but I have no jurisdiction there."

"I wish you did," I said. "So it's all wrapped up then? But what about Brendan? Did he know the paintings were fakes?"

"It doesn't look like it," Nick said. "We think they deceived him so they could use his good reputation to make the sales look a little cleaner. Maybe he didn't ask all the questions he should have, but it wasn't criminal. Just over-eager. Many experts have done the same thing, like you said about those Vermeer forgeries years ago."

"I'm glad about that. I like Brendan. And was Diana really Ramona Katorsky of the Bronx?" I asked.

"Yep. I got confirmation just when everything started going down. She was going to take her cut of the money they got from Jim for the forged paintings, and take off with her boyfriend. I hope you're not planning to go comfort her husband."

"He's on his own," I assured Nick. "Once it all dies down, I think he'll find life without Diana to be a lot easier to take, maybe even without liquor. But one more thing-- how did your men get involved with the plan to kidnap me?" I asked.

"We'd had them cultivating a friendship with the museum guards for a while, and they let it be known that their professional services were available in 'times of trouble.' Eventually Leighton heard, told Diana, and when she convinced him that you were onto them, they decided to leave it to my guys. We figured we'd keep close to you, make sure nothing serious happened."

"You know I almost fell into that damned sculpture pit? I could've been killed."

He pulled me close to him and held me tight. "Okay, we didn't expect that. We had no idea you'd be able to get away and go running through the museum, but at least my guys were right behind you. If anything had happened to you..."

I looked into his eyes, and I swear I could almost see his painful memories of Nancy disappear from them.

ABOUT THE AUTHOR

Ronnie Levine is an artist and writer based in Tarrytown, New York. Like Lissa, she paints in a traditional style influenced by the French Impressionists. With a degree in psychology but an overriding passion for art, she attended the Art Institute of Boston, The International Center of Photography, and the Art Students League of New York. Her training continued with an informal, independent study of the masters, as she copied many of her favorite works in the Metropolitan Museum of Art. Her original oil paintings and prints are in many private collections. She has written numerous non-fiction articles about art and people in the arts, which have appeared in *Westchester Magazine* and local newspapers and news websites. For more about her art and journalism, see www.TheIceCreamShopDetective.com.

Made in the USA
Middletown, DE
24 November 2021

52524471R00196